Love, Composed

Sometimes love deserves an encore.

Michelle Tibbs-Brown

To all the girls who outgrew the bonds of bitterness of what they expected from life and embraced the messy, unscripted, real life they were given.

CHAPTER 1

Lucy Hall
June 2019

He grabbed Lucy's hand as they walked through the Notting Hill neighborhood, and her heart was racing by having this new man, Jack, so near to her. She tried her best to remain calm by having him do that simple, loving gesture. This man acted so comfortable around her, but he was a little shy when it came to showing affection because they really were getting to know one another.

I think he is new at this dating thing too, Lucy thought to herself. *He seems to be as nervous around me as I am around him. Normally, teens have their first love moment, but not me, I am twenty-three years old, and this is my first real relationship. Well, I think it is moving to a relationship. This "dating" situation is so new. It feels like I have known him much longer than the short time I have been dating though. It feels like I have known him forever, not just four weeks. Spending time with him seems so easy, much easier than anyone else in my life.*

Lucy smiled over at Jack as they walked, doing her best to be casual, but her stomach was doing flip flops, and her cheeks were warm. *Lucy, you need to get control of yourself.* Her free hand held her ice cream cone steadily as she tried not to show her excitement just to be around him. It may have been a little cool in the morning in late

August for ice cream, but he insisted on treating her for her favorite dessert while they ran errands, preparing for their upcoming trip.

"Where else do you want to go today?" he asked her.

Lucy took a quick lick of her ice cream. "I need to review my list."

"Well, review your list," Jack said, leaning down and whispering in her ear while staring at her mouth, taking in every inch of her in the moment. She loved this new side to him. He was a bit reserved, shy at first, but was slowly becoming more secure in their new connection. *I adore the flirty side of him*, Lucy thought, hiding a smile by taking another quick lick of her ice cream.

"My list is in my pocket," she stated, feigning confidence around him. She kept her mouth close to his, daring him to come closer. Lucy was testing him to see if he would kiss her as they walked through one of the most charming neighborhoods in London. This kiss would be idyllic here in the middle of the charming bustling market. *Come on, you shy fool, kiss me here.* He didn't seem to be overly affectionate normally, so this was almost a dare. Lucy stood staring at him playfully, her ice cream in one hand and her other hand in his.

"Ok, I will give you your hand back," he replied and let go of her hand, clearly proving that he was still the shy guy who caught her attention a month ago.

Lucy tried not to show her disappointment, realizing he didn't take her bait. She wanted to see if he would offer a small, sweet kiss in her neighborhood, showing some public confidence in what seemed like a mutual connection. Despite their conversations being so easy, almost familiar, he did seem to hold back sometimes.   He admitted he was inexperienced and hadn't dated much, but still, it seems like he was holding back sometimes too.

Lucy, get out of your head. You are about to go to one of the most romantic cities in the world with this man, she reminded herself.

After pulling the list out of her pocket, Lucy unfolded the rather crinkled piece of paper that was her to-do list before they left for their trip.

"Ok, I need to go pick up some toothpaste, granola bars, some money, and one more thing." Lucy quickly attempted to hide the list after stating what she needed.

"What do we have there, miss?"

Jack was trying to work his way around her arm. Lucy did her best to hold her list high in the air, while dodging his ridiculous attempt, to pretend he was trying to see the very list that she was keeping so secret.

"There is nothing to see here," Lucy said, pretending to keep strolling on the street, still doing her best to keep the contents of the list from him.

"Not so fast." He took a long stride with his long legs and stood in front of Lucy, stopping firmly in front of her to stop her mid-step.

Ok, dishy bloke, I like where we are going here, Lucy thought to herself.

Again, they were standing facing one another. His tall frame kept him about one foot taller than her. Lucy looked up at him with her hand behind her, hiding the list and that secret thing she didn't want him to see on it. The secret thing—she wanted to surprise him with his favorite treats for the trip.

Lucy started collecting a few things for him when they agreed they would go to Paris together. Of course, they made this big decision only five days ago, but she began thinking of a way to surprise him on their train ride.

When she told Jack about how she wanted to take the train to Paris from London instead of taking a short flight, her new man seemed almost crestfallen. Lucy ignored this fact about the seemingly nearly perfect man standing before her. His one red flag, the one detail she couldn't ignore, was he didn't love the best mode of transportation, the biggest feat of engineering—traveling in a train. She loved it and wanted to take this mode of transportation with him—the first man to take her to Paris. *Hopefully, he will be the last too,* she admitted only to herself. Lucy was hoping the four weeks of dating would blossom into something long-term.

Sure, some think that trains are slow and time-consuming, but I think it is one of the most authentic modes of travel. Plus, how romantic is it to ride side by side with a special someone? Lucy even dreamed up the perfect scenario for them when they left for Paris. Instead of going to the train together, she wanted to meet him at the train station, wanted to arrive early and watch him look for her. Their eyes would scan the train for one another until their eyes met. He would smile at her once he saw her waiting expectantly and greet her with a sweet kiss on the cheek, present her with some flowers, and have a seat next to her while taking her hand. Of course, this entire scenario had been fabricated all in her head, but she was so excited about the possibility of it.

Jack was standing in the street facing her while teasing that he was going to steal her list that she was trying to keep top secret, and then he did it. He gently put his hands on either side of her face and gave her the sweetest, most tender kiss while standing in the middle of a market on one of the most charming neighborhood streets. *In this moment, I am in a romance movie,* Lucy thought. Her heart turned into a puddle. He actually did it … he kissed her in front of God and the world. Normally, he was so shy about PDAs. Her heart was pounding in her chest as they shared their kiss.

Afterward, Lucy smiled at him and whispered, "I can't wait to spend some time in Paris with you this weekend."

"I can't wait to spend time in Paris with you this weekend," he echoed her words while their eyes met for a beat.

Their moment was interrupted when his phone dinged. He pulled the phone out of his pocket and stared at the screen.

"I have to get going. Are you ok with the rest of your errands?"

"I just have a few things left to pick up," she reassured him.

"Are you sure you don't want to take a flight? Here is your last chance to take a modern mode of transportation," he teased.

"I am absolutely certain," she stated with a smile. "Trains are one of the biggest feats of engineering."

"Ok … ok." He smiled. "I will see you at the train station at eight a.m. sharp."

"You've got it," she whispered back.

"Will I find out in the morning what is on your super-secret list?"

"Maybe." She smiled conspiratorially.

"I'll see you in the morning," he said, then stood there admiring her. "You are so beautiful." He gave her a quick peck on the lips goodbye and began walking away while looking back at his phone again.

Lucy smiled as she watched him walk away. *He is so cute,* she thought. *I have just one more stop to pick up these items on my list to surprise him, but I am so thankful to spend a few days with this beautiful man in Paris.*

Then, Lucy watched him slowly turn around and look back at her, as he was just a little farther away, surrounded by the chaos of the market. A smile spread across his face, then he lifted his hand in a tiny wave.

The two looked at one another, and Lucy's heart felt like it was going to pound out of her chest.

I am so lucky to have met this guy. He literally checks all the boxes. Tomorrow morning can't come early enough, Lucy thought as she walked down the street, finishing her errands. Little did she know this would be the last time she would see him again.

CHAPTER 2

Louis

June 2019

"John, I think you have a chance to win." Louis pushed his brother's shoulder as he sat next to him on the piano bench.

"I think you are my crazy brother who needs to realize we live in the real world, and we are competing against all kind of bloody talent," John replied.

"You are right. There are some gifted jazz musicians who are in contention for these awards, but none of them composed one of the most popular songs of the year in the jazz industry," Louis added.

"We composed the song," John emphasized. "Remember, my brother, you were there too. It was a collab-oo-ration." He emphasized the last part, doing his best to playfully remind his brother how much their work together meant to him.

The two men grew quiet, appreciating their work together. They were almost in awe that God blessed them with this opportunity. Not only were the two brothers best friends, but they were also lovers of all things jazz. Even John's wife, Cathrene, tolerated their late-night jam sessions when Louis came to visit on the weekends. They didn't get to have jam sessions like they used to do when they both lived in London.

Louis tapped a key on the piano.

His brother matched a complimentary note.

Louis nodded slowly and added more keys to his original note.

Again, John returned but added a little jazzy riff. He was so taken by the music, he leaned dramatically away from the keys, deep in the moment, his eyes closed, finishing his small riff to Louis's original notes.

Louis slowly began, trying to remember the pure genius that his brother had just come up with moments ago. It was their own version of a copycat game they had played since they were boys, sitting at the piano for hours at times. Sure, just like any boys, they both imagined themselves playing "cooler" instruments instead of the piano, but soon they found themselves playing together all hours of the night. They started writing music by mimicking one another; one brother would play keys and the other would return but put their own spin to it. John, being the older brother, was the first to play the piano, but Louis always followed after his brother. As adult men, they could still spend hours playing this familiar game, given the opportunity.

This old game was what they were doing even now. Louis continued playing slowly, mimicking his brother's original notes but adding his own to it. The next thing he knew, he wasn't having a musical conversation with his brother, but he was taking the music somewhere else. He suddenly heard some New Orleans jazz come from somewhere in his mind. In that moment, Louis was in another world. He wasn't thinking about playing music any longer—music just happened while his mind was in a different universe experiencing the notes. Music took him to another realm in his mind. Many times, John would stop playing and began taking notes of what Louis was playing because during these improvisations, Louis wouldn't recall everything he played; he would just feel the music.

John always thought it was almost magic to behold, a gift to watch God empower him in these moments.

John loved watching this happen because, personally, he was a student of the music. He trained in college and studied how to make his technique better; for Louis, music was part of his DNA. Although John had been recognized more than Louis for his musical prowess in the professional world, Louis was a natural musician.

Suddenly, Louis returned to the piano and realized that he had been lost in the music again. He slowed down his strumming and slowly played his final notes. After years of doing this with his brother, he still almost became embarrassed by getting lost. He took his hands off the keys and rubbed the tops of his legs with the palms of his hands awkwardly.

"Sorry mate, I didn't mean to take over," Louis said shyly.

"Don't be sorry." John pushed his brother's shoulder, the same way Louis had done earlier.

There was a beat of silence.

"Are we going to talk?" John asked Louis.

"You can tell I am nervous?" Louis put a nervous hand on his well-trimmed beard. He pushed his glasses up with his other hand.

"You shouldn't be nervous. We aren't going to be gone long," John reassured his brother.

"I know," Louis added. "Why do you want to go right now?"

"I promised my bride when we got engaged seven years ago that I would take her there and I am a man of my word. We have a small family now, and I want to meet her family in Mali. I know the area can be unpredictable, but her family has lived there for years, and they know how to navigate the country. Plus, we have this opportunity to have some of our costs paid for while delivering some of the aid to help the community. It is a win-win," John insisted.

"Why not wait until the kids are older?" Louis added. "Perhaps they want to come too?"

"Actually, I would like to take them some time, but I want to go first. If it is safe, then I will bring them when they are older, but traveling with our 2-year-old and 5-year-old is not ideal yet. Plus, it was serendipitous that this organization needed help in getting some supplies to her region. Isn't it crazy how God does that?"

"Yes, it is," Louis said quietly.

"Are you nervous about watching the kids for us? Is that it?" John smiled and put his hand on one of his brother's shoulders.

"No, I am not. I love the kids, and I am here so often, I love being here. I miss living near you. I would love to live here but rent in Paris is crazy. I don't have the extra money working jazz gigs like some of us do, Professor Durant."

"I tell you what, once we get back from Mali, let's have a conversation about getting you to Paris full-time. I am sure Cathrene would love some extra help around here if you lived with us until you get on your feet. You won't have to keep coming back and forth from England every weekend to visit. Plus, Paris has such a great jazz scene here too."

Louis stood up from the bench in excitement. "That would be bloody amazing." He ran his hands through his hair and walked over to his brother and gave him a big hug. He slapped him on the back loudly as they embraced, his way of making the moment less emotional.

"Let me talk to Cathrene about it, but I think she will love the idea. She would love having family here in Paris. Since I took the job at the university here, I know she has been lonely, which is why I want to take her on this trip too."

"You are right. You married way out of your league, so you better keep your wife happy," Louis joked.

"I have to get going. I need to catch the train back to London. I'll see you next weekend for your trip and to watch the kids."

Louis gave his brother one more hug before leaving the music studio in the back of the house. He was so excited about this opportunity because London hadn't been the same since his brother moved to Paris for his professorship.

Carthrene is all heart, and I know she will agree to letting me move in temporarily so I can relocate. Finally, I am going to be able to move to Paris and start getting some proper music gigs. I will be able to stop my teaching job during the day and work random gigs at night. I can focus on my music and give it a proper try, if I move here.

Louis shouldered his coat and quietly walked out the front door of the flat with a hopeful attitude regarding this new opportunity.

John and Cathrene's return from their trip can't come soon enough so that my life in Paris and my music career can finally begin, Louis thought to himself.

CHAPTER 3

Lucy Hall - Skye Reynolds
2026

She looked at the empty piece of luggage, sighed, and ran a frustrated hand through her hair. She blew out her breath. *Why was this so difficult? Going to Paris with her soon-to-be sister-in-law was her idea.* Now, she was second-guessing the trip. *Why did you agree to this trip?* Lucy continued to stare at the luggage while mustering motivation when she heard a knock at the door.

"Come in," she said, while softly clearing her throat from lack of use this morning.

"Good morning, Miss Reynolds." Dottie Pemrose entered the space almost cautiously.

Dottie was Lucy's new assistant, like really new, like she was just hired yesterday new. Dottie had auburn curly hair and tortoiseshell thick-rimmed glasses and was a small 5' 2". Although Lucy didn't know Dottie well yet, she would guess that Dottie read in her free time. She had a bookish feel about her, which Lucy found endearing, for some reason.

With Liam's, Lucy's brother's, recent engagement, he instantly found an assistant to help Lucy ease into her new work life without him as he planned to step away from his role as driver, bodyguard, and makeshift assistant for Lucy. However, he wanted to begin making Dottie a part of Lucy's life before he officially stepped down from his position.

"Would you like some help with packing some things?" Dottie offered with a quick smile.

Lucy stood looking dumbfounded by the question. She literally couldn't wrap her brain around the idea that she had her very own assistant now. *Lucy, get it together. The woman is staring at you, and you need to give her something to do.*

"Absolutely," Lucy said with a warm smile.

"Well … let's see." Dottie took out her tablet from her oversized tote that was on her shoulder and began taking notes.

"Do you prefer to pack an outfit for each day, or do you like to just have a certain number of pants, shirts, and shoes?" Dottie asked expectantly as she looked at Lucy with bright eyes.

"I prefer to have options. We are going to be gone for 5 days, so will you pack 6 pants, 2 dresses, 8 shirts, and undergarments? You are welcome to look through my drawers so that you can get acclimated with my layout in my closet." Lucy led Dottie to her walk-in closet.

Dottie stood in awe at the sophisticated space. There was a settee in the center of the space that was illuminated by a chandelier in the center of the room. Dottie tried not to look shocked by the grandeur of Lucy's closet or, most likely, a dressing room.

"What are your plans? I mean, do you have any special plans

that would require specific attire?" Dottie asked, almost nervously, while attempting to find her confidence in her new role.

"We are doing some typical sightseeing and will walk around most of the city, so I will need some comfortable shoes. Being in Paris, I usually go for a more sophisticated look, so please pack some black, tan, cream, and white colors if you don't mind. I do have to read for a movie, but I can still dress casually. I will be seeing a voice coach too, but again, that won't be anything special. Also, I like to wear hats and sunglasses when we walk around town, just to help stay a little incognito as we do some sightseeing. If you don't mind packing a couple of options for me," Lucy said with a smile.

There was an awkward silence between two people who were just learning to work together.

"I'd better leave you to it," Lucy added, trying to end the discomfort.

"Right-o," Dottie replied a bit nervously and a little too enthusiastically.

"Do you see my bag over there by my bed? I will pack that myself because I have some work materials that I need to bring with me. If you can help me remember to actually bring the bag with me when I leave, that would be great." Lucy smiled.

"I am glad you are here," she added warmly.

"Thank you so much. I am so excited to be here." Dottie suddenly found herself almost speaking in a different accent when she answered.

Lucy chuckled and walked out of the changing room. She began gathering her items for her trip and looked at the song lyrics that she had been given by her agent. Just looking at the paper of lyrics made her stomach knot. This page reminded her of the other reason why she was hesitant about the trip.

Lucy had finally agreed to attempt to do a singing role for a new movie. *Why did I agree to this role? I am not a singer! I can't even read music! Why would my agent think this is a good idea? I am known to be in action movies, not for my singing skills. I can't believe I have agreed to move forward with this idea. The only solace is that I am supposed to work with a singing coach while I am in Paris. These indecipherable musical notes are just another reminder of why I am not feeling like heading to Paris. I feel like such a high-maintenance diva with these thoughts!*

Lucy shoved the pages in her bag, trying to get the nagging doubt out of her mind. She grabbed her passport, and a ticket fell out of the back of the booklet. She looked down at the paper on the floor, bent over, and studied the piece of paper closely. Lucy saw that it was the train ticket from the last time she was in Paris for pleasure.

"Ghosty McGhosterton," Lucy said to herself; well, that was what she called him now instead of Jack. He was all talk leading up to their trip to Paris and seemed so charming and attentive. They spent the day before the trip preparing and shopping in Notting Hill. The trip was his idea. "Let's go take a quick trip to Paris. It will be so romantic," he said, but Lucy showed up to their meeting spot on the train, and he didn't come. She went to Paris alone and spent the entire time by herself inside the rental she arranged. Lucy made light of it now with his well-earned nickname, but honestly, she was heartbroken. She literally waited on the train—looking out the window—waiting for him to arrive. "Sorry"; that was it. The only message she received from Ghosty McGhosterton, the first guy to break her heart, which was nearly five years ago.

She never told anyone about what happened that weekend, especially her protective brother.

Lucy looked back at the ticket in her hand, ripped it into pieces, and threw it into the garbage, fighting the trembling pressure that started in her chest and moved to her throat. *Bloody hell, Lucy, get a grip. This was five years ago,* she told herself. She couldn't stand when a guy wasted her time, and Ghost McGhosterton was just one of the guys who disappointed her, which was how Liam ended up being her driver-bodyguard-assistant.

With her mind returning to her brother and his fiancé, it made Lucy smile. Her amazing new friend, Elle Bennett, who jumped at the idea of coming for a little girl time in Paris was going to marry her brother!

I am so fortunate to have a brother who loves me and a new sister-in-law who is more of a best friend than a sister-in-law. I need to take control of this negative self-talk!

Lucy smiled to herself, thinking about the adorable couple when her phone dinged with a text message. Lucy saw a message from Elle.

Elle

Have you packed your passport, your best red lipstick, and your tolerance for eating some of the best food in the world for the next few days?

CHAPTER 4

Elle

2026

Elle looked at her small piece of luggage and was impressed with her organization and ability to fit everything she wanted to bring in such a tiny bag. She had carefully curated outfits for every day, planning and placing them together to avoid confusion when traveling. Elle had a general idea of the itinerary, a term she was using loosely because they were not planning to be super-structured, but she chose her wardrobe based on their plans.

Elle packed some loungewear for casual days but picked up something new to wear while in Paris. One thing that Elle had learned during her short time in London was that loungewear in Europe was much different than loungewear in the States. Although Paris was generally a safe city, she knew several people who had been pickpocketed at tourist attractions during their visits. She wanted to do her best to not only live the cafe life for a few days but also keep her travels without incident. Elle was there to live like a Parisian for a few days, too.

As she double-checked the contents of her luggage, Elle referred to her list on her phone to make sure she packed all that she wanted. Sleeping mask - check. Travel fan - check. Euros - check. Makeup and hair products - check and check. Deck of cards - check. She hoped that Lucy would be surprised that she thought to bring a game to play on their train ride to Paris. She was so shocked that Lucy wanted to take public transportation to Paris, given her status as a world-famous actress. Lucy did, after all, reserve a private cabin for them to travel with first-class accommodation, which would allow for some privacy too.

Elle was also surprised that Lucy didn't ask her brother to drive them to Paris, but Lucy usually had a reason for things, Elle was beginning to learn.

Elle was triple-checking her packing list on her phone when she felt an arm slowly come around her neck, presenting her with a take-out coffee.

"I am going to miss you so much," she heard Liam's breath whisper in her ear as he stood behind her.

"Coffee!" Elle squealed, teasing Liam that she was more excited about the coffee than seeing him one more time before the trip to Paris.

"Wow, that hurts. You just love me for my coffee delivery services?" Liam whispered in her ear as he put her arms around her waist, once handing over the coffee to her.

Elle slowly turned around, put her coffee down on the nightstand, and put her arms around Liam's neck.

"Oh, there is so much more I like about you." Elle moved her face closer to Liam's face. She gently kissed Liam on the neck and began a trail of soft kisses that led up to Liam's mouth. She closed the space between them even more and deepened the kiss, warm, lingering, and threaded with the ache that they didn't have much time together. They slowly pulled themselves apart and kept their gaze just a moment longer until the world pulled them apart.

A sound came from Liam's phone.

"Oh, I almost forgot, I was a bit distracted." Liam pulled out his phone and stared at a notification. "I was being notified by this Bluetooth tracker I bought you."

"What is it?"

"It will help you keep track of your bags once you place it inside. Because you are traveling with my sister, I think it is a good idea that you keep one in your carry-on. She always has to be very cautious due to 'fans.' I don't want something to happen to your things. Would you like me to download the tracker app to your phone?" Liam asked with a hopeful expression. "I gave a go at it and connected it to my phone to see what it does."

"Can you just keep it on your phone and give me updates if need be?" Elle asked. "I just don't want to keep your sister waiting."

"Of course, I will just place the tracker in your bag for you. Are you sure you don't want me to put it on your phone? I bought my sister one a few years ago, once her fan base started to grow. You wouldn't believe the crazy things people want from their favorite actors as a token."

"You are such a good brother, and driver, fiancé, and kisser." Elle moved in closer to Liam to give him another kiss when there was a ding on her phone.

"Ugh," Elle said as she checked her phone.

"Selfishly, I want to beg you to stay, but you both deserve this so much," Liam encouraged Elle about her trip with his sister.

"Lucy said she will be ready in about ten minutes, so we can head her way to pick her up," Lucy explained to Liam.

"I am ready when you are." Liam's reaction emphasized that this newly engaged man was having a very hard time staying away from his fiancée at this point in their relationship.

"I am ready. Ugh, why is this so hard? I am going to Paris for a few days. I should not be acting like this!" Elle confessed as she turned back to Liam and looked into his eyes, putting his hands in her hands.

Liam touched Elle's long brown hair and looked at her blue eyes and answered, "It's hard because we don't want to say goodbye to each other for a few days. We love each other, and it's hard." Liam's Adam's apple bopped up and down, showing a bit of emotion while speaking to Elle. "Soon, we will be married, and we won't have to say goodbye to each other anymore."

Elle was surprised by the emotion in his voice and his reaction. He was normally in protective mode and incredibly attentive, but not emotional, always a bit reserved emotionally. She found his confession endearing and vulnerable, and it made it hard for her not to grab him and kiss his soft lips again and again.

Instead, she put her arms around Liam, looking at his blue eyes and dark hair, soaking him in one more time without saying a word. He captured her feelings perfectly; this was why it was hard. He nailed it, and she didn't need to say anything else but one more thing.

"I love you," Elle whispered.

"I love you, too," Liam returned and pulled her in closely to give her one more hug before Elle left for Paris.

CHAPTER 5

Louis

2026

Louis stared at the empty to-go coffee mug, almost willing the machine to begin its initial brew, waiting for it to sputter to life.

"Where are my school socks?" Noemie called from upstairs.

Louis continued to stare at the machine, hoping that the stare-down with a coffee machine would make it work more efficiently.

"Where are my school socks?" Noemie appeared from around the corner, finally making Louis realize she was asking him about her socks.

"Oh darling, I am so sorry," Louis said, hugging her. "I didn't realize you were talking to me."

Noemie continued to stare at Louis, waiting for him to answer her question.

"I think I saw them on your dresser," Louis said while smiling at her.

"I put my laundry away already. They must have been put with

Theo's laundry." She huffed and walked up the stairs to find her socks in her brother's room instead.

I have got to get better about helping in the morning. He chastised himself for not remembering to put the school clothes together last night. *I need to get better, but then again, I did get home late after I worked my second job. When did I become the makeshift maid?*

"Theo," Louis called from downstairs, but knew better than to expect him to call back. Given that Theo was a young man of very few words and most likely wearing his noise-cancelling headphones, he would not answer him.

Louis took the narrow steps up to the bedrooms of the flat. He picked up toy trains that had been left on the stairs as he walked up the wooden staircase, the boards creaking after each step.

"I still don't see the socks with Theo's stuff either." Tears were beginning to well in Noemie's eyes, which could only mean one thing: they must be running late for school.

"Ok, love, I will find them for you," Louis reassured her as he approached the top of the stairs where Noemie was standing. Her arms were folded, and she had a crease between her eyes.

Louis bent down and looked eye to eye with Noemie, placing his upside-down hand on her chin and reassuring her.

"I will find your socks. We won't be late, ok?" Louis tried to use a tone that sounded the most reassuring, but inside his stomach was in knots.

Why did I have to be the one to do this morning routine? They deserve so much more than what I can offer for sure.

"Do you mind helping your brother get ready while I find your socks?" Louis again tried to sound reassuring, but once he glanced at his watch, he could easily see that they were pushing their time in order to get both kids to school on schedule.

Louis felt almost guilty for asking Noemie to help with her brother. She already crossed a line from time to time, trying to be another adult in the room, always advocating and protecting her brother, maybe a side effect of their circumstances. Noemie often matched the conversation of the adults in the room, and, many times, acted as a mother figure to her autistic brother rather than his ten-year-old sibling. Louis chastised himself for asking her to step again into an adult role by getting her brother together this morning, but he had to find those socks.

He began going from room to room, scanning the rooms for any sign of the missing school uniform socks. He was trying to move quickly but didn't want to induce panic in the already-stressed Noemie. She always had a watchful eye, reading the room and picked up on the small things.

Louis checked every usual spot where his scattered and overworked brain could have left the clean socks. He checked the tops of dressers. He opened typical drawers. Then, he remembered that he had done other laundry that day and feverishly began looking for the missing socks in the closet where extra linens were stored. Still nothing. Finally, he went to the bathroom, where extra bath towels were placed just yesterday, though it felt like days ago. He opened the vanity door, and the socks were sitting adjacent to the freshly laundered bath towels.

"Bingo," Louis yelled and held up the socks as though he had won a trophy.

"Nice job." Noemie appeared in the doorway with a newly dressed Theo, who was staring at the pile of toy trains that Louis had absentmindedly collected last night and left at the top of the stairs. Noemie put on her socks with her shoes, clearly ready to leave for school.

"Thank you." Louis was suddenly self-conscious of the fact that he acted like a hero by just finding misplaced socks, and here stood sweet Noemie, standing with her brother, the real hero of the morning.

"Good morning, Buddy. Do you want to take two trains to school with you?" Louis suggested.

"His teacher suggested he keep his toys at home so he doesn't lose one. He can have a meltdown if he loses one," Noemie added, again, just crossing the line of older sister and trying to be the adult.

"How about I take the two toys you would like to bring to school, and I will keep them with me?" Louis smiled at Theo, who seemed to think that it was a good idea too.

Mentally, Louis was chastising himself again for his poor planning with the morning shift.

I really need to do better. Life has been different for years with this routine, and I am still struggling. Every morning, I am tasked to get the kids off to school and I feel like it is chaos. I am stressed in the morning—I can't imagine how my high-strung Noemie feels. I need to do much better for them. They deserve better.

"Are you ready?" Louis asked hopefully, trying to hide the shame he felt for being so inconsistent in the morning.

"Yes, let's go," Noemie replied, with a slight impatient edge to her voice.

"Ok, ok," Louis said, while grabbing his vest to pair with his button-down and 1920s style trousers. He slipped on his Oxford shoes and grabbed his glasses to complete his look. With most of his clothes inspired by the 1920s, he felt like he was born in the wrong era.

Finally, they made their way down the steps and were finally out of the door of the Parisian flat, closing the door behind them and leaving Louis's forgotten hot cup of coffee sitting at the coffee machine.

CHAPTER 6

Elle

2026

"I am so excited." Elle smiled at Liam. "I will admit, though, I am a little nervous too."

"What makes you say that?" Liam was driving and continued to keep his eyes on the road while glancing from time to time to speak to Elle.

"I adore your sister, but I have only been around her in small time frames. I feel like we clicked instantly when we met in my hair salon in New York. Then, she invited me here to lead the fashion show in London, and I saw her here and there, but in all honesty, we haven't spent much time alone together." Elle hesitated before saying, "I don't want her to think I am dull."

Liam let out a guffaw, which did not please Elle, and she paused, almost waiting for an explanation for his laugh.

"You are far from dull, my love." Liam took her hand and kissed the back of it. "I know that I may be biased because I am head over heels for you, but you have to know that you are a force. You make a room brighter just by being in it. You are so genuine and kind and are such an incredible person. My sister is going to be thankful to have someone so kind and authentic with her for a few days."

Elle didn't know what to make of Liam's outpouring of love. She was so thankful for him.

"I love you," Elle replied to Liam, and she kissed the back of his hand this time while she sat in the passenger side of the car.

London was a blur as they were talking and driving through the city. Soon, Liam slowed down and pulled in front of Lucy's building. Liam stepped out and greeted the doorman by shaking his hand. A little pang of guilt hit Elle, as she could see that Liam was such a big part of Lucy's life … even befriending the doorman of her building. Just this gesture of greeting the doorman made some guilt enter Elle's head about bringing Liam to New York with her after the wedding. Bringing Liam to New York meant she was pulling him away from his sister and from this community here in London. It was a conversation they never really had, but it began with Liam applying for jobs in New York. Then, it just made sense for him to make the move, but his life was here too.

Elle felt a pull in her chest as the reality seemed to setting in with her moving him away from his life in London. Then, a sound interrupted Elle's thoughts.

Lucy

On my way! 👯

Elle was smiling at her phone when Liam returned to the car.

"I was going to tell you that Lucy is on her way, but I have a feeling she already messaged you." Liam smiled, then leaned over and kissed Elle on the cheek.

"After I drive you both to the train station, do not ever hesitate to call, text, or video chat me or any of the above." Liam held Elle's hand, smiling at her while meeting her gaze. His eyes slowly made their way to her lips, which were like magnets to him. He leaned over and brushed her lips with his own, then kissed next to her mouth. He slowly moved to the other side of her mouth and kissed her gently there. He wanted to cover her in kisses before she left.

"I cannot leave you two alone for a minute without buying a ticket to the Love Fest!" Lucy joked as she opened the door to Liam's car. "Don't mind me, I've got my bags," Lucy deadpanned. "My sweet brother worked for me for years, but suddenly he finds the girl of his dreams, and I am like an old dishcloth."

"Ladies and gentlemen, Love Fest will be closing its doors for the next few days, so please make your way to the exit," Elle returned the joke, which made Lucy cackle in laughter.

"Hello, bird, or do I call you my soon-to-be sister-in-law?" Lucy was on a roll with the jokes.

Lucy's playful nature made Elle feel more reassured about their time together. *After all, Lucy is a well-renowned actress with fans all over the world. It's easy to get a little intimidated by it as a friend, but Lucy is just a regular person who needs good people around her,* Elle reminded herself. *Plus, she is hilarious.*

"Just call me Elle. I am so excited. I have been to Paris one other time, but it was years ago. Do you have any must-see items on your list?"

"I have a few things in mind, but I do have to do some work while I am there," Lucy mentioned to Elle as Liam was putting her bags into the car and saying goodbye to the doorman one final time.

"What kind of work do you have to do?"

Liam reentered the car and sat behind the wheel.

"Ok, ladies, let me do the honor of driving the most important women in my life to the train station."

"Wow, my brother has become quite the open-hearted, love-affirming man," Lucy teased. "We were just talking about the little bit of work I am going to be doing in Paris."

"Do you need me to arrange for Dottie to come to Paris too?" Liam offered.

"I don't think so. I am just not that used to having someone help me like having a personal assistant. I will get used to it, but for now, I am used to doing things myself," Lucy explained.

"I can understand that. I would debrief with her at a certain time each day, just to help give her purpose." Liam tried to be helpful.

"Thank you, big brother," Lucy said with emphasis, almost teasing her brother for being so caring.

"So, what kind of work do you have to do?" Elle tried to change the subject because she could see that Liam was going to struggle with stepping away from the role he had with Lucy's professional life as driver, modified assistant, and makeshift bodyguard.

"I agreed to do a new movie…" Lucy hesitated "…that requires me to sing." She said the last part and practically hid behind the seat to conceal her announcement.

"You are going to sing in a movie?" Liam clarified, with a clear shocked expression on his face.

I could pick up on the unspoken words between the two of them. Clearly, Lucy isn't considered a singer by anyone, it would appear. It sounds like this is a big risk for her professionally, but I could be reading it wrong, Elle thought while trying to follow the secret language of siblings.

"I don't know what made me agree to it. I just wanted to try something new. I wanted to expand my repertoire, but the burden of this decision is getting real," Lucy confessed.

"So, what work are you doing in Paris?" Elle clarified.

"I am working with a voice coach there. Supposedly, he is the best in the business. After working with him, we will have a better idea if I need to move forward with this crazy idea of mine." Lucy smiled and shrugged her shoulders, attempting to feign confidence.

"I'll pray about it, Lucy. I am so proud of you for stepping out of your comfort zone professionally." Elle smiled conspiratorially. Elle had just taken a big risk by accepting the job opportunity in London while leaving her new business in New York, so she could relate to taking professional risks. Although the position Elle took was temporary, the impact on leaving her business for a few weeks could have long-term effects.

Lucy returned the smile, understanding what Elle meant in her comment. "Yes, you do understand, don't you?" Lucy patted Elle on the hand not only in acknowledgement of her point, but also for that extra boost of confidence.

"Ladies, we are just pulling up to the train station, so Lucy, you may want to put on your hat and sunglasses. I am going to get the porter that Dottie hired and load your luggage for you. You two can head to your private cabin to make sure you maintain Lucy's privacy," Liam explained.

Lucy, who was used to this way of life, hopped out of the car and quickly began heading in the direction of the train. Elle, on the other hand, was having to say goodbye to her fiancé for the first time since becoming engaged, but he was busy taking care of the luggage.

Elle watched the direction in which Lucy was headed and wanted so badly to say goodbye to Liam, but she knew she needed to stay with Lucy. She felt so conflicted for a moment.

It's ok, this is life to them. This is new to you. You said goodbye five times to him this morning with hugs and kisses. Just keep moving and make sure to stay with Lucy because you have been told that fans can be crazy.

Elle was just now beginning to realize what her life might look like and beginning to really appreciate what Lucy had to deal with every day as a famous actress.

Maybe the guilt I felt earlier for taking Liam away from Lucy after the wedding may have been misguided. Maybe this will be an opportunity to distance himself from this life, Elle considered.

She watched Lucy step up into the train and was just a few steps behind her, finally heading to Paris for a much-needed break.

CHAPTER 7

Dottie

2026

"Hello, Dottie Pemrose speaking," Dottie answered her new work phone and could not possibly understand who would be calling this number.

"Hello Dottie, this is Lucy's agent, Clara Whitmore. Do you know the best way to contact her?"

"Based on her schedule…" Dottie paused to pull out her color-coded schedule and scanned the itinerary. She already had the day's plans memorized, being new to this job and wanting to get everything right.

"She is en route to Paris on the train at this point, so I don't believe you will be able to reach her for at least another hour." Dottie glanced at the time to confirm.

"We have a situation," Clara continued, almost dramatically. "Her voice coach cancelled that she was scheduled to work with in Paris. We need a replacement as soon as possible. Lucy doesn't like to be bombarded with last-minute decisions, so we need to find her a new voice coach in Paris and give her the information like things never changed. She didn't know the person anyway, so we just need to come up with another voice coach without burdening her with the stress of this last-minute change."

"Okay…" Dottie replied, completely unclear of what this meant to her as the new assistant.

"You need to find someone else," the agent replied, "within the hour. Lucy needs to get the information when she arrives in Paris, so you better work quickly. Find someone not crazy, incredibly talented, and reliable. Oh … and send me the information once it is confirmed. Also, her budget is $500 per hour."

"Right-O," Dottie replied. *Why did you use that word right now? Are you giving her a welcome mat to walk over you? Confidence, Dottie, confidence,* she repeated mentally to herself. *Plus, five hundred Euros an hour? What on earth?*

"One more thing. Lucy is incredibly nervous about this work she is doing for this movie. She wants the challenge for adding vocal experience, but this is very new for her. Do not let her know that I told you that so you need to find someone good who can make her feel at ease."

"I have it covered. I'll make some quick calls, then Bob's your uncle." Dottie tried to mask her nervousness in her voice.

She paused to hear a response, but the agent had already hung up the phone.

"Steady on… steady on…" Dottie repeated aloud to herself, white staring at Lucy's beautiful color-coded calendar she created with each color highlighting details for the coming days.

Ok, Dot, what are you going to do? This is the first real task for Lucy, and you can do this. Dottie looked for a mirror in the room at Lucy's flat. *Do not second-guess yourself, missy. You have got this! I will admit, bird; this doesn't sound like something that should fall into your job description, but it is now your job. Think.*

With feigned confidence, Dottie looked at herself in the mirror, *You can do this. You are capable and smart. You will find the right person.*

With renewed confidence, Dottie pulled out her phone and began searching music schools in Paris. *No, this seems too obvious. I think Lucy would want someone more specialized because her itinerary mentioned a voice coach for jazz music.*

She then searched jazz and Paris in the search bar. Dottie educated herself briefly by scrolling through the history of jazz in Paris. *Ok, Dottie, where could you find a voice coach that specializes in jazz?*

Then, Dottie began searching historic jazz bars in Paris.

"Ok Pemrose, I think you are getting closer."

This looked like a historic place, and she clicked on the hyperlink and saw the charm of this historic bar with photos of several artists performing.

She hit the call button. After ringing for some time, finally, a gravelly voice answered.

"Le Chat Bleu."

"Bugger … English?"

"Yeah, I speak English."

"Oh lovely, thank you."

There was a beat of silence.

"What do you need?" the gravelly voice responded.

"I have a strange request. To make a long story short, I am looking for a voice coach who specializes in jazz music. My boss needs a reliable, kind, and talented person to work with her this week."

"Who is your boss?"

"My boss is Lucy—er … I mean her name is Skye Reynolds. She is an actress who is interested in preparing for a new role that will require some vocal work." *Dottie, why are you telling him Lucy's life story? Also, you almost used her real name with him. You've got this … be confident. You have been hired to be the assistant to a world-famous actress. Act like you know what you are doing! Say something convincing to Mr. Grouchy Pants.*

"We can pay handsomely for the work if you have someone in mind. Plus, we need a nice person who is going to not only do a great job but also show up for this work. Do you know someone who would fit the bill?" *I suppose this guy is going to say that he would be the perfect candidate because she already told him about the pay. Dottie, next time, don't put all your cards out there.*

"I think I have the perfect musician in mind. He is a talented jazz pianist, but he is an incredible singer. He is a full-time music teacher during the day, so he would be a great coach."

"She may need to meet him tomorrow, based on her schedule. Will that be a problem for him?"

"Look, lady, I am sure whatever you may be paying handsomely will help out this guy. I don't like many people, but I like him, and he is talented. Plus, his family is going through it right now, and he could use the money."

"That sounds lovely. Will you give me his contact information?"

"Actually, let me reach out first and make sure he is interested. I'll call you back on this number. What is your name?"

"I am Dottie Pemrose, Skye Reynolds's personal assistant.

"I am sorry, what is your name, sir?"

"My name is Cap. I am the manager of Le Chat Bleu."

CHAPTER 8

Louis

2026

"What are you looking forward to most today at school?" Louis asked Noemie as he walked next to her on the way to school, while she insisted on holding her brother's hand.

"I don't know." Noemie bit her lip as she considered the question. "I like that we are learning more English."

"Why are you enjoying it so much?"

"Well, it is easy. We already speak English mostly at home. Plus, I will never tell my teacher that much of my family is from England, so that will be my little secret."

Louis let out a laugh. "That is very strategic of you."

Guilt hit Louis again. *Should we be speaking more French at home? I just feel more comfortable with English. Am I doing her a disservice? I know things were much different before...*Louis paused and returned his thoughts to Noemie.

"So, is your plan to hide it because you don't want to get any unwanted attention for your giftedness from the teacher?"

"No, I don't want to be given more work because I know more. It is like a hand of poker."

Again, Louis chuckled and marveled at just another example of how Noemie was older beyond her years. *She really needs to begin to relax more and just be a kid. She is even double-checking on her brother while we are talking. Should I have insisted on holding Theo's hand instead of hers? Should I have asked for her help in getting him ready for school today? I really have to get more organized for our morning routine. I feel like I can't get ahead; I feel like I am barely treading water.* Louis watched Noemie straighten the hood of her brother's jacket and smiled to himself. *What if she enjoys doing things and caring for her brother?* Deep in thought, Louis had the urge to take a sip of his coffee and just realized for the first time he must have left his coffee at home.

"Bugger, I left my coffee at home." Louis ran his hand over his head.

The three continued to walk quietly for a moment.

Noemie took her phone out of her jacket pocket and checked the time.

"I think we have time to stop and get a coffee if you like," she encouraged.

"Are you sure you won't feel rushed this morning?"

"No, I think we will be fine," she reassured him, again partially making him feel like the child and her the adult.

"Here is a little cafe on the corner, let's stop here. Would you like anything?"

"No, we are good," Noemie answered for her and her brother. He was contentedly wearing his noise-cancelling headphones.

Louis's phone rang just as they continued their walk toward the cafe.

"I need to get this. Hey Cap." Louis recognized the number to the manager of the jazz bar where he had regular gigs, which was one of the reasons he couldn't seem to get home early enough to get organized for the next morning for school.

"Everything ok?"

"I just had a strange phone call from the personal assistant of a celebrity who is going to be in town and who needs a voice coach for the next few days. Their pre-scheduled voice coach cancelled, so they called our world-renowned jazz bar and asked for a recommendation for another voice coach," said Cap.

"First, I am a musician who happens to sing sometimes. Plus, I don't know if I will have time to do this kind of work and work gigs at your bar."

"The assistant, whose name is Dottie Pemrose, said she would pay you $500 an hour for this gig. I think you should take it. I can schedule someone else to play your gigs for you this week. I think it may help, given your situation," he said.

Louis looked down at Noemie and Theo, who were standing on the sidewalk, off to the side, out of the way. Noemie was scrolling on her phone with her other arm around her brother. If he does this gig, it will give him some extra money, and he can be around more. It would also give Noemie a chance to just be a kid.

"I'll take it." Louis ran his hand over his head again, trying to process this opportunity that fell into his lap at the perfect time. *Thank you, God, I could use this right now.*

"Cap, thank you for thinking of me for this," Louis said, trying to fight back tears, sounding emotional.

"Don't mention it," Cap answered in a gruff tone.

"I just …"

"Really, don't mention it," Cap said again. "I don't want word to get around that I am a nice guy and giving you some favors. Call me later to let me know your plans for your evening gigs."

Louis smiled to himself, thankful for his "tough guy" manager at his second job for thinking of him for this gig. *Thank you, God, for this opportunity,* Louis said quietly to himself again.

"Thanks for your patience," Louis said, hugging Theo and Noemie, "Can I interest anyone in a croissant this morning?"

Louis placed his arms around both of the kids, finding his way between the kids and holding both of their hands, feeling lighter after getting some good news.

CHAPTER 9

Elle

2026

Elle took in the French countryside as the train swayed back and forth in a constant rhythm. She refused to be distracted by her phone and wanted to enjoy the experience during their train ride and for their girls' trip. Elle may live in New York at home and have access to all kinds of transportation, but she was always too busy working to really enjoy much downtime. This girls' trip was exactly what she needed after the demanding fashion show in London.

Elle looked over at Lucy, who was also quiet and taking in the views of the countryside. Lucy returned a content smile when she noticed Elle looking at her. Being in their private cabin, Lucy had taken off her sunglasses and hat to relax a little.

"Can I ask you a question?" said Elle.

"Sure."

"What does the train mean on your baseball cap? It is a designer or something?"

Lucy chuckled. "It is the farthest thing from designer. It is a cheap cap that I picked up on a trip because I love riding trains. I love trains, period."

"Really?" Elle asked surprised. *This famous actress could ride on any mode of transportation, and I love the fact that she adores trains,* Elle thought to herself.

"They are a feat in engineering, iconic and classic. They force me to slow down and be present. Afterall, most of my technology is spotty during the ride. I love the slow swaying back and forth on the train ride. It is relaxing. I just love trains," Lucy said with a smile. "I know it is a little quirky."

"It is a little quirky," Elle admitted, "but it is so endearing really. It makes me like you even more."

Lucy smiled. "Did you wonder why Liam didn't try to convince me to let him drive us?"

"Come to think of it, you are right. I was a bit surprised that he didn't try to negotiate his way into this trip by driving us." Elle smiled, thinking of her thoughtful, protective fiancé.

"Liam knows I love taking the train. I can't always use this mode of travel though, but this is a short enough trip that it isn't wasting too much time traveling like this. Plus, it has this secure cabin that allows me to travel safely, without the attention of potential fans. I have taken this train a few times, and I even know this porter too." Lucy smiled again.

"I am learning more about you every day as my new sister-in-law. I love that you enjoy this so much, and I am really enjoying it too. I love how you are so intentional about slowing down because I really need to do that too, but I have to ask you a question." Elle paused. "Is everything ok? You seem … I don't know …reflective."

"Well, I am actually a little reflective. I can't believe you noticed it. What I am about to tell you cannot leave this cabin."

Of course you can tell me anything. She must know that we are nearly family now, but please don't tell me something that will make me concerned about your well-being. I want us to be close, but please spill, Elle thought to herself, feeling a bit conflicted if she wanted to know something that shouldn't leave the cabin.

"Absolutely. You … Liam … Margaux are really the closest people in my life. I don't have many friends in which I can confide, so your secret is safe with me."

"I was just sitting here thinking about the last time I was supposed to be in Paris for just a fun weekend. I go for work sometimes, but it isn't like just going and seeing the city and enjoying the culture."

Elle nodded in agreement, even though she had no concept what it would be like to have a job that required you to travel so much. Doing the fashion show in London with Lucy was such a rare, spontaneous occurrence—it was not the norm for Elle at all. Elle has been tight on money for years with her new business and paying back her parents for the cost of school. Working the fashion show finally gave Elle some financial freedom. *Lucy, your offer to hire me for the fashion show gave me financial freedom that you will truly not understand,* Elle thought to herself.

"I found a ticket in my passport that came from five years ago, and it brought back some unexpected emotions. I was dating, let's call him Ghosty McGhosteron. He and I had been dating for a month and planned a few days in Paris. We were scheduled to meet on this train. I scheduled the private cabin, not because I was really well-known professionally yet, but I did it to be special for us. I arrived to the station early because I was so excited about our fun plans and the potential for our relationship."

"So, what happened?" Elle asked.

"We even spent the day before our trip running errands for our first trip as a couple. I was really excited about going to Paris with him."

"What happened?" Elle pressed, waiting for her answer.

"I went to our private cabin, and I waited for him, and I kept texting him and calling him several times when our train was about to depart. Then, he missed the train."

"Did he catch up with you in Paris? Did something happen to him?"

"Of course, at first, I was in panic mode. I was convinced something terrible happened to him. After some time on the train and time to think rationally, I knew he must have a good reason because he was such a good bloke. For the month we dated, he was nothing but lovely."

"Did he find you in Paris?" Elle was on the edge of her seat with anticipation.

"I made it to Paris and called and text him again, but this time, everything went to voicemail. I checked into our rental and tried contacting him again, but still no word from him. So, I paced the floors of our rental the entire evening, thinking something happened to him. I decided to distract myself by reading over a script, and I pulled out my tablet. That's when I saw his email." Lucy's face filled with indignation.

"What did the email say?" Elle was fully committed to this story. *Was he okay? Was he hurt? Did something tragic happen to someone he loved?*

"It said 'Sorry, can't make it,' as the subject line and that was it. He sent me the email two hours after he was supposed to meet with me on the train too. I didn't even know he had my email! Naturally, I replied to his email, but nothing."

"So, he didn't reply with a reason? What did you do?"

"I stayed in the rental the entire weekend and ate junk food and drank wine."

"Did he ever explain his reason?"

"No, my love; that is why he earned the nickname Ghosty McGhosterton. I never heard from him again. The email was the last time that I heard from him."

"I bet Liam was furious about what he did to you." Elle looked out the window as she noticed that the train was beginning to slow down slightly.

"He never knew about it; no one knows about it but you. You are the only person I have told about him. Honestly, it hurt so much. He broke my heart. I hadn't had someone I cared about be so cruel for no reason to me before."

"I am so sorry that happened to you." Elle reached across and put her hand on Lucy's hand.

"Love, don't feel sorry for me. Clearly, he wasn't the man for me. It's just that." Lucy paused, almost getting emotional. "He wasted my time. If you don't like me … fine … but don't waste my time.

We literally spent the day before the trip shopping together. I put a bag of his favorite food together to surprise him on the train. I hated that he wasted my time."

"I am so sorry."

Both were quiet for a beat, lost in their thoughts.

"I think we are getting close to Gare du Nord." Lucy's demeanor changed with her response. "There are plenty of fish in the sea." Lucy smiled back at Elle, a sudden shift from her reflective mood from moments ago.

"Yes, there are, and I hear the single men in Paris are next level," Elle joked as an encouragement to Lucy.

"We will have to find out if that is true … well, just me," Lucy joked.

"I'll be your wing man," Elle deadpanned. "Do you mind if we go to a cafe once we arrive? I could really use a pick-me-up coffee."

"I don't need a man; I need a latte the size of my emotional baggage!" Lucy quipped.

"Ohhh… that was good. So, a venti with a side of therapy?" Elle shot back, and both women rolled with laughter, ready for some sisterly fun in Paris.

CHAPTER 10

Lucy
2026

"Isn't it crazy that even the trains stations smell better in Paris?" Lucy quipped. "It smells like a perfumerie in the train station! I am always mesmerized by the sophistication of this city. I have been in some cities that treat their train stations as an afterthought."

Both women were looking for their way to the "sortie," the French term for exit, but Lucy was making sure to be discreet. "Parisians never make a big deal out of my celebrity status, it is the tourists here who do," Lucy whispered to Elle.

"Let's go out of this exit, and I know a cafe down the street. I am going to lead the way, if you don't mind, because I am trying to get a feel of the crowds here today. I am trying to be discreet," Lucy added.

"Yes, please. Also, let me know if there is something I may be doing to inadvertently cause attention or if I can help you more. I don't want to make it harder for you, so just let me know," Elle whispered back to Lucy.

In a short time, both women entered a nondescript cafe on the corner just as Lucy described.

This is perfect. It looks small and not too crowded. Plus, it looks local, so fewer tourists to recognize me. Goodness knows that I love my fans; it is just the super fans that get a little scary.

Elle's phone dinged once they stepped into the café, and she was convinced Liam was probably aware that they were in Paris now, but instead Elle was pleasantly surprised.

Elle was staring at a text message from Margaux as she entered the cafe. Lucy was heading to the bathroom while donning sunglasses and a baseball cap, trying her best to remain in disguise in the City of Lights.

Elle smiled at her phone as she replied to her friend Margaux, who was having the time of her life celebrating in Italy.

"Hey there, I want to grab a coffee to go," Elle explained to Lucy when she returned from the bathroom. "Do you want anything? This place is so charming." Elle admired the quaint but charming cafe.

"Let's be clear about this … you will never have to ask me if I need coffee," Lucy joked.

"Duly noted. What would you like to do first now that we are in Paris?" Elle asked Lucy.

"I do have a reading for a movie some time tomorrow, but it won't take too long. For today, I planned for us to go to the Eiffel Tower," Lucy said while smiling conspiratorially.

"Yayyyy." Elle's usually quiet demeanor suddenly became more gregarious after hearing about the Eiffel Tower being in her near future.

"Let's stand over here out of the way while we wait for coffee." Lucy pulled Elle aside to allow for other patrons to order their coffee and not notice them.

Meanwhile, Lucy had noticed two children waiting near them. One young boy had on his headphones, and the other older sibling was holding his hand. *I noticed the dad with them moments ago, but he wasn't with them now. He must have gone to the bathroom.* Lucy saw that the younger child had on his headphones and swayed rhythmically to what Lucy assumed was music while the slightly older sibling held his hand.

"Un cafe pour Louis," the barista called.

No one arrived to take the coffee or even shifted their feet to get the coffee.

"Un cafe pour Louis," the barista called more loudly this time.

The slightly older girl must have realized the takeaway coffee was for her dad and attempted to reach for it. Before reaching it, she accidentally pulled the cord from her brother's headset, causing it to fall and splinter on the ground of the cafe.

"It's ok. It's ok," she whispered to her brother after noticing what she did.

Just then, the espresso machine screamed to life.

The boy suddenly had panic in his eyes, once hearing the screech from the machine. He covered his ears and began swaying back and forth as he started to whimper. The sister leaned down, attempting to pick up the pieces of the shattered headset with her hands shaking. She was looking around in panic, as though she were looking for her dad, who was just there five minutes ago. The brother began to wail louder, and his swaying became more erratic and pronounced. His sister tried to quiet him, but he started tapping his ears with both hands, almost to protect them from the noise that filled the small cafe.

Lucy was starting to pick up on what was going on even though it was happening so quickly. This was something she'd seen before in her work to prepare for a role where she needed to understand the autism spectrum.

His noise-cancelling headphones are his only barrier between him and the noise of the outside world, Lucy realized. *He is getting overstimulated, and his dad is nowhere to be seen. His sister looks like she is about to panic, now that his headphones are destroyed. I can't just stand here,* Lucy thought was she started to prepare to take action. *I hope the boy responds to my attempt to help.*

Lucy, quickly and smoothly, calmly leaned down and was nearly face to face with the boy. She gently, almost masterfully, placed her headset on the boy's ears.

Suddenly, he was still. He was content, then he saw his dad.

His sister, looking emotional about having accidentally broken her brother's headset, walked over to her dad and buried her face in his stomach.

"Sorry love, I was in the bathroom. Are you okay?"

The dad looked around the space while checking in with both

kids. The little boy was content with a seemingly new headset while the sister appeared shaken for some reason unbeknownst to him. There was a woman squatting in front of his son.

"Your daughter accidentally yanked on your son's cord, which caused his headset to fall on the ground and break. I gave him my headset after he became upset, which seemed to work," Lucy answered and smiled, looking down at the young boy.

She stood up and was suddenly staring at the boy's stunning father, and a pang of guilt hit her as she questioned herself as to why she would be admiring this beautiful man, who happened to be a dad. The father did a double take once he saw the woman who had intervened on behalf of his kids.

Lucy's mind was a flood of thoughts—*I need to get out of here. I don't want to cause a scene that may attract any unwanted attention, but wow, that dad is absolutely gorgeous with his hazel eyes and sophisticated style. Lucy, why were you looking to see if he had on a wedding ring? What is wrong with you? He doesn't have on a wedding ring, but are you finding dads attractive now? I mean, he does look like he is your age, but get out of your head, girl, and start walking now!*

"I don't know how to thank you," he said to Lucy with such a rich, velvety voice that this time, Lucy did a double take once she heard his silky voice.

"It was no problem. Keep the headphones. Have a good day." Lucy grabbed Elle's arm, signaling that she was stepping outside the cafe.

Elle followed Lucy, knowing that Lucy was probably uncomfortable or saw something that she didn't like.

Is my sudden departure due to remaining incognito with my movie star status or because I am trying to avoid the beautiful dad who was returning her gaze, if ever so briefly, and not wearing a wedding ring?

CHAPTER 11

Louis
2026

"Hey, love," Louis said in the cafe and continued to hug Noemie, doing his best to make her feel better. "It's ok." He continued to reassure the protective older sister, who was shaken up after seeing her brother get so upset when his headset splintered on the ground.

"I am going to have a backup headset in my work bag that I will always keep with me from this moment forward." Those words seemed to encourage Noemie more than any reassurance or even the hugs.

She nodded and sniffed. This little girl was tough on most days, but the thing that had shaken her was because she was not feeling like she could help her brother in that moment.

"Are you ok, now? Are you ready for school?" Louis asked as Noemie sniffed again, feeling reassured and ready to go to school.

"Come on, Theo, let's get going." Theo took his sister's hand and made his way out of the cafe.

"It was so kind of that woman to help and offer her headset," Louis said to no one.

"You do know that the Decibell headsets are the top-of-the-line headsets, right?" Noemie replied as they made their way out of the cafe and onto the sidewalk.

"Really?" Louis was surprised.

"One of my friends at school said that they wanted some for their birthday, and they cost about one thousand euros. That is expensive, right?"

Finally, something that showed Noemie is a little girl, and not an adult. On most days, she took the role of older sister very seriously.

"Yes, love … a thousand euros is quite a bit of money for headphones. We will have to make sure to take care of those."

"I doubt if they will break if they drop on the ground because they are so nice," Noemie added.

"You are probably right." Louis smiled as they walked down the sidewalk with his arm around her. Still, she was holding her brother's hand as the trio walked.

"Let's not find out how breakable these headphones are," Louis joked.

"Agreed." Noemie smiled.

They arrived outside the kids' school.

"Have a good day." Louis gave Noemie's shoulders another rub of encouragement.

Louis leaned down so he was face to face with Theo.

"Have a good day. Be sure to take care of your headphones, ok?"

Louis smiled at Theo while straightening the collar of his red shirt, Theo's favorite color.

"I love you," Louis said to Theo.

"Okay," Theo responded.

"I love you too," Louis said, standing up and hugged Noemie.

"Okay," she teased Louis.

"Not you too. Will anyone tell me they love me?" Louis joked.

"Have a good day," he relented, knowing Noemie's response was her way of teasing him.

Noemie and Louis made their way through the front gate of the school building.

I am so thankful we made it to school on time, he thought to himself as he watched his kids enter the building, as he was near the gate to exit. *I have got to get better at this whole morning routine. It cannot continue to be this chaotic every morning,* Louis mentally berated himself.

Louis turned on his heel and began making his way to his own school, where he was a music teacher. He took a sip of coffee and could not help but think of that beautiful woman in the cafe. *My man, why didn't you respond more to that beauty? Why didn't you offer her some money for the headphones? There is no way I could afford to give her any money, but I should have offered something for her kindness. Why did the hero of the morning have to be one of the most beautiful women I've ever seen in my life? How did she know how to respond to Theo?* Louis continued to be consumed with thoughts as he approached his own school, which was just a short walk from his kids.

"Mr. Durant, I need to talk to you about starting a jazz club after school. Do you have some time to talk?" a student said while approaching Louis as he arrived at his building.

"Mr. Chevalier, how are you this morning?" Louis called all his students mister or miss.

"Oh, good morning, I meant," the student replied, realizing his manners.

"Let's talk later today after class to brainstorm some possibilities," Louis replied with a smile.

"Thank you so much! I need a good club on my Uni applications. I knew you would help me. Thank you, Mr. Durant." The student did a quick snap and shake with Louis before walking away.

Louis continued through the door and down the hallway, hoping to find his boss, Miss Poulain. With the news that he received this morning about doing some one-on-one tutoring at the jazz bar, he may need to take some time off work this week. This money would help tremendously. Plus, if it wasn't for his boss, he wouldn't have made it through the past few years. She has been the one who recommended the babysitter that he used in the evenings for his jazz gigs.

He made his way to Miss Poulain's door and took a deep, reassuring breath because he hated to think about having to miss work this week to do the voice coaching. However, this gig may help him get financially ahead … finally … well … maybe.

Louis knocked on the door of his boss's office.

"Enter, Mr. Durant, because you are the only person who knocks on my office door."

"Good morning, Miss Poulain, how are you today?"

"Ok, what is going on because you rarely call me by my last name. Did you need something because you are never quite that formal with me, especially since I do help babysit your children from time to time?" She smiled at Louis.

"You are correct again. You know me like a book, don't you?" he responded nervously. *She is a friend, but he doesn't want to appear to be taking advantage of her kindness either, especially since she is his boss after all.*

She sat expectantly at her desk, waiting for Louis to explain his purpose for the morning visit.

"I will need to take some time off this week," he said nervously, finding himself straightening his sweater vest. He continued, "I have been offered a voice coaching job for a client at the jazz club, and well, it may help me financially; it has been an unexpected offer. I should know something tomorrow when I meet with the client. I don't think it will be a regular thing, but this will be a lucrative gig that may allow me to cut back on my evening work."

"You know that I would never tell you no, especially in the best interest of your family. The students adore you, and I know you will juggle both your first and second jobs well. By the way, how are things going?"

"This morning was a train wreck. I have got to do better in the morning, and I think I rely way too much on Noemie to help me with Theo." Louis sipped his now lukewarm coffee to help him stop talking. *Overshare much?* Louis thought to himself.

"Hopefully, taking some time off will help you find your routine with all of the working you do. Don't be too hard on yourself. I know you are trying very best." This time, Miss Poulain stood up and walked to the front of her desk. She stepped closer to him and put an encouraging hand on his shoulder.

Louis sipped his coffee again and took a deep breath.

"It will get easier," she reminded him, with her one encouraging hand remaining on his shoulder, just as he had done for Noemie this morning.

"I have to get going." Louis had a hard time accepting what felt like pity but really was just concern. *She means well,* he told himself, *but it is so humiliating to be in this situation.*

"Thanks so much. I will be sure to have my lesson plans on your desk this afternoon for tomorrow."

I hope this gig helps me free up some time. I pray that this opportunity opens some doors for me and takes off some financial pressure off the family.

Louis prayed as he walked to his classroom for the day. He took a moment while standing at the desk, just as the starting bell rang.

Please, God, I could use a break right now. I know You have plans for me, but I am at Your feet. Thank you for Your faithfulness.

"Who is ready to learn one of the songs that changed my life?" Louis called to the students as they entered his classroom.

CHAPTER 12

Elle

2026

"You were amazing in the cafe with that little boy," Elle said to Lucy as they walked down the sidewalk.

"I suspect he is on the autism spectrum, and I had to study a character on the spectrum for one of my roles. I was just fortunate with having that experience, and the very little that I knew worked out for the little boy." Lucy shrugged. "If you will excuse me, but I think our rental is coming up around the corner."

Lucy slowed down while staring at her phone for directions.

"Here we are … 403." Lucy stopped and stared at her phone for further directions. "Let me enter the code, and we should be all set. Here we are…" Lucy led Elle into a huge two-story flat in the heart of the Latin Quarter in Paris.

"Do you always stay here?" Elle looked at the huge space. There were variations of white and tan furniture scattered throughout the open space. A baby grand piano sat in the corner of the huge living room area that lined the wall. Elle was drawn to the windows and looked down at the Seine River; Notre Dame was just across the river from this rental. Elle watched the boats glide across the river at a slow pace, then she could see several people sitting along the river while enjoying the late summer day.

"I usually stay in this neighborhood because it is so close to everything, and I can get food delivered if I wish. I requested this location because of one reason." Lucy smiled sheepishly.

"The view?" Elle answered while still standing near the window, soaking in all the activities that reflected Parisian life.

"The piano actually." Lucy smiled. "I have to start practicing for a new role."

"Are you playing the piano for this new role?"

"I am trying out for a role, so it isn't mine yet. However, the director knows that I am interested in trying something new. So, I am extremely nervous and out of my comfort zone, but I want to give it a try," Lucy said with a confident smile.

"You are giving main character energy, and I am here for it! No wonder you make the big bucks!" Elle teased.

Lucy pretended to flip her hair and grabbed her luggage and made her way toward the stairs to the bedrooms.

"I am going to check out the bedroom situation. Do you have any preferences?" Lucy called as she began up the steps.

"I would just like a bed," Elle called back to Lucy while still staring out the window and taking in the views.

"Elle … Elle!" Lucy called with such urgency that Elle began a mad dash toward the stairs and began skipping steps to make it to Lucy.

"What is it?" Elle busted through the door.

"Look at this balcony!" Lucy smiled, just now realizing that she scared Elle out of her wits.

"You scared me to death because I am a little worried about your safety. On the other hand, oh yayyyy … a balcony!" Elle squealed like she was a teenager.

The quick switch with her demeanor made Lucy chortle.

"Come here, I want to show you where I would like to go this evening. Do you see the church there, Sacre Coeur? It's a church in the Montmartre neighborhood, and there is a world-famous jazz club that I would like to visit again. I think I need to hear some jazz in one of the most iconic locations in the world to help me get some motivation to move forward with this crazy idea for a new role.

"I am going to make some calls, but do you want to relax for a bit? We can go out around 7 or 8 this evening for dinner. Does that work for you? I have a cute, little restaurant I want us to try for dinner tonight."

"Of course; meanwhile, I am going to sit out here and enjoy the views from our balcony," Elle said with a smile.

After Lucy stepped out of the room, Elle took out her phone and hit the video chat button.

"Hello there, beautiful," Liam answered the call.

"Look at this view." Elle flipped the screen so that Liam could share the view that Elle has been admiring.

She turned the screen back to her. "Isn't this view amazing?"

Liam smiled. "I couldn't think of anything more beautiful, and I don't mean Paris."

CHAPTER 13

Lucy

2026

"Elle, I am going to be ready in a few minutes. Does that work for you?' Lucy called from the adjacent room.

"I am ready when you are … meanwhile, I am going to continue enjoying the view."

"You really are in love with this city, aren't you?" Lucy entered the room.

"It is amazing to me to think of how intuitive Parisians were when they designed and built so much of this city hundreds of years ago. The style that they chose for their buildings is so stately. It is still beautiful. They knew what they were doing when they began imagining this city." Elle shrugged her shoulders, despite the fact that she was sitting by herself on the balcony, as she continued admiring the view.

"Then, we better go explore this beautiful city." Lucy always had a timely quip, as she poked her head into Elle's room.

Both women packed up their things and walked out of the door of their rental as the afternoon turned to evening.

"I wanted us to try this cozy, little place in Montmartre called La Belle Legume. It specializes in farm-to-table fare but also, they have many vegetarian options. My brother mentioned that you tend to eat vegetarian." Lucy smiled.

"Thank you for thinking of me," Elle said, returning the smile.

"I hope you have walking shoes because we are going to be taking several sets of stairs to reach the charming neighborhood. It also has some of the best views of the city too."

"Even better views than our rental?" Elle teased.

"I know it sounds impossible, but yes, even better," Lucy joked as they walked down sidewalk, heading to the metro.

"Excuse me. Excuse me," a man said, approaching the women as they walked.

Keep walking, Elle, Lucy thought to herself. *We don't stop for strangers in a city because it could get us in a proper kerfuffle, especially if a fan recognizes me.*

Elle turned to the man who now had gently touched Lucy's arm.

"Are you Skye Reynolds? I am a huge fan."

"Would you like an autograph?" Lucy wore a pasted smile, while she tried to remain discreet.

"No, I just wanted to tell you how much I love you," the man gushed.

"Thank you. Enjoy your evening," Lucy said with a smile.

"But you just have to know how much I admire your work. You

are such an inspiration."

"Thank you, I have to get going."

Suddenly Elle intervened, "Look, my job is to project, deflect, and occasionally intercept bad behavior. So, if you are as big of a fan as you say you are, then you know it is time to give her some space." Elle paused as she stood between Lucy and the pushy fan. For melodramatic effect, Elle added, "Did you get all of that?"

The "fan" stood somewhat taken aback by Elle's aggressive comments.

"Skye, let's go," Elle called to Lucy as though she was truly on official business.

Both women began walking away from the fan, while Elle kept watching him to make sure he wouldn't be a bother any longer.

"Where did that come from?" Lucy asked, on the verge of laughter, after they were a distance away.

"I have no idea, but I wanted to ditch him. It was really making me feel very uncomfortable, and I didn't want him to take his fan-guying any further than he already had. I am beginning to see some of the behavior you have to deal with," Elle said.

"I was just beginning to think he reminded me of a guy I talked to for a little while, Talky McTalkerson. I could never get a word in during a conversation. He was constantly talking over me or interrupting me," Lucy joked.

If Elle only really knew what a complete hassle these guys have been in my life, wasting my time, playing games. If I didn't give them goofy nicknames, I think I would cry about the time I wasted with these random blokes.

"You have had a Ghosty McGhosteron and a Talky McTalkerson in your life?"

"Just wait … I have so many more stories to tell you." Lucy smiled. "Here is our metro that will take us to Montmartre."

"I have got to hear more!" Elle said as they entered the subway.

"Let me tell you a wee bit about Handsy McHanderton," Lucy began as they found their seats on the train.

Elle guffawed, "I don't know if I should laugh or cry with some of these guys."

You have no idea, Lucy thought to herself.

CHAPTER 14

Elle

2026

"That was the most amazing meal that I have ever had in my life," Elle continued. "I had no idea that you can make mushrooms look and taste like steak. The chef said he used Lion's Mane mushroom, right?"

"I think that is what he called them," Lucy answered. "Do you mind if we walk around this little arrondissement for a bit? I love the charm of it." Lucy smiled, slowed her stroll, and took in the allure of the neighborhood.

"I am so happy you enjoyed the meal."

"I plan to go back during our next visit," Elle added.

"Absolutely." Lucy smiled, loving the fact that Elle was already considering another visit.

During our next visit, I will most likely be your sister-in-law and be a Mrs.

"Let's take a turn right here." Lucy was guiding the duo as they walked the cobblestone walkways through the Montmartre arrondissement that was known for its arts and music scene.

This is so quaint and charming, Elle thought as they turned the corner to see an evening market. Various vendors were set up in the center of a small square that was surrounded by buildings on all sides of the square. The buildings were not only historic but had cafe tables dotted across the sidewalk in front of each business. Several planters dotted the area to add a splash of summer color among the vendors.

"I read that this market is here on most nights," Lucy added. "There are various types of artists who choose this venue. You will only find one-of-a-kind items at this spot."

Elle approached a vendor and perused their handmade bookmarks that were designed out of pages of books. Art was intricately drawn on each bookmark, revealing some magical aspects of Paris.

Meanwhile, Lucy was looking at the adjacent vendor with the build-a-bouquet vendor. "Some beautiful flowers for a beautiful lady?" the man standing behind the counter added in French.

"No, thank you," Lucy added. She did know some French but didn't want to start a conversation.

"No, please … take these … no charge," the man added, as he continued to hold a bouquet out for Lucy to take.

"No, I couldn't possibly take some flowers. Thank you though."

"It would be an honor to have such a beautiful woman carry around my flowers," he added.

"I'll take them," Elle chimed in and handed over some money.

"Oh … ok," he added with a shrug.

"Merci," Elle added, again trying to intervene when someone

was becoming a tad too assertive with Lucy. In some ways, Elle felt responsible for Lucy without having Liam with them. Elle walked with her arm in Lucy's arm as they continued through the market.

"You are the bloody best," Lucy added.

"He was actually really cute and kind of charming, I will admit. He was a bit too pushy though," Elle added.

"He reminded me too much of The Fluffernator that I dated. He was all talk and no delivery. I mean, look at the bouquet. If you are really trying to impress a girl, can you choose more than two flowers pretending to be a bouquet to woo her?" Lucy added.

"That is a good point," Elle added. "He could have been trying to just get your attention though."

"Maybe?" Lucy shrugged.

Wow, Lucy can be so harsh about men. Is she kind of bitter or just hurt? Is she making up the nicknames or are there so many men who have been unkind to her? I mean all the little nicknames are funny, but something makes me sad too. I just want her to find a nice person for her if that is what she wants.

"Do you mind if we go listen to jazz music after this? I need some inspo for my work. There is a place called Le Chat Bleu that I want you to see."

"Of course, I read online today that Paris is known for its jazz history." Elle was always a student of new experiences and eager to learn.

"It isn't far from this market," Lucy added.

"Is that it over there?" Elle pointed toward the sign.

"It is … shall we?"

Both women left the charm of the outside market and walked into a dark space with small lamps that adorned the green tablecloths on each table. Bench-style seats outlined the perimeter of the room. A jazz musician was playing the piano as they entered the room. Lucy entered the space first and looked for available seating toward the back of the venue.

I assume she wanted to sit in the back for security. Personally, I would have picked a seat in the center of the room to experience the ambience of the room. I am always learning more about Lucy and her life as a well-known actress, Elle thought to herself.

Lucy scooted into the booth that was slightly illuminated by a small gold table lamp.

"This musician is really good. I love piano jazz," Elle added.

"Do you want a glass of wine?" Lucy asked. "A red?"

"Sure," Elle added, "I think you know what I like."

Lucy ordered in French when the waitress arrived.

"Wow, you really can speak French." Elle was surprised.

"Just a bit. I know the important stuff, like ordering food and asking where I can find the loo," Lucy joked.

The pianist then began singing, and his velvety voice practically brought the room to a standstill.

"He just went from good to amazing," Elle whispered. "His smooth voice could slice butter." Elle waited for a chuckle from

Lucy, but Lucy was turning her head, trying to get a better view of the musician from her seat. Lucy was no longer engaged in a conversation with Elle because she was distracted by the musician.

"Hello?" Elle called.

"Sorry … he is outstanding. I just wanted to get a better view of him from here."

"I can't see him either … want to move?"

"No, that's ok." Lucy sat entranced as she listened to him finish his song.

"Thank you, ladies and gentlemen, I am going to take a short break, and I will be back soon."

"The wine is good and the music is even better," Elle whispered to Lucy. "If you like this place, we could come again during our trip."

"I would love that." Lucy smiled. "However, as much as I would love to stay longer, I am exhausted."

"I completely understand. We have had a full day," Elle said, smiling with exhaustion.

"Do you mind bringing the bill?" Lucy asked the server.

"Your account has been settled," the waitress added.

"I am sorry?" Lucy looked at her in confusion.

"Yes, Louis Durant paid for it. He told me to tell you thank you for your help this morning at the café."

"Who is Louis Durant?"

Just as the waitress was about to answer Lucy's questions, her voice was muffled by the sound of the musician, who returned to the piano and played a short riff as a subtle introduction.

"Ladies and gentlemen, thank you for sticking around while I took a quick break. I am Louis Durant, and I am so glad you came tonight."

Lucy looked at the stage and saw the man from the cafe this morning. The man whose son she gave her headphones. The most beautiful man she has ever seen in her life.

Then, she smiled in her direction, and he began singing "Postcards We Never Sent."

Lucy was entranced and slowly sat back down.

Elle was completely entertained by Lucy's reaction to the man's gesture, but more surprised by Lucy's reaction to the man.

Elle thought, *If this guy is single, we may have a new nickname for a man in her life, and that could be … Mr. Right.*

CHAPTER 15

Lucy
2026

"Good morning, Sunshine," Elle said, entering the rental, after a quick trip to a local patisserie. She entered the space with coffee and pastries for the girls to enjoy. Elle slipped off her shoes with both hands full of drinks and treats.

"What a lovely surprise," Lucy cooed. *If only Elle knew how upset my stomach is this morning before I am doing my reading, well … singing. Literally, my stomach is in knots just thinking about working with a voice coach for the project. Come on, Lucy; what were you thinking to even consider this job that included singing? You have a celebrated career in the movie industry, so why did you feel like you needed to expand into music?* Lucy was determined to get her spiraling thoughts under control. *Get it together, Lucy; enjoy this time with your sweet sister-in-law.*

"I know it can be tricky for you to get out and about in the city. So, I brought a little bit of the city to you."

"You are the bloody best," Lucy said with a smile.

"I will meet you up on the balcony for breakfast. Give me a few minutes to set it up for us. Sound, ok?"

Elle took the bags into the kitchen and began searching the cabinets for a vase. She pulled a beautiful purple vase out of the cabinet and took the flowers that she had hidden as a small surprise for Lucy. She arranged the small bouquet in the vase, which would fit perfectly on the bistro table on the balcony. Satisfied, Elle smiled at her little surprise for her soon-to-be sister-in-law. Taking the stairs, Elle made quick work for setting up the breakfast and flowers on the balcony.

"Breakfast is served," Elle called to Lucy when she was done.

"I am on my way," Lucy called back from the other room.

Elle sat down at the table and was eagerly waiting to see Lucy's face when she saw the surprise breakfast.

"Wow … just wow," Lucy smilingly stated, her eyes filling up with tears. "Bloody hell … you are going to make me cry."

Elle hopped up from the table and gave Lucy a hug.

"I am so sorry. I just wanted to give you a well-deserved treat this morning before your big day with your reading." Elle held onto the hug and gave Lucy's back a rub for encouragement. She could sense that Lucy was beginning to relax during their long embrace.

Elle made her way back to the small table.

"Isn't this view just beautiful?"

"It really is." Lucy finally took the time to sit and enjoy the view of the Seine River, and the quiet of the Parisian morning. The light gray and tan stone stately buildings that had endured years of history. The apartment was located at the tip of Isle Saint Louis where you could see the river split and surround both sides of Notre Dame. The tops of the green trees outlined the water but allowed the perfect view. Small boats, moored to the land, outlined the river while some early morning explorers glided slowly down the water on a flat riverboat. Lucy took a deep breath and smiled at the view as both women sat at the bistro table.

"How are you doing? I know that you seem a bit nervous about your reading today. I can sense your apprehension." Elle smiled encouragingly after her statement.

"Honestly, I am second-guessing my decision to try this singing thing. Why would I even try doing something like this when I have a pretty successful career doing what I am doing now? Why would I even take the risk? This is where my head is currently with my big project," Lucy confessed.

Lucy, why are you being such a downer during this trip? Why are you telling her all your feelings? You need to keep the visit light, Lucy chastised herself for her honesty.

"I think you put yourself out there because you like to constantly improve what you do. You have mastered this part of your career currently, and you want to take on a new challenge. Your decision is commendable," Elle encouraged her.

"You are very sweet," Lucy said quietly, taking a nibble of a croissant.

"I mean it. For many people, they wouldn't even try something new, but you are always diving into new experiences. Plus, if I know you, you will dive full-force into this new project, and you will master it too."

Lucy seemed to begin feeling better since Elle offered the encouragement.

"You may be the next Coco Lush," Elle added, which made Lucy cackle in laughter. Coco Lush was the lead singer to one of Elle's favorite bands, Femme Frequency. She was a music icon, which made Elle's comment poignant and comical.

"You, my dear, are a master at giving a pep talk." Lucy then smiled and sipped on her coffee. "This reminds me of my old love interest, Sir Boost-a-Lot; he was great at the pep talk, but no delivery."

Elle laughed at yet another well-timed nickname for one of Lucy's former love interests.

"You have the best names for your former loves," Elle stated, "but what is the story behind this? Do you want to talk about it? I know you make light of it, but it must also be very frustrating too."

"If I don't make light of it, I would be bitter about it. I just have to realize that having my job that I do, it is difficult to find someone who is not looking for some angle when they get to know me. It's difficult to find someone who is willing to be authentic; it comes with the territory, I guess." Lucy shrugged, but Elle could sense that there was more to the story than that for Lucy.

"I can understand that." Elle tried to say something reassuring to Lucy but had difficulty saying more to her. She knew that being newly engaged may seem insincere to offer any advice or kind words.

"I will be honest … you know, the thing that bothers me most about these guys?"

Elle shrugged her shoulders, trying to express some kind of

reassurance, nodding to encourage Lucy to say more.

"They wasted my time. They waste my time to find someone else. I don't care about money I have spent on them or gifts I have purchased. I hate the fact that I wasted time on waiting for them to show up and be the person they made me think they were when we first began talking." Lucy sniffed, trying to hold back that fact that she was getting emotional.

Elle put her hand on Lucy's hand. Elle's eyes began to brim with tears in feeling for Lucy.

"I am so sorry," Elle offered encouragement again.

Lucy, get yourself together. Elle means well, but she is looking at you in pity! Your life isn't that bad. Get over it, she thought to herself.

The women sat quietly for a beat while they sipped coffee or nibbled on pastries.

"I am sorry I went crazy with the pastries," Elle broke the silence. "I wanted to try everything when I was standing in the bakery."

"You are so sweet for going out for us. Thanks again for the breakfast," Lucy sipped on her coffee and smiled at the thoughtfulness spread.

"Did I ever tell you about the guy who was addicted to coffee that I dated? It was so short-lived that I literally never came up with a fun nickname for him," Lucy joked. "The guy was literally buzzing from caffeine half of the time." Lucy chuckled, thinking about the short-lived relationship.

"He sounds like a bit of Caffeinstein," Elle quipped.

Lucy cackled in laughter.

Elle was on a roll. "What about Java Junkie or Captain Caffeine?"

Lucy laughed out loud.

"One more, how about Sir Buzz-a-Lot?"

This one made Lucy wipe her eyes because she became teary-eyed from all the laughter.

"I love you, Elle. I am so happy you are joining our family."

"To Java the Nut," Elle called and held out her coffee cup to cheers with Lucy, who continued to giggle.

"Now, how about to making music with someone who helps you hit all the right notes with your new music venture?" Elle continued.

"Now that is perfect," Lucy answered.

They cheered their coffee cups together and enjoyed their breakfast from the veranda of their rental, looking over the beautiful city of Paris as it was coming to life.

CHAPTER 16

Louis

2026

"Breakfast is ready," Louis called upstairs as he could hear Noemie and Theo getting ready for school.

"Pardon?" Louis heard Noemie ask from upstairs, then heard the sound of small feet taking the stairs down to the kitchen. "Did you make breakfast?"

"I did." Louis smiled proudly, suddenly a little self-conscious that he may not be able to make this endeavor an actual habit.

"How does toasted baguette, jam, butter, warm milk, and juice sound this morning?" Louis beamed.

Theo could be heard taking the stairs now and saw the spread that Louis had prepared for them.

I hope I am able to do this every morning, Louis thought to himself. *This wasn't that difficult. I have got to get better. The kids have been through enough and the least I could do is give them a good breakfast to start their day. Louis, you will make them breakfast before school from this moment forward,* Louis thought, making a promise to himself.

The normally quiet Theo entered the kitchen, grabbed a piece of the toasted baguette, dipped it into butter, and sat down at the table. He began humming as he sat chewing quietly with his feet swinging.

Look at my sweet boy sitting so contently here for breakfast. I had no idea how much they missed their morning routine.

Noemie followed Theo's lead and joined him at the table, swinging her legs as she nibbled on bread dipped in jam. She and her brother looked at one another and smiled as they downed their breakfast. Noemie took a sip of warm milk as she chewed, while smiling at Theo who was sitting contently at the breakfast table.

Louis repeated Theo's action and joined the kids at the table, nibbling on a baguette, smiling contently as well.

"How did you find time to make some breakfast this morning?" Noemie asked.

"I am taking the day off of school today."

"Can I take the day off of school today too?" Noemie tested Louis.

"I am actually working, but I am working at the bar today." Louis took a sip of his coffee.

"People go to a bar during the day to listen to jazz?" Noemie asked incredulously.

"Not exactly," Louis answered with a smile. "I guess there is someone looking for a music coach."

"A coach? Who hires someone to teach them to sing or play music?"

"Honestly, I don't know all the answers yet, but I think it is someone who is a celebrity and needs a voice coach. They are paying me well enough that it might be a little easier around here."

"Really? How easy?" Noemie asked.

Theo sat quietly while still eating his baguette and butter. He followed the conversation with his eyes, still swinging his legs contently.

"Don't worry, I don't think life will be completely different, but maybe a little easier for a bit. I hope that I won't have to work so many evening gigs for extra money. Hopefully, I can be home more in the evening." Louis sipped his coffee and smiled at the kids, looking at him hopefully.

"I don't know, our sitter lets us eat most anything we want for dinner," Noemie teased that his absence hasn't been noticed.

"The truth is finally out," Louis stated with a smile.

Theo held up a bite of baguette for Louis.

"Thank you … the perfect bite." Louis opened his mouth for the welcome bite.

Louis stood up and began gathering the dirty dishes. "Will you finish getting ready? I will clean up here."

While standing up from the table, Theo put his arms around Louis as a quiet thank-you for breakfast. Then, both Noemie and Theo went back upstairs to finish getting ready for school.

You have got to find time to do this, Louis, he said to himself. *This morning was such a pleasure and a completely different change of pace compared to yesterday. I want every morning to be like this. My heart nearly melted when Theo offered me a bite of food and gave me a hug. I want this every morning. I hope this opportunity offers us a chance for these slow mornings.*

Louis finished the dishes and went into the living room to finish getting ready himself. He put on his usual style: sweater vest over a button-down shirt, with pleated brown pants. His ensemble was complete with a pair of leather spectator shoes. Finally, he slipped on his round brown glasses. This was his usual "uniform" for school and for his jazz gigs. He looked like his style came right out of the 1920s, but he loved it; Louis's look almost solidified his love for jazz music. He gave himself one more glance in the mirror before leaving, almost a nod of encouragement for this new opportunity.

"You look great," Noemie said, while standing by the stairs.

"Thank you for the encouragement." Louis hugged Noemie.

"I love you, kiddo," he told Noemie, feeling thankful for the kind words she offered to him this morning.

"Ok," she teased.

"Not you too," Louis asked, while giving Noemie another hug.

The trio walked out the door, this morning with a peaceful attitude. Each of them feeling hopeful and ready for a day of new opportunities.

CHAPTER 17

Lucy
2026

Lucy exited the metro station and began her ascent up the long steps into the Montmartre neighborhood. She loved being back in this neighborhood, and after her time last night, it made her realize this was another one of her favorite areas in Paris. She loved being among the creative people who called this area home. Lucy walked the winding stairwell that led riders off the metro and into the eighteenth arrondissement.

The brightness of the day made Lucy's sunglasses feel almost useless. She had a baseball cap that was pulled down just above her eyebrows and wore a versatile outfit for her work this morning. Lucy didn't know what to expect, so she wore a black cotton pant set that was casual and yet could be chic if accessorized well. She also wore black and white trainers to give the outfit a more casual look with her baseball cap, yet it could look smart with the light blazer that she packed in her bag once she got a feel of the work environment. Lucy's blonde hair would normally be styled, especially given that Elle just gave her an amazing new rocker hair cut about a month ago, but today, she was being discreet while she traveled to this gig alone. Plus, she might keep her glasses and hat on during her work today if it didn't go well.

Lucy was not confident with dipping her toe into the musical world professionally, but she was excited for a new challenge.

Lucy took in her surroundings as she walked to Le Chat Bleu. *This city is so charming. The city is just waking up, and I love being here to witness it,* Lucy thought as she continued her walk. Then, she suddenly realized her coach was standing outside of the jazz club.

Lucy took a cleansing breath. She paced a bit outside of the bar, rethinking her choice to be here. *I could change my mind. I could text Dottie to have her change the details of my plans, and no one would know any different. No one would know.* She continued pacing, then stopped suddenly. Lucy picked up her phone and stared at the screen. She scrolled to Dottie's name.

"Hi there, are you Lucy?" a familiar face stood behind her, holding two cups of coffee.

Lucy clicked the button on the side of her phone, and the screen shut went black.

"Hello," Lucy replied nervously.

How could this be happening? This is the guy … the dad … the musician from last night. He can't possibly recognize me. Then again, I am wearing the same hat that I wore yesterday morning in the cafe when I helped him with his son. I wonder if he is going to say anything to me about yesterday morning? Does he recognize me?

"I didn't know what kind of coffee you would take, so I picked up two cafe cremes—one with milk and one with oatmilk. Which would you prefer?" He held out the coffees as though it was a game.

"Oh … don't worry … I didn't sample the coffee first," he said honestly.

"I'll take the oatmilk," Lucy said smiling. "Thank you."

"Normally, I would not suggest dairy before a voice lesson, but in this case, we can start slow. Based on the pacing I saw you doing outside of this building, I think you may be a little nervous."

Lucy was sipping her coffee, so she nodded emphatically. For some reason, she wanted to cry when he noticed her apprehension.

"Don't worry, I am here to help. Do you mind if we go inside to chat? I want to get to know you a bit better."

Oh … I want to get to know YOU better too, Lucy said to herself. *Lucy, what is wrong with you? You need to focus on work … do you hear that… work? You are not here to meet another Mr. Wrong. You are here to work and try something new. You are not here to look at his beautiful hazel eyes and stare at his golden-brown skin, or his hair that is cut in a modern fade, with a textured top with warm tones highlighting the top.* Lucy fought the intrusive thoughts and the urge to start pacing again. *Focus, Lucy, focus.*

"Sounds great." Lucy suddenly found herself tongue-tied.

"Oh … I am Louis, by the way," he said as he opened the door of the Le Chat Bleu.

Lucy stepped inside, but paused, allowing Louis to lead her to their location.

"Let's sit at one of these tables. I want to hear about your experience and your goals for this work we are about to do,"

Lucy sat down and blurted out the first thing that came to her mind, "My goal is to not suck."

Louis rolled with laughter. "You sound like my students."

"You call your clients your students?" Lucy asked, a bit confused.

"No." Louis laughed again. "I am also a music teacher."

"I see." Lucy smiled. "I didn't know if I was expected to raise my hand if I had a question."

"Talented and funny," Louis said.

"We will see if you think I am talented when you hear me sing."

"Let's start with this … half of the battle with conquering any kind of voice work is your mental game. You need to feel like you can do it, and you will learn techniques that will help you do it. Make sense?"

Suddenly, Lucy's shoulders began to relax a bit. *This strategy must work on his students too because I am feeling a bit better already.*

"Tell me about the project that brought you here."

"I have a reading for a movie that is coming up soon. I don't have to do any voice work for the movie, but I could. The movie is based on the work of Vivienne St. James. Normally, I do action movies, but I want to try this type of film. I want to try some of the singing parts. I mean, I sing at home and my voice isn't terrible, but it isn't Vivienne St. James either," Lucy stated with a shrug.

"Again, you are wanting to try it, so your willingness helps you conquer fears. I will show you some techniques that she used while also teaching you some basic vocal techniques. I may give you some homework too."

"That sounds fair," Lucy said.

"I love 1920s jazz, so I am very familiar with Vivienne St. James's work. I actually have some of her albums at home that I love listening to on vinyl. There is nothing like it." Louis smiled while talking.

He is so captivating. Can you find someone incredibly appealing just listening to them talk about their passions? Lucy thought to herself.

"I can only imagine what that sounds like. I have been listening to her music recently to become more acquainted with her work. I am a novice though."

"Here is my phone number. I hear you have an unpredictable schedule while you are here in Paris, so I will have you speak to me directly to schedule our sessions. I can work early or late this week if you like." Louis took out his phone and held out his contact information for her to add to her phone.

"You can share my information with your assistant if you want her to schedule things with me."

"It's ok, you can have my contact information. Just don't share it with paparazzi," Lucy joked and text him back after she added his contact information to her phone.

"Got it. Let's practice some breathing first. Let's stand up. Do you feel more comfortable with your sunglasses and hat on because I don't think anyone is in here," Louis added. "I think it is secure throughout the day."

Lucy took off her hat and sunglasses, her blonde hair cascading down from her hat, and Louis's eyes actually widened when he realized who he was standing face to face with.

Clearly, he knows it is you. He either recognizes you as an actress or the person who helped with his son. I am going to pretend that none of it happened and continue on with our work together as though it is an average day meeting someone new.

"You need to engage your diaphragm when singing. Inhale deeply for four counts, hold for two counts, then exhale like a motorboat." Lucy focused on the breathing but was struggling to relax her lips to make the sound.

Louis stepped closer to her, pursing his lips, then relaxing them.

Lord, please get this gorgeous man and his moving lips away from me. I do not have the strength to learn how to sing and not be distracted by his charms.

"Stick out your lips and relax them," Louis demonstrated. "Try it again. Now, breathe."

Lucy finally made the sound.

"You did it. Now, you need to engage your diaphragm."

Lucy looked at him confused.

"Look at me." Louis touched just below his ribs and above his belly button as he did the breathing.

Lucy repeated but still had a confused look on her face.

"May I?" Lucy nodded, and Louis gentled touched her stomach so gently, while breathing in and out steadily with her.

"You will feel your stomach expand when you do it correctly. Do you feel it now?"

Yes, I certainly feel it now! Lucy thought to herself. *What I am feeling is not related to this exercise.*

"I feel it," Lucy answered, trying to hide the fact she was feeling flustered, and her voice may have been shaky.

The two practiced breathing exercises and vocalizing.

"Here is your homework. Practice these exercises. Then, I am going to text you this app that has the solfeggio scale … you know the do, re, mi scale? I want you to practice matching the chords by singing them." Louis text her the app. "Does this sound like homework you can do?"

"It does." Lucy paused. "So, I don't have to sing today?"

"No, I think you were too anxious about it. Let's try in our next session. I'll wait for you to text me with your schedule, or I can go through Dottie, if you prefer."

"No, I will text you if that is ok. I'll try to schedule out some time in advance, so you can plan time with your kids." Lucy let the last part slip, alerting him to the fact that she did remember him.

"Thank you. I look forward to hearing from you." Louis held out his hand. "Thank you."

"I will be in touch." Lucy stood there longer than she intended, staring at Louis, suddenly realizing she had delayed a bit too long. Lucy began walking toward the exit while putting back on her sunglasses and hat.

Move, Lucy, move … have you never met a beautiful man in your life? Get a grip!

Then, she walked out the door but turned before stepping outside and saw Louis watching her as she exited.

CHAPTER 18

Louis
2026

I think my hands are actually shaking since running into her again! What are the chances that I keep running into this beautiful woman? First, she helps me in the cafe by assisting with Theo. She comes to Le Chat Bleu while I am performing last night. Then, she is the celebrity who needs coaching. I just can't believe I get to work with this clever, funny, and beautiful woman. Well ... I hope she does call me back for more sessions at least.

"Hey, Cap," Louis called for the manager as he was moving his things up to the piano on the stage. "Are you sure it is no trouble having me off this week while I do this coaching?"

"It's no problem at all, but I don't want you telling everyone around here that I am a nice guy and recommended you for this extra job. I have a reputation to keep," Cap joked with this gruff voice while he was working in his office.

"Do you mind if I play around on the keys for a bit?"

"Nah, go ahead," Cap called out of the office without bothering to enter the room.

Louis sat on the piano and pulled out a notebook. He took out a pencil and sat it next to his notes. He looked at the lyrics that he began recently.

Oh, it's midnight on Bourbon Street,

Where the moon and music meet,

Horns sound and lovers sway,

Louis paused to think about his next line. He reread the lines, singing them aloud, but then touched the keys, trying to get the right note.

"Sounds pretty good," Cap yelled from the office again.

Louis tried it again and thought about the lyrics again.

Horns sound and lovers sway

Music, taking all the pain away

"I didn't know you wrote music too." Lucy was back in the venue, listening to Louis attempt to write some new music.

"I … um … didn't know you were there." Louis seemed completely vulnerable.

I am happy to see you again so soon, but just not right now, Louis thought to himself. *Writing my music is one of my most unguarded moments.*

"Sorry, I didn't mean to interrupt you." Lucy was able to pick up on Louis's apprehension.

"No, it isn't that. When I write music, I try ten wrong lines before I find one that sounds good. All that to say, I feel vulnerable when I write my music." Louis was candid, but honest, and Lucy found that refreshing.

"No, I get it. It is like putting yourself out there to sing for the very first time but doing it in front of the entire entertainment world," Lucy quipped.

"Touche," Louis said, acknowledging her feelings.

"It's great to see you again, but did you forget something?"

"I did actually." Lucy returned to where they had talked about thirty minutes ago. "I forgot my backpack, which doesn't really have anything important in here, but I hate the feeling of losing things."

"I know, that is the worst feeling, isn't it? I lost my coffee mug one day, and I think I went manic for a day," Louis joked.

Lucy smiled at Louis and found herself lingering again. "I better get going."

"Hi there, what are you doing here?"

Louis and Lucy turned to see Noemie and Theo walk into the bar.

"Hello there," Lucy said, completely shocked by seeing the kids again.

Noemie walked up to Lucy and gave her a hug. "Thank you for your help yesterday. You saved the day. I am Noemie, and this is Theo."

My sweet Noemie, Louis thought, *you act so much older than you are. You sound so grown-up speaking to Lucy about her help yesterday. It makes my heart swell with pride and breaks my heart that you have grown up so quickly.*

"You are so welcome. I am Lucy, by the way," holding her hand out to Noemie. The gesture clearly pleased the young girl, who felt a little more grown-up with this formal introduction.

"Hello, young man." Lucy bent down and faced Theo at his eye level and smiled at him. She didn't attempt to shake his hand, knowing that he most likely only kept these gestures to those people he knew and trusted. Much to everyone's surprise, Theo held out his tiny hand to Lucy to shake her hand.

"Hello, good sir. It is a pleasure to meet you." Lucy tried to keep the moment light, but she could tell by Louis and Noemie's expressions that they were shocked that he offered a handshake.

"Would you like to come for ice cream with us?" Noemie asked. "Our favorite ice cream place is in this neighborhood, so we decided to meet here after school."

"I don't know … I don't want to impose on your plans. I think Louis was working on some music."

"He works too much anyway," Noemie pressed, again sounding like an adult. "We would love the company." Noemie could sense her hesitation. "You do like ice cream, right?"

"What kind of question is that? Do you think I am a monster? Of course, I like ice cream!" Lucy joked.

"It is settled then. You have to come with us for ice cream. I think it may become your favorite place too."

"You should be a lawyer; you are quite convincing," Lucy continued.

"It is the least we can do to thank you for your help at the cafe,"

Noemie said.

"It is settled then. How could I say no?"

Did Noemie just talk the most witty, beautiful woman for ice cream with us? Now she will never call me back for more work. Oh well, at least I get to spend some more time with her today.

Noemie, Lucy, Louis, and Theo walked out of Le Chat Bleu and began walking down the street. Instead of taking his sister's hand as they walked down the sidewalk, Theo took Lucy's hand instead, leaving Louis and Noemie complete shocked by it. Theo never opened up so quickly to anyone, and this small gesture made Louis intrigued by Lucy even more.

CHAPTER 19

Elle

2026

Walking through the streets of the Latin Quarter was an experience of a lifetime. While Lucy was out for work, Elle took advantage of the opportunity to enjoy the city. Elle began her walk, heading in the direction of Notre Dame, strolling through the grounds that surrounded the historic cathedral. The gray of the stately building, recently renovated, was a sight to behold with its prominent spire and the chiming bells.

This is incredible. I need to take photos to send to Liam, just of Notre Dame. Then, Elle walked around the cathedral. First, she started in the courtyard in front of the church where the tourists seemed to gather. Then, she walked to the Rive Gauche side of the building, which had a makeshift park and benches that sat adjacent to the old building. After walking around the entire perimeter of the building, Elle made her way inside the cathedral to take more photos. *I am only taking a few photos of the outside of the church. As a Christian, it feels almost disrespectful to use a working church as a tourist's spot,* Elle thought to herself.

After exploring the inside of the cathedral, Elle wanted to wander and take in more of the city. *This city is a feast for the senses. I should really explore New York City more often like a tourist when I return home. After all, the world travels to my own city, I need to look at the city with fresh eyes, especially if Liam moves to the States with me when we are married.*

Then, that gnawing guilt that had been sitting at the pit of her stomach returned. *Elle, are you really going to take Liam away from the world he knows? Are you going to take him away from his sister? Are you going to move away from your new bestie and soon-to-be sister-in-law? Do you really have a large community in New York to return to after this trip? Are you sure you don't want to call London home?*

Elle continued walking, determining to shake these intrusive thoughts. She hadn't even told Liam about her doubts yet. With their Christmas wedding coming up in December, she had time to get comfortable with the decision, but for now, she was going to enjoy this city and time with her sister-in-law.

After walking away from the grounds of Notre Dame, Elle took the steps down to the cobblestone walkway that overlooked the Seine River. This view reminded her of her first date with Liam. Although she didn't realize it became a date, but that was the night that she knew she was having feelings for Liam. The night they nearly shared their first kiss and the night that they slow-danced by the Thames River in London.

Thinking of her fiancé, Elle took a photo and sent Liam a picture.

Elle

Missing you so much! XX.

Liam

I was just thinking about you too.
Everything ok?

Yes, Paris is beautiful, but not the same without you. I am just exploring right now, but I will call later.

Liam

Sounds great. XX

As she continued her walk, Elle saw another spot that piqued her interest, Shakespeare and Company. Elle walked up the historic steps from the river and crossed the bridge to make her way to the historic bookstore. Before spending her time as a hairstylist, she was a medical student who spent most of her time in libraries studying. She had always been a bit bookish and always carried a book with her.

Elle approached the iconic green-and-red entrance and entered, immediately overcome by the comforting smell of books. *No e-Readers for this girl,* Elle thought to herself. *This girl likes a physical book. Strangely, I find the smell of books comforting.* Elle perused the small shop and was determined to find one book. She scanned the shelves and shelves of books until her eyes landed on The Hunchback of Notre Dame. *Perfect,* she thought to herself and took one finger to pull the book off the shelf and into her hands. *When shopping at a bookstore across from Notre Dame in Paris, one MUST buy this book.* She smiled to herself, clutching her newfound treasure close to her chest as she walked up to the attendant to pay for it. *Now, you need to go live like a Parisian.*

After paying for her book, Elle was now strolling to Luxembourg

Garden in the heart of the Latin Quarter. Elle perused the street vendors as she was making her way up the hill from the river to the nearby park. She stopped at one vendor who was selling vintage postcards because one of the postcards caught her eye that seemed to be in Italy, which made her think of her best friend Margaux, who was celebrating in Italy. Elle pulled out her phone and decided to call Margaux.

"Do you miss me yet?" Elle, Margaux's boss and dear friend, joked.

"I do miss you. I wish you could experience Italy with me. The villa, the friends, and …" Margaux paused. She was tempted to mention something about Evan but thought better of it.

"…And what…?" Elle dragged out the last part of her word to see what kind of reaction Margaux would have to her question.

"Nothing … this trip has been amazing in so many ways. How is Paris? How long have you been in the city?" Margaux wanted the scoop about their girls' trip to Paris to celebrate the successful conclusion of the fashion show.

"Paris is beautiful. I wish Liam was here. I miss him already." Elle's cheeks burned thinking of her fiancé, who she left back in London for this quick girls' trip.

"You poor girl, how can you manage life without constantly being around your fiancé?" Margaux teased.

"Actually, I am kind of worried about Lucy," Elle whispered. Margaux could tell by the volume of Elle's voice and the whisper that she was attempting to be private about the conversation.

"You are worried about Lucy," Margaux responded with a hint of sarcasm. "Lucy, also known as Skye Reynolds, the world-famous actress. The wealthy, beautiful, and talented women who will soon be your sister-in-law once you marry her brother? You are worried about her? It sounds kind of impossible."

"I know it sounds crazy, but yes, I am worried about her," Elle again replied in almost a whisper.

"Is she nearby?" Margaux returned the whispered tone over the phone.

"No, she had to go to a reading for a script this morning. She told me about her work here before we left for Paris. I feel guilty saying anything. I guess I don't need to be whispering about it." Elle chuckled at her own behavior.

"Sorry to sound so insincere, but Lucy has everything she could ever want. She has people who adore her; she is financially independent; she has a job she loves; now she has a soon-to-be-sister-in-law/ bestie who will be added to her family. How are you worried about her? Is she dating a creep again?" Margaux joked.

"No, it isn't like that." Elle seemed to pause before saying more.

"What is it?" Margaux pushed. "It isn't like I am going to run and tell her about what you said. You seem to genuinely care about her, so you aren't gossiping about it. You are just concerned about her. Now, that you mention it. When we were working with her in London during the fashion show, her brother did seem to worry about her often, like she needed someone to watch out for her sometimes." Margaux was speaking out loud her stream of thought.

"It isn't really like that either," Elle just said what she was thinking.

"Lucy is bitter."

"She is bitter?" Margaux asked, completely confused.

"Yes," Elle said, again feeling guilty about having the conversation with another person. She had just been thinking about it and felt awkward to even say anything to Liam about it.

"What could she possibly be bitter about?" Margaux asked.

"Men," Elle said bluntly.

"Ohhhhhh…" Margaux said. "I got the impression that she hadn't been very lucky in love … that is based on all the tabloids I used to read. Come to think of it, you will be proud of me. I haven't read any of that stuff since I have been in Italy. I have been living life," Margaux said in triumph.

"Congratulations, you are growing up so fast." Elle teased Margaux like an older sister would. "With Lucy, she is so bitter that she acts like she hates all men. On our way here, she made comment after comment about how every man we encountered had some kind of flaw that related to a former love interest. Literally, like every man, she has been so negative with any interaction we have had with any man at all. It is like she hates men."

"Maybe she needs some time," Margaux encouraged Elle. "She did just have a breakup when you met her, right?"

"She did, but I had a feeling that they weren't very exclusive based on what she has said. Plus, Lucy is such an encouraging person. I want to be that for her right now. I just feel bad for her. Plus, I am in this new relationship, so I know that I am annoyingly in love right now," Elle joked. "I may not be easy to be around if you are feeling a little jaded by love."

"I'll pray for her. I am sure she is struggling right now, and I wish I could come up and help you distract her," Margaux added.

"I am sure Lucy would love to have you with us. Plus, the place we are staying in is huge. I think Lucy used her fancy-movie connections to get this place. It is stunning," Elle replied.

"I want to let you girls have time together, especially since you will be family soon once you marry Liam. Hopefully, you will be able to distract her and encourage her so that she is back to her old self. If that is one thing I know about my boss and bestie, it is that you are the ultimate encourager," Margaux said while smiling over the phone.

"I love you, friend," Elle said softly, finally feeling better about the situation with Lucy. Margaux could almost hear the smile over the phone with Elle's reply.

"Let's chat later, ok?" Elle said, a tone of gratitude in her voice.

"Love you back," Margaux said. "We will absolutely chat later. Hugs."

Elle pressed the red button to end her call and found that she was only one block away from the garden. She continued her walk and took in cafes, which seemed to be preparing for the evening crowd while still being early afternoon. Most of the outside tables were empty at this point in the day, but soon they would be filled with residents who used the city as their own living room.

After walking through the open wrought-iron gates of the entrance, Elle continued walking through the park. She walked past the stately tan-and-white building that sat adjacent to the Grand Bassin. Families were surrounding the pool of water ready to send their toy sailboats gliding across the water. Elle continued walking the well-curated grounds, with patches of grass, meticulously-maintained gravel, and pockets of vendors scattered throughout the space. Finally, she found the place she was looking for … the lawn area.

Elle joined the lawn's inhabitants who were dotted throughout the grassy area, where some were laying quietly and others were chatting over prepared snacks that were laid out on blankets. Elle took out her own small blanket she brought with her, although many people lounged directly on the grass. She sat down on her blanket and took a deep, satisfying breath. *I can't believe I am sitting in the middle of Paris, living like a local. The sounds of the city are just a quiet whisper while sitting in this park. Lord Jesus, I am so thankful to be here. Thank you for the beautiful opportunity. Amen.*

Elle came to do one thing in this park. She sat down, crossed her legs, and took her takeaway glass of wine out of her bag that she brought from the rental. After opening the wine and sitting it down beside her, she took out her new book and began reading, lounging among the locals in the heart of Paris. This was the life!

CHAPTER 20

Louis

2026

"This is our favorite ice cream place, but it also has another benefit," Louis said while walking with Noemie, Theo, and Lucy.

"They give Noemie a discount because she is so cute," Lucy deadpanned, while Noemie glowed from hearing the compliment.

"They really should do that, honestly, but sadly no. It is a very small place and off the beaten path. Hopefully, you won't have any fans recognize you." Louis smiled.

"Thank you for thinking of that." Lucy looked genuinely surprised at his thoughtfulness.

I haven't made a big deal about your celebrity status, but I think most people in the free world would recognize your beautiful face, Louis thought to himself.

"I would like to make your time with us as pleasant as possible," Louis stated, his stomach fluttered by just being around such a beautiful woman.

Louis, stay cool. *This is just some friendly ice cream. Don't overthink her kind gesture. She is just a really nice person. There is no way she is interested in you. Plus, you haven't been on a real date in forever. Plus, what deranged person would consider taking your kids with a beautiful woman for ice cream an actual date? Man, I am out of practice! Just relax and enjoy this.*

"Everything ok?" Lucy could see that there was something on Louis's mind.

"I am a little nervous, honestly," Louis confessed.

"Me too." Lucy smiled.

How could this beautiful woman be nervous? Louis asked himself. *Maybe she is still thinking about her music. I am nervous about being here with her.*

"It is normal to feel nervous about trying your hand at singing," Louis reassured her.

"I don't mean that," Lucy said, as they continued to walk.

Louis's cheeks flushed with heat. His heart sped up, and he swallowed hard to keep his breathing even and steady.

Louis, don't get your hopes up, he chanted to himself.

"Here we are." Noemie was leading the group as they walked, eager for a sweet treat. She held the door open.

"Why, thank you, miss," Lucy joked with Noemie. "You, my girl, have more manners than most of the guys I have dated,"

"Keep your expectations high," Noemie quipped.

"Wait, what?" Louis responded. "Where did you hear that?"

"I think someone famous said it, but it stuck with me," she mentioned with a shrug.

"I love you," Louis laughed.

"Ok," Noemie teased.

"Bonjour," they heard from a familiar face.

"Bonjour, Matheo!"

"This is my friend, Lucy. Lucy, this is the world's must innovative ice cream chef. No kidding, he will come up with the most unique flavors, and it will be everything you ever wanted in your entire life."

"Everything I have ever wanted." Lucy feigned shock.

"Well, maybe not everything," Louis said, staring too long at Lucy.

"Let me get you some samples," Matheo said. "I have rose raspberry for today's featured flavor, but I plan to make lavender honey later this week if you want to come try it."

"This is incredible," Lucy said unexpectedly after tasting the sample. "This combination is so clever and unexpected. I would like a single scoop, please."

"I'll have the same," Louis replied.

"Same," Noemie added.

"Theo, would you like to try something new, or would you prefer the usual chocolate?"

"Chocolate," he whispered while looking away, but still taking in the conversation.

"Chocolate for Theo," Louis repeated, if Matheo could hear

him.

"No way!" a voice shouted from the door as they entered the business.

"Skye Reynolds, I am a huge fan." A man and his friend walked up to Lucy with their camera recording.

Without thinking, Louis found himself standing between Lucy and the two young men.

"You need to put your phone away," Louis said, calmly.

"No man … I just want to get some photos with her. You are beautiful, by the way," one of the men called to Lucy.

"Hey guys, I am so glad you love her work. She has had a rough day today. Being a super fan, I am sure you understand." Louis remained between the fans and Lucy. "Really, she appreciates your support." Louis ushered the two men out of the door, strategically, almost without them noticing. Louis continued to talk to the two men outside of the business. He shook their hands, and they waved goodbye to Lucy as they walked away.

Louis re-entered the business. "I hope you didn't finish your ice cream."

Everyone was staring at Louis in surprise.

"What?"

"What did you say to them?"

"Nothing really. I just thanked them for being great supporters, and they needed to delete their video due to some safety issues you have had." Louis joined the group at a table. "They seemed to understand." He tasted his ice cream. "Hmmmm … Matheo, you have outdone yourself."

"I think I need to hire you for my security team." Lucy marveled at Louis's calm demeanor and skill. "I just … wow, you were incredible."

"It must be a teacher thing. I can talk to anyone." Louis shrugged but felt his face turn hot just thinking that he may have impressed Lucy.

"I have to say that we have decided ice cream fixes everything, well … ice cream and Jesus," Noemie explained. "If we are ever having a bad day, we come see Matheo, and our day is so much better. If we have a good day, we celebrate with Matheo too."

"You have wisdom beyond your years because I completely agree," Lucy added. "It took me into my twenties to realize the magic that ice cream has on me though."

"I learned pretty quickly when my mom…" Louis began coughing, trying to avoid that conversation. *Louis, you will cry if we have that conversation today.*

"I feel bad, we should have invited your mom to have ice cream with us," Lucy said conspiratorially so that she can find out their "situation." Lucy could think Louis was cute, but she would never, ever flirt with a married man.

There was a beat of silence when Louis answered, "She has moved on…". *Man, this is such a vague answer, but I do not want to get into it here in the ice cream shop. It is too much. Hurry, change the subject … change the subject.*

"How are everyone's treats?"

"Amazing," Noemie answered as she continued eating ice cream.

Theo nodded in satisfaction, while seated and swinging his feet.

"Do you mind if I try your chocolate?" Lucy asked Theo.

Much to Louis and Noemie's surprise, Theo held out his cup for Lucy to try some of his ice cream. What happened next shocked them both even more.

Lucy took her spoon and took a small sample from Theo's cup. "That is so good. I think I may try that next time. Are you sure you don't want to try mine?" Lucy helped out her ice cream, and Theo dipped his spoon in her cup and tasted a tiny sample.

Wait, how did Lucy get Theo to try something new? Theo is my precious autistic boy who orders the same item each time during their visits there, and he never has tried something new. How did she do it? Louis, my man, don't start crying. Don't cry in front of this beautiful woman the first day you meet her.

"What do you think?" Lucy asked Theo about his opinion on her ice cream.

Theo responded with a thumbs-up.

"Let's cheers." Lucy held up her cup and showed Theo how to hold up his cup, and they clinked them together.

"I think I need to come back with you during your next visit," Lucy whispered to Theo.

"What does your day look like tomorrow? I think I can find time in my schedule to come back," Noemie joked.

The group laughed at Noemie's joke, even Noemie. Louis looked at Lucy sitting between Noemie and Theo with so much gratitude that Lucy decided to join them.

This woman is incredible. Theo takes a long time to warm up to anyone, and he just seems to adore Lucy. My heart is so full seeing the kids so happy right now. I wish… Louis stopped and reminded himself, *there is no way a woman like her could be interested in a man like you.*

CHAPTER 21

Louis
PARIS • MARCH 2021

"Bonjour Louis," Matheo called in his thick french acccent as he welcomed Louis back into his new ice cream shop.

"Hello, you are always so cheerful," Louis responded.

"May I be honest?' Matheo asked.

"Of course," Louis responded.

"It looks like you could use some cheer," Matheo said with genuine concern.

Louis wanted to hug him. He could use a friend and would have never thought that one of his only friends in this city would be the owner of one of his favorite ice cream parlors. *I just haven't had time to make friends and build many connections outside of work and family.*

"It has been a rough week," Louis said honestly.

"Do you want to talk about it?"

"I had hoped to move here for a long time, and it is not at all how I thought it would be," Louis added solemnly.

"You don't like my city?" Matheo sounded almost slightly offended.

"No, it isn't that. Paris is beautiful actually and amazing in its own special way."

"What is it?"

"I thought moving here would have been easier. I would get some help from my family to help me get on my feet, but it hasn't been like that at all."

"You are a British, no?"

"Yes, I am from England, but it has been my dream to be here in Paris because I wanted to be near family. I wanted to grow my jazz career. The jazz scene is promising."

"What is the problem? Should you go back to England? Would you feel better there?"

"I need to work jazz gigs at night, so I am gone every evening. My family needs me too. So, I am not there for them. They need more help."

"I am sure they understand the expectations of your work."

"It is not only that," Louis added.

There was a beat of silence. Louis contemplated how to say that last part without getting too emotional or too detailed.

"Getting the better gigs at the jazz clubs are really difficult, even after winning an award with my brother for a song we wrote."

"Congratulations, you must be very proud."

"Sure, I am so thankful for the recognition, but I thought it would help open some doors in the musical community a bit. I am still struggling."

"Do you want to continue doing it?"

"I can't imagine my life without having music in it. I have realized that I have to get another job in addition to my gigs. With COVID that hit last year, I was in limbo with my gigs because nothing was open. I lived on my savings mostly during that time while I … adjusted to life in Paris."

Louis, don't tell this man everything about your life right now. Sure, the shop is empty, but you don't need to go into the details of your relocation. Not now; you aren't ready to talk about it yet.

There was a beat of silence.

"I thought the award may have given me more opportunities, but I have found that I am just like any musician here in the city, and I have to start at the bottom, which means I have the worst hours for my gigs, which makes it hard on my family. Do you have a family, Matheo?"

"I do have a family. They are the reason I opened this shop." Matheo grabbed a photo from behind the counter and showed Louis his photo of his wife and children.

"You have a beautiful family," Louis added.

"This is my wife, Marie-Claire, my daughter, Michele, and my son, Claude. He is autistic, which is why he wears noise-cancelling headphones in the photo. I feel like I need to explain that for some reason."

"My boy, Theo, is autistic too, and here is my girl, Noemie." Louis pulled out a photo on his phone to show Matheo.

"Do the headphones work?" Louis asked with hopeful expression.

"They were a game-changer for us because it was difficult for us to take Claude out very often without him getting overstimulated. It wasn't good for him or any of us if he was overstimulated. He goes where we go now."

"Matheo, you are a genius. My boy has been going through the same thing, and I feel guilty not taking him all the places he should go, but I know he wouldn't enjoy it either." Louis looked at the photo on the phone. "I am going to try that with Theo."

Despite the burden that Louis carried into the shop about his work and family situation, he felt so much lighter. *My man, you have some options for your boy. You need to go get a headset on your way home. This is going to change things for Theo!*

"Do you want some ice cream now or just therapy?" Matheo joked.

"I have to admit … ice cream seems to solve everything. What is your featured ice cream?"

"I have saffron and orange blossom."

"One scoop of your featured ice cream, please." Louis sat at the counter and felt so much relief. *Your problems aren't solved, but you have a new idea to try with your sweet boy.*

As Louis waited for his ice cream, he asked, "Matheo, does your son collect things? I am noticing my boy seems to love trains."

"My son loves watches. He loves to take them apart and put them back together."

"Watches, huh?"

Matteo nodded and placed the ice cream scoop on the counter in front of Louis. "We usually go to the markets around the city looking for old watches. It is our thing we do together now." Matheo smiled, clearly thinking about his son and their time together.

"I need to think of how I can connect with Theo with his interest in trains."

"You know what, I had a customer leave these 2 toy trains in the shop 2 weeks ago. I thought they may come back for them, but after two weeks, I don't think they will. Take this, and you can give them to your boy."

"Thanks man," Louis added.

"If you will excuse me, I need to go to the back for a couple of minutes."

Meanwhile, Louis sat at the counter, feeling a tad overwhelmed with the prospect of getting another job. More importantly, he was hopeful and excited about how he could connect and better help his sweet boy, Theo.

CHAPTER 22

Lucy
2026

ucy, you have got to keep yourself together. Do not trust the flutter in the pit of your stomach. Do not trust the feeling of warmth in your cheeks and the punch of adrenaline that is coursing through your veins. You do NOT, and I repeat do NOT, need to get excited about this guy. Reason one, you don't know him. He absolutely took charge of the overzealous fan situation like a professional and even shook hands with the guys as they left. They were happy, he was happy, I was happy about the situation in the end. How did he do that? I mean, how? Most fans get offended when you want privacy, and he was shaking their hands in the end? Again, how?

Keep it together, Lucy. Reason two, you do not really know him. He is probably like the other men you have dated or talked to, which resulted in wasting your time. Plus, he was really vague about the kids' mom. Is there momma drama? Is there a sad story? If it's a sad story, I will want to run into this man's arms to the sounds of his smooth-like-butter baritone voice. No, Lucy no, do not get lost in those hazel eyes.

Reason three, he has Noemie and Theo. I adore them already, and they don't need to be around someone who may not be around for long. Plus, Lucy, you have never dated anyone with children. What makes you think you are equipped to navigate those tricky waters? Oh, I know, Lucy, you are not equipped. You can barely take care of yourself. Plus, the kids only deserve the best.

A ding from Lucy's phone brought her back into walking the streets in Paris back to her rental.

Louis

Thank you for meeting us for ice cream. I think you are Noemie and Theo's favorite person. Message me when you want to rehearse again. Don't forget your homework. 😉

Lucy

Sir, yes, sir!

Lucy

By the way, my assistant should have sent you money. Did you get it? I don't want you to think I tried to dip on your payment. 🤣

Louis

Why did you send me $1000 euros? We only worked together for an hour!!

Lucy

You were forced to tolerate me for another hour for ice cream.

Louis

I think it should be the other way ... you tolerated us.

Lucy accidentally sent send before finishing her message. *Oh my gosh, Lucy, he is going to think you are in love with him.* Lucy had to stop her walk and slow her shaking hands.

Lucy laughed out loud with Louis's response. She sat smiling at her phone.

Oh my gosh, is he asking me on a date? He just requested dinner and I would love to go, but this seems ... sudden. On the other hand, he is so cute and charming. Lucy, do not overthink this. What if he could be the one God is waving in front of you, and you are too jaded to say yes?

"Hey there, what are you doing?" Elle asked Lucy as they both stood out in front of the rental. "Is there a reason you are smiling at your phone?"

"Oh … a friend said something that made me smile. How was your day?" Lucy hugged Elle in greeting.

"I am great. I lounged in Luxembourg Gardens like a local," Elle said triumphantly.

"That sounds lovely." Lucy smiled. "I am going to send a message really quickly. I don't want you to think I am being rude."

"Oh … no worries. We can talk about any plans for tonight once you get upstairs," Elle mentioned as she unlocked the door to the rental.

"I was thinking La Tour Eiffel tonight? What do you think? We kind of missed it last night." Lucy smiled but still seemed distracted by her phone.

"Yay … it sounds amazing. I will see you upstairs."

Lucy looked down at her phone and felt awful for delaying a reply after Louis mentioned it. *He probably thinks he offended you. You need to say something that lets him know you aren't offended.*

Lucy

Dinner is fine, but really, I don't mind paying a little extra. Plus, you acted as my security when we did ice cream.

                                                    Lucy

Also, do you mind if we meet tomorrow evening for lessons? It will be later in the evening, if that works for you.

Louis

Sounds great. 👍

Louis

Also, where did you get your baseball cap with the train on it? Theo is obsessed with trains.

                                                    Lucy

I bought it a long time ago. I am obsessed with trains too. I will look for one for him.

Louis

You don't have to do that.

                                                    Lucy

Train-obsessed people must stick together. 🤝

Lucy didn't know what else to say. She could see three dots that suggested that Louis was writing more. So, she waited.

Louis

Thank you for being so great with my kids, especially Theo. I saw Theo open up more to you in a short amount of time, more than anyone I have ever seen. It means so much to me. 🩶

Lucy stared at his message and had no reply for this text message. She hit the heart button on the message, then stood outside of her rental. Holding the phone close to her chest, thinking of the kind man who sent her a lovely message, and allowed herself to get a little excited about seeing him again, trying to rid her mind of the constant doubt that he was going to be another man who was going to disappoint her.

CHAPTER 23

Lucy
LONDON • 2021

"Liam, pick up your phone. Pick up your phone. Pick up your phone," Lucy was whispering to herself as she listened to the phone ring.

"I know it is midnight in New York, but that isn't too late on a Friday night. Right?"

Lucy paused to think for a minute. *You are thinking about your boring brother, so he probably is in bed.*

No answer, she thought.

He probably has his do not disturb on and if I call him back, then it will not go through.

Lucy stabbed the call button with her finger; her need to speak to her reliable brother was too much.

Come on, Liam, pick up.

Tears welled up in Lucy's eyes the moment she heard a groggy, but familiar voice.

"Hello," Liam answered, clearly awakened by Lucy.

She couldn't respond yet, just hearing his voice brought a flood of tears.

"Lucy." Liam's British accent could be heard, and she knew that he probably was sitting straight up in bed.

"Wait," Lucy croaked out, just to let him know she was fine and not in danger.

"Take your time," Liam responded.

Lucy and Liam had always been close. Liam most likely understood that something was wrong if Lucy chose to call him instead of texting him. Plus, things had been going really well professionally for Lucy since everything reopened after COVID. Lucy's circumstances had changed since she first began acting. She was earning more money, and people expected more from her. She was underwater with all that was expected and felt like no one was truly on her side in her professional life.

You need to tell him, Lucy told herself.

"I need to have you closer," she croaked out the words and was trying to steady her breathing. *Lucy, you are asking for too much.* She knows that this request isn't helping Liam professionally and personally and could cause him some personal stress too. Knowing this, she tried to hold back, but her tears pushed forward anyway. Tears fell down her cheeks, but she inhaled deeply to steady her breath.

"What is happening? Are you safe?"

"I am," she said, the one thing that was going ok for her at the moment. She looked around her beautiful London flat with all the amenities. Just looking around her beautifully decorated flat, it was something she never thought she could afford on her acting salary, but there we were. Professionally, she was thriving.

"What happened?"

"I trusted the wrong people," she finally let out.

"What has someone done?"

"Well, first, I was talking to Handsy McHandserton, a guy I sort of dated for a short period of time. I don't know why I tolerated him, but for some reason, I did date him. Now, I found out he is 'Handsy' with everyone in town." Remembering she was talking to her brother, she added, "Don't worry, I didn't let him get too handsy. I am a good girl." She chuckled through tears.

"I am sorry," he said quietly.

"No, that isn't just it."

"There is more?" Liam asked.

"Yes, I found out my bookkeeper has been taking money from me," Lucy said and got emotional again.

"Bloody hell … are you sure?"

Lucy, your brother is in finance, so you need to tell him the truth. It isn't much money, but it was taken secretly, and he has betrayed your trust.

"I am sure. I checked my accounts, which I don't do often enough, but I could see several withdrawals from my account into his account for no reason. I confronted him about it, and he had no rationale for it. Then, he became defensive about it, so I took him off everything immediately. I haven't fired him, but he has to know it is coming."

"What a daft prick," Liam whispered.

"I need your help," Lucy whispered. "I just can't trust my circle. I put my faith in people that I find that I can't actually trust them." Lucy paused. "I need you in my circle."

"What has been going on with you? What can I do?"

"I just need your help. You are the only person I can trust right now. As my brother, you have always looked out for me. Currently, it feels that no one in my life is reliable or trustworthy."

There was a beat of silence. *Lucy, you need to tell him what you want. Tell him what you need.*

"I can hire you to do my bookkeeping and what-not. I will match your current salary," Lucy trailed off quietly.

There was a beat of silence.

Lucy, you have done it. You have asked for too much. Your brother is not going to move back to London after settling in New York to work in finance. He hasn't been there for too long. He doesn't seem to like it after all, but he also doesn't give up easily. Maybe this could be his way out of his miserable job, and it is helping both of you. Lucy's thoughts were all over the place.

There was still a beat of silence.

"Did I tell you how much I miss England, and New York isn't what I thought it would be?"

Lucy smiled over the phone, and tears came again.

"Are you serious?"

"Of course," Liam said. "I will always come to help you, Lucy. I can't help you now though."

"Why? What happened?"

"I need more sleep before we have a real conversation about this," Liam deadpanned.

"Oh … I am so sorry. I know you are working so much right now. Let's chat soon, ok?"

"Absolutely."

"Liam, you are the best brother a girl could have."

"I know," Liam joked.

"Bye."

Lucy heard Liam end the call.

She held her phone close to her chest. She needed this. She trusted all the wrong people, but now, she would have someone reliable in her corner. Finally, Lucy felt peace overcome her and finally hope for her future.

CHAPTER 24

Elle

2026

"This is incredible," Elle whispered to Lucy as they stood on the second level of the Eiffel Tower, standing shoulder to shoulder, taking in the view of the city.

"Sorry we missed it last night," Lucy mentioned as she continued to stare out at the city. "Do you know much about Paris?"

"Not really," Elle confessed.

For most of my formative years, I had my nose in a book, trying my best to get into medical school. I didn't think of much of anything else besides that, Elle thought to herself.

"I prefer the second level more than the summit because I love to watch the city come alive at night," Lucy said as she looked out at the City of Lights.

"That is the Champ de Mar, the green space that surrounds most of the Eiffel Tower. Do you see the soccer stadium over there?" Lucy pointed with her chin, her arms folding in front of her, resting on the metal grating that surrounds the structure. "Can you imagine being a child and have the Eiffel Tower overlooking your soccer field?"

"You sound like Margaux. She is very dreamy like that ... I adore that about both of you," Elle added. "I am not joking when I tell you that I spent most of my childhood in a book or studying. I was determined to get into medical school." Elle shrugged, standing there in Paris, a far cry from medical school.

Life is stranger than fiction, Elle thought to herself. *I am standing on the Eiffel Tower with my soon-to-be sister-in-law, who happens to be a world-famous actress, and now a friend. God always surprises me in the best way. He always does exceedingly more than I could have imagined.*

"I am so happy you changed your mind. After all, if you hadn't changed your career path, I doubt we would have ever met." Lucy smiled, looking at Elle, who had become very dear to her.

"God knew what He was doing," Elle said with a smile, thinking about all the blessings in her life.

"I don't know how you would have met my brother either," Lucy said in almost a coo, teasing Elle about her newfound love.

"I know," Elle said, almost in complete awe in how her life had unfolded recently.

"Let's walk over here, so we can continue your tour," Lucy joked while she led Elle on a small tour of the views from the Eiffel Tower. "There is the Sacred Heart in Montmartre, which is near where we went for the jazz music." The women were quiet for a beat while they enjoyed the views.

"I love watching the riverboats float down the river ... from here ... it looks so peaceful." *Lucy sounds like she is thinking about something more than just boats. She sounds like she wants some peace in her life, too.* Elle attempted to stop her cycle of overthinking. *There is probably nothing to it, she redirected her thoughts.*

The women looked out at the city, no words spoken between them; they just enjoyed this moment.

After a few minutes, Lucy asked, "Do you want to explore the city using one of the telescopes? I brought some change to pay for it." Lucy smiled playfully.

"Of course," Elle answered, as though that was a question that would always be a yes.

Lucy walked up to one of the telescopes that had two people using it. She stood near them, suggesting that she was waiting to use it next but didn't appear pushy or impatient.

After a couple of minutes, one of the men mentioned to Elle and Lucy, "Hey mates, you can take a go at it if you like." Then, something in their demeanor changed once they saw Lucy.

"Bloody hell … no way," one of the men said, literally jumping up and down, putting a closed fist over his mouth in excitement, as though he was attempting to quiet himself.

Elle watched Lucy's demeanor change too. Then, her voice became a whisper.

"Thanks mates for being such loyal fans, but I need for you to take your voice to a whisper if you don't mind."

"Could we get a photo with you?" one of the men asked in a whisper but was already raising his phone in the air for a .5 selfie.

"Actually, I can't take a photo with you sadly. What are your names?" Lucy asked.

"This is Geoffrey, and I am Liam."

"Hi, Geoffrey and Liam. Do you know my brother's name is Liam, too?" The man beamed to being privy to learning something about one of the most beautiful and talented actresses in the movie business.

"You see, if you take a photo with me and post it, it alerts the world to the fact that I am in Paris right now. Plus, it could draw unwanted attention to me. Potentially, drawing attention from weirdos too. I could be put in danger. You don't want me in danger, do you?" Lucy asked.

"Oh no … you are um … my favorite actress. I have seen every movie you have ever done," Liam answered, and Geoffrey nodded enthusiastically.

"I hear a British accent. Are you from England as well?"

"Yes."

"Here is what we will do. You will come see me in London at one of my premieres. We will get a proper photo there. You will ask for Dottie at the premiere. Sound, ok?"

"Dottie?" Geoffrey asked in confirmation.

"She will make sure you get to see me. Plus, you won't be putting me in danger with your post." She paused for melodramatic effect. "You can do that, right?"

"Yes, of course," they answered enthusiastically.

"It was a pleasure meeting both of you, Geoffrey and Liam … I will see you in London," she added and turned to the telescope.

"Allow me," one of the guys insisted on paying for their telescope fee.

"Oh…" Lucy smiled politely, "thank you. Have a good evening." Lucy's subtle way of asking the men to move along with their evening.

As they walked away, Elle could hear one of them say, "That was bloody crazy. I can't believe we met the Skye Reynolds, and she was so chill."

"They are going to be talking about meeting you for years." Elle smiled. "By the way, you handled that beautifully. I wanted to get in their face about it, but you handled it. Where did you pick up those smooth techniques in handling fans?"

"It's funny you asked that because when I was with my voice coach, we had an issue with some fans. I watched him do what I just did. He was calm and collected. I tried to mimic what he did, and it worked … and I did it … much to my surprise."

"That is impressive. So, do you want to show me how to use this telescope thing?" Elle asked Lucy.

Grasping the handles, Lucy maneuvered the telescope to point in one direction while looking through the lens. "Look through here, you will see Notre Dame."

"Oh wow … it's beautiful."

Lucy moved the lens of the telescope again. "Now, you can see the Louvre."

"Wow, you know your way around this city. I love how it is bathed in lights. I understand why Paris is called the City of Lights."

"I love this city. Generally, the locals won't approach me out on the street. I do get some fans from time to time who will approach me, but usually, I don't have many problems being out in the city. I feel 'lighter' here." Lucy smiled as she continued to stare out at the city. "I know the City of Lights reference doesn't mean that to most people, but to me, it does."

"Lucy, I want to give you the biggest hug right now." Elle reached out and pulled her close to her.

"Hey girl, don't feel bad for me," Lucy said as they stood hugging. "I have been blessed in so many ways in my life, but the lack of privacy and finding someone who wants a relationship with a real person is difficult."

There was a beat of silence.

"I am thankful for my life, but I do wish I had someone special too and just a bit of privacy sometimes." Lucy's smile widened.

Elle reached out and grabbed her hand; she didn't know what to say but just wanted to remind Lucy how much she cares about her.

"Speaking of feeling lighter, how do you feel about doing a bike tour tomorrow? I started researching some things to do, and I hear we can tour Versailles on bikes. Plus, there is a market to buy items for a picnic. What do you think about this idea ... picnicking on the grounds of Versailles?" Elle said the last part dramatically.

"I feel lighter already, just thinking about it," Lucy deadpanned.

As the women quietly looked out at Paris, Elle said a silent prayer, unbeknownst to Lucy. *God, thank you for this time with Lucy. I finally understand my fiancé's protective nature with her. I want to protect her too from people who have betrayed her trust. If it is Your will, please bring Lucy someone special into her life. I think she wants someone trustworthy and godly to add to her life. Please help restore her faith in men and to let go of her hurt. She has so much to offer. Amen.*

Their quiet admiration was interrupted by a ding on Lucy's phone.

"Oh sorry, this is work stuff." Lucy felt the need to explain using her phone, "My voice coach is sending some materials to study." Lucy let Elle peer over her shoulder to look at her phone, too.

Louis

> Here is some musical inspiration for your evening.

"He sent a playlist he made for me with a bunch of jazz artists. He even called the playlist 'Lucy's Next Big Thing.'"

Lucy

> Thank you so much. I'll add this to my homework. 😉

Louis

> Think of it as something to brighten your evening, not work. 🙂

Lucy

> That I can do. 

Elle watched Lucy stare smiling at her phone after typing a quick reply. Elle was beginning to think there is more to this than meets the eye.

God, if this is how quickly You work after a prayer, I am speechless for the first time in my life, Elle thought to herself.

CHAPTER 25

Lucy
2026

"I hope you don't mind that I booked the tour with a group. So far, everyone seems friendly. If anyone has recognized you, they aren't acting like it," Elle reassured Lucy as they were on the train to Versailles from the city.

"Have you ever been to Versailles?"

"I haven't been here, but it is on my list. Plus, I would love to go to their fete sometime. Have you heard of that?"

"That is where everyone comes for the evening dressed up in their period attire and parties all night, right?"

"That it is. Doesn't that sound fun?"

"Is that even a question? Let's add that to our list for one of our next adventures," Elle added, thinking about how hard it was going to be when she went back to New York. She wasn't going to see Lucy as often as she did now, and it was going to be difficult to pull Liam away from this sister.

"Here we are," the tour guide added. "We are going to get off the train at the next stop, and we will walk about two blocks to pick up our bicycles."

"This is so fun!" Elle added. "I am going to be riding a bicycle around France! What is this life? I think Margaux is rubbing off on me because she always sees life as the next adventure. I am starting to get excited about all these new experiences. Plus, I want to get a baguette for our picnic so I can have it in my basket of my bike!" Elle pointed to herself with a shocked expression. "Literally, I am sounding just like Margaux."

"You really are…" Lucy laughed. "I am excited too."

After stopping to choose their bicycles, the small group of ten were ready to embark on the beginning of their ride. Elle noticed that Lucy seemed to be uncharacteristically checking her phone.

"Is everything ok?"

"Yes, sorry I keep checking my phone. My voice coach is supposed to contact me today about our plans for rehearsal tonight. I am a little nervous about it."

Am I lying to Elle? I don't want to tell her that I have literally been thinking about this guy all day, and I can't wait for him to text me again. As a matter of fact, he and I spent most of the evening texting about nothing after we got back from the Eiffel Tower last night … and it was the most fun, pointless communication I have had with a man in a long time … no maybe ever.

"I would be nervous getting that far out of my comfort zone too." Elle was trying to sound encouraging and validating about her nerves.

It really is out of my comfort zone, Lucy thought to herself, realizing her comment had multiple meanings to her personally.

"Please follow me," the tour guide announced. "We are going through the small town of Versailles on our bikes. If I stop, please stop as well. This is the trickiest part of your tour today because we are navigating just a bit of the city streets here in the small town. Don't worry, it won't be too bad. Then, the rest of our day will be exploring the French countryside by bicycle," he said triumphantly.

Soon, like ducklings following their momma, each of the ten participants dutifully followed the tour guide on their bicycles. Lucy and Elle were coasting through the streets of Versailles. Much of the buildings looked the same as in Paris in the town center. The tones of the stonework were monotone; it was almost sophisticated, despite the years. The garden areas were beautifully maintained.

The tour guide stopped. "You are going to see a vast change in architecture once we enter the grounds of Versailles. You notice that right now, you see the Haussmannian style, which has wrought iron balconies, neutral facades, and the distinctive mansard roofs."

Lucy could feel her phone vibrating in her pocket.

I bet it's Louis again, Lucy thought to herself. *I want to check the message, but I don't want to worry Elle either. I'll check it discreetly later.*

"You will see a vast change in opulence as we enter the grounds of Versailles, but first, you will need to prepare your picnics. We are going to walk our bikes to the area just to the right of this building. In this building, you will find any kind of food you can think of, and it is farm to table. All the items in this market are made and grown locally," the guide said with enthusiasm. "Buy what you want and place them in your baskets. We will take our food with us and stop for our picnic. Does anyone have questions?"

Elle raised her hand. *Always the eager student,* Lucy thought fondly. "Do you have any food recommendations or favorite items?"

"That is a great question." The guide seemed pleased with Elle's curiosity.

"We are close to the Brie region here in Versailles. You are going to find a variety of Brie cheese, so I would recommend that." He smiled widely.

"Please tell me you like Brie." Elle turned to Lucy excitedly.

"Again, is that even a question?" Lucy teased Elle.

Lucy felt her phone vibrate again.

"I would like to go to the loo after we park our bikes," Lucy added. *And I want to see why my phone keeps buzzing, but I really hope it is Louis again, she thought to herself.*

After parking their bikes, Lucy went to the bathroom and checked her phone as Elle began selecting items for their picnic.

Once in the privacy of the bathroom stall, Lucy pulled out her phone and saw some messages from Louis, and her stomach was filled with butterflies.

Louis

I hope you have a great morning. ☀

Louis

I added some songs to your playlist that will help you stay inspired during your bike tour today!

Lucy stood looking at her phone while standing in the stall of the bathroom. *I like the messages, but don't want to reply because I know he will reply to me, and it will start an entire five minutes' round of more texts. He is so easy to talk or text with,* Lucy thought to herself. *Most men play games for a few days and try to hide their enthusiasm. It is kind of refreshing even if nothing comes from this … it is nice to see a guy who seems … nice.*

Lucy put her phone in her backpack, determined to be present for the day. She walked outside and joined Elle, who was chatting with other sightseers. Some had their baskets already loaded with food.

"So, what do we want for our picnic?" Lucy asked Elle.

"I know I have bossypants tendencies, but I picked out several things and set it aside. Let's go see what you think about it." Elle led Lucy into the building that housed the market.

"Tada," Elle said with jazz hands.

Lucy's smile widened. "It's like you read my mind."

"Really?"

"Yes, but did you get the baguettes for our baskets?" Lucy joked.

"Is that even a question?" Elle teased and pointed to the baguette in the basket next to her.

The ladies paid for their items and strategically placed them in their bicycle baskets for the perfect French aesthetic.

"Ok crew, we are now heading into the gates of Versailles. Stay together and follow me. We are going to be riding our bikes for about thirty minutes. Let's stick together."

Dutifully, the group followed the guide. In a short amount of time, the group was gliding down well-worn paths that have been used for centuries. Water fountains and buildings dotted the huge expanse of land. There were beautiful flowers, curated and designed in various configurations that showcased the vision behind this place called Versailles. There was a small village that was a model of Marie Antoinette's home country that was built for her by the supervision of her husband. There were gardens. There were rustic buildings that showed some reflection of years past. Everything about Versailles was curated and intentional, much like Paris.

After exploring for thirty minutes, they stopped for their picnics. Elle was so encouraged by the change in Lucy's attitude, but for some reason, there was something that made her hesitant too. As they sat and ate, Elle and Lucy decided to send some photos to Liam.

Elle

Wish you were here!

Liam

I love that you two went on a bike tour. I don't know if Lucy has been on a bike since she was little.

Then, Elle and Lucy thought about Margaux in Italy and sent her a few pictures.

Elle looked over at Lucy, who was also checking her phone. She had gone from smiling to having a crestfallen expression on her face.

Elle looked at Lucy and mouthed, "You, ok?"

Lucy waved her phone slightly to Elle, so to protect her privacy while sitting among the other people on the tour.

Lucy text Elle so that no one else could hear this part of their conversation.

CHAPTER 26

Louis
2026

Louis

I'm so sorry. 😔

Louis

Did you get my message?

No response.

Why isn't she replying to my text messages? It's not like I can help this. Is she mad? Louis, think. Just think for a second about how to problem-solve.

First, you could just go ahead and meet her to practice.

My man, what are you thinking? What kind of dad leaves his son with a babysitter when he isn't feeling well? You know he doesn't communicate like other kids, and it isn't fair to him to not feel well with someone else at home with him.

My boy never gets sick. Why did he have to come home sick today from school? Literally, I haven't ever had to pick him up from school for being sick. Today has to be the day that he gets sick?

Then again, it is just a stomach thing. He doesn't have a fever. You could go work with her. You can absolutely trust Gabrielle to watch him for a couple of hours…

It doesn't feel right to leave him, though. Leaving Theo with a sitter when he isn't feeling well.

Think, Louis. What is another idea? You have got to have some other options up your sleeve?

Should I bother telling Lucy why I am changing our plans? Is that oversharing? Am I going to seem like one of those unprofessional blokes who are unreliable?

Or, is she just going to think I am an unreliable man in general? I am not even thinking about professionally. I don't want her to think I am that kind of dodgy geezer. That is even worse. I do care what she thinks about me.

She even mentioned casually last night how difficult it is to find reliable people in her personal life. Dude, you are doing it to her too!!

There was a beat of silence. Louis was overwhelmed with options, and none of them seemed to be ideal.

Fine, I will text her and tell her why.

Louis picked up his phone and stared at it. He was acting as though holding his phone and staring at it would help him come up with the right words to not sound like a complete, dodgy geezer, or a player, or just a general jerk.

Another idea hit Louis. He held his phone up to his head, thinking.

Dude, no … just no. She is not going to go for this idea. I think this idea is even worse than appearing unreliable.

Louis put his phone back down again. He just sat, staring into space, trying to figure out what to do.

You want to see her again. If you don't figure this out, you may never see her again.

Then again, if you overwhelm her with the reality of dadhood on the second day of knowing her, she is going to run away. There is no way a woman as beautiful, talented, smart, and sophisticated will want to deal with your personal dad stuff.

But I am a dad, and this is my reality.

Finally, Louis made a decision. This was one of his gifts; he was best at being honest. He needed to stop having his self-doubt cloud his mind.

Louis picked up his phone and took a deep breath. He began typing.

Louis

> Theo got sick at school today. I have never had to pick him up from school for being sick. It is a stomach bug. I can't leave him tonight, especially because he doesn't always verbalize on a regular day. It is not fair to him or a babysitter. I am so sorry. I understand if you need to find someone else.

Louis hit send and put his phone down and exhaled. He didn't even realize he was holding his breath until he exhaled.

He stood up and tried to busy himself, fully realizing that this woman would not want to give him a second chance. Louis grabbed his phone and couldn't resist the urge to see if he could see the magic three dots … and there they were.

Louis jumped up from his sofa and had to fight the urge to shout in triumph. At least, she was responding.

Ok, you don't even know what she is going to say. Calm down, man.

Lucy

Why didn't you just tell me that from the beginning? It made you seem flaky.

See dude, you should have just been honest, Louis said to himself.

Louis

I thought it may have made you think I was too much trouble.

Lucy

So, you need to stay home?

Louis

Yes, I don't think it is fair to Theo that I leave him if he feels worse.

Lucy

Would it be weird if I just came to your place to rehearse?

Louis saw the message and stood up and walked in a circle. His hands started shaking. *Calm down, dude, you need to relax.*

Louis

Would that be weird for you?

Lucy

Would that be weird for you?

Louis

A little strange, but that's ok. 

His last comment made him laugh when he sent it.

Lucy

So, does that mean you will be on your best behavior or not? You didn't answer.

Lucy

Just pin me your address. I'll see you tonight.

Mate, you are in deep trouble because you really do like this woman.

CHAPTER 27

Lucy
2026

I am sure this is a good idea. You don't need to worry about Louis being anything but a gentleman. He seems professional and courteous. Plus, the kids will be home for pity's sake. Lucy, quit getting into your head so much.

Lucy continued to walk toward the address that Louis had pinned her to come for a rehearsal. The streets in the fifteenth arrondissement were much more spacious and updated compared to being closer to the city center. While standing on the sidewalk, Lucy was surprised by the size of his flat as she arrived. Suddenly, Lucy felt a nervous flutter in the pit of her stomach as she stared at the house number while confirming what he sent her on her phone.

For a teacher's salary, this place is really big. The neighborhood seemed very family-friendly with several families walking the neighborhood as she approached the outside of his place. She looked around a bit more before knocking. There was a cute cafe across the street, but there seemed to be mostly homes in this section of the city. Street lanterns dotted the sidewalk while warm lights provided additional light from the windows. Lucy continued to study the area and felt a warmth overcome her. *I bet the kids love growing up here, Lucy thought to herself. This is such a charming neighborhood.*

As Lucy lifted her hand to knock on the door, the door slowly opened to a very pleased Noemie.

"Welcome to our home," she cooed, clearly pleased to have Lucy come to their house. "Can I take your jacket?"

"Yes, of course, thank you." Lucy looked around the home as she walked in. She also felt a sense of reassurance, knowing that Noemie answered the door.

Lucy wasn't sure why she was so nervous about coming here. *Lucy, my dear, I think you just don't trust yourself around Louis.*

"You are quite the lady of the house," Lucy teased. Noemie looked adorable. She was in pink pajamas with bows. Her curls were tied up into two little puffs with bows that matched. *She is adorable,* Lucy thought.

"I try," Noemie added. "Sadly, this lady of the house has to go to bed because I have had an exhausting day at school. I like to read before bed; it helps me wind down from my day."

It took everything for Lucy to stifle a giggle. Noemie spoke like an adult and apparently acted like one too.

"Do you have trouble sleeping?" Lucy asked.

"Not really, but my mind likes to think of everything when I go to bed for some reason." Noemie shrugged.

"What are you reading?"

"The Bible," Noemie answered without allowing much time to

pass before continuing. "I am reading the book of Ruth. I just love that book. Two strong women helping one another." Noemie stood nodding, just thinking about the inner workings of the women in the book of Ruth.

"If you like strong women, you should read about Deborah in the Bible. Do you know much about her?"

"Noted," Noemie quipped.

"Well, good night, I hear you have a big audition coming up."

"I do … that is what your dad and I are working on tonight. If you can keep a secret," Lucy leaned in and lowered her voice to a whisper, "I am a bit nervous about it. I have never had to sing for work before now, and it is a bit scary."

"I'll pray for you tonight when I go to bed." Noemie smiled. "I am sorry I have to go to bed and can't stay up to talk to you. Good night." Noemie leaned in and put one arm around Lucy for a quick hug.

"Good night." Lucy returned the hug. *That little girl is not only like an adult, but she is all business.* It was so funny how she thought to greet Lucy and announce she was heading to bed. *What great manners.* Lucy felt almost a protective feeling when she thought about Noemie.

"I am sorry, but Theo will not be down to add to the round of good-night hugs." Louis came from behind Noemie, giving her a hug and a kiss on the head before she began her way upstairs.

"I am glad you agreed to this," Louis added, his hazel eyes on Lucy. Although it was the evening, Louis still dressed like he was born in the wrong era. He had on tan trousers, but a cream-colored short-sleeved shirt without a tie, slightly unbuttoned, which was enhanced by the matching suspenders. Lucy loved his style. His round tortoise-shell glasses completed his look … a look that he wasn't trying to create but was his style.

Lucy, you are here to practice music, you are not here to get distracted, Lucy said to herself in affirmation for her real purpose here.

"Would you like anything to drink?" Louis offered. "Water is a good idea to have when you are pushing the limits of your voice. Hot tea would work too." Louis ran a nervous hand through his tight coils, giving way under the pressure of his touch.

"I will take a water," Lucy added. "You have a lovely home. I love the quaint neighborhood."

"Thank you. It is a bit to maintain, but the kids love it here. I don't think I could move them … even if I wanted to." Louis smiled.

That was a strange response, Lucy thought to herself. *Did he want to move? Was he putting her on notice? The kids will not be moved. Interesting comment.*

"Are you ready?" Louis asked, almost nervously, rubbing his hands together. "Come back this way." Louis led Lucy down a long hallway that took them past the kitchen and living room. There was a door at the end of the hall.

"This is where we will be working … my music studio." Louis opened the door and stepped aside so that Lucy could see the studio.

"Wow, this is impressive," Lucy added as she looked around. "What are all of these awards?" Lucy walked around the room where she could see several certificates displayed.

"Who is John? It looks like you both like to do collaborations?" Lucy asked as she continued walking around the room, studying the awards.

"That's my brother," Louis answered, but he was also busying himself with straightening up the space.

"That's impressive. Does he like jazz too?"

"Yes," Louis answered with a bit of hesitation that even Lucy could sense.

"I am sorry. I don't mean to pry. I could just see that you both are bloody talented," Lucy explained and took the hint to stop asking some questions.

"Oh no, it's ok," Louis answered, still holding something back.

There was a beat of silence. *I can tell that he didn't really want to talk about his brother; I am waiting for him to lead the conversation. Then again, he could just be nervous because to be around me because looking into those hazel eyes again did something to me,* Lucy thought.

"Are you ready to start?" Louis looked up at Lucy, his eyes meeting hers, and Lucy found her resolve weakening.

Then, Louis surprised her.

"My brother passed away," Louis explained.

"Oh, I am sorry," Lucy added. "You don't have to talk about it, unless you want to."

"Thank you, it is difficult to talk about. I appreciate your understanding."

There was a beat of silence because Louis wasn't ready to offer more than that.

"Are you ready to practice?"

"What songs did you like from the playlist I sent you?"

"I think my favorite was 'Train to Nowhere.' I loved the message the most. Then again, I don't know how difficult it is to sing." Lucy smiled shyly.

"Have a seat here. Give me a moment while I pull up the lyrics." Louis was quickly working on a tablet. "Here you go." He handed Lucy the tablet.

"Now, I am going to pull up the instrumental music for it. We are going to sing this together to start. If you did your exercises, it will make singing much easier. If you didn't do it … well…" Louis teased her moving his hands across his throat.

"Oh my gosh," Lucy responded. "Are you teasing me about that because I am already nervous?"

Louis pulled up a stool for himself and one for Lucy so that they could face one another. Their knees were touching so that they could sit closely to harmonize together.

"I am joking. Let's start with these lines … we are just going to read them a few times…"

Now I am riding empty tracks with no way to yesterday

This train already left the station but your love decided to stay

They read the words together at first. Then, they began singing them over and over again. Slowly, Louis would back out of sections of the song.

"Let's add the next two lines of lyrics…"

Now the trails twist and wander, I've got no place to go

I'm on a train to no where, since you left me all alone.

The last lyrics, Lucy closed her eyes and felt these words. She didn't feel heard or understood for so long. She felt the music. Lucy swayed and let go of the worry of doing it correctly. She felt these words in the moment and found herself doing a little riff of notes to emphasize the last of the words.

"That was bloody brilliant." Louis jumped up from the stool in which he was sitting.

"Lucy, this was amazing. You were actually singing," and she jumped up too. She wrapped her arms around Louis's neck, and he picked her up and twirled her around in a circle.

Louis and Lucy suddenly realized their closeness, their proximity. Lucy could feel his hands around her, gently touching the small of her back. Her hands were wrapped around his neck and slightly resting on his shoulders. Louis was just a few inches taller than Lucy, so their eyes met. They didn't say anything but stared at one another. Louis licked his lips and didn't dare say a word at this moment. Lucy's heart was racing, being held by this beautiful man with the baritone voice, making her feel unsteady but also safe. When she was with him, Lucy felt like a magnet being drawn to him.

She kept staring at Louis's lips, soft and inviting. Sparks seemed to race underneath her skin, awakening her entire body. Lucy fought the urge to pull him closer despite the fact that they were still in an embrace. It was Louis who moved first; he gently brought one hand on the side of Lucy's face and met her gaze.

Suddenly, they heard a soft knock at the door and nearly jumped away from one another.

"I wanted to say good night to Lucy again." Noemie entered the room, her eyes looking tired, and she let out a long yawn.

"Of course, dahling." Lucy opened up her arms to receive Noemie.

"How about me?" This was Louis's way of asking for a hug. Noemie walked over to him, burying her face into his stomach, and Louis began scratching her back. He kissed her on the head and whispered, "I love you."

"Ok," Noemie whispered, making Lucy smile, being privy to their inside joke now.

She quietly walked out of the room.

Lucy and Louis looked at one another, and suddenly their attraction was more than Lucy could resist. *Lucy, you have got to get out of here.*

"I should get going." Lucy suddenly felt like she could no longer trust herself with Louis in this room. She wanted to kiss him so badly.

"I think you are ready." Louis offered reassurance, ignoring the moment they just shared.

"I would like to practice one more time before I run the song by the director. My assistant said the director is in Paris and will be scheduling something soon."

She was walking toward the door and started gathering her things, almost trying to make her escape before things could escalate with Louis any further.

Lucy, get out of here. You just can't resist his charms, and he isn't even trying to charm you. His charming nature is just in his DNA!

"Is something wrong?" Louis followed after her, almost sensing her urgency, convinced he had offended her. He tried to keep up with her.

"Do you want me to call you an Uber? I am so sorry. You must have thought I was completely out of line," Louis continued, finally realizing that he may have misread Lucy's attraction.

As she was walking out the front door, she stopped. *He thinks he is the problem. The problem is that I can't resist you, Louis. You aren't the problem, Louis. It is me.*

"Again, I am so sorry if I offended you." Louis appeared almost crestfallen.

Just as she opened the door, Lucy paused in the doorway. She then turned on her heel toward Louis, who was still following her, causing him to stop just behind her. Previously, she had kept him at a distance, but in that moment, distance was the last thing she wanted. She closed the gap between them, and she slowed, looking at his face and his soft inviting lips again.

Lucy moved her lips to his … soft and certain. She slowly brushed her lips against his. His lips were soft and inviting. Louis placed his hand on her waist, so gently that it could have been unnoticed, but Lucy's body responded any time Louis was near here. She pulled away from him——it was a quick kiss, but not careless. It was tender. She slowly put her hands around him gently on the small of his back. There was a sense of control now, but there was the harsh reality that suddenly overcame Lucy too.

"I have to go because I don't trust myself when I am alone with you," Lucy whispered as she stood, still holding Louis, standing face to face in his doorway.

Lucy stepped away quickly, moving out of the door, making her way toward the metro. Taking huge strides to distance herself from Louis, passing people on the sidewalk. *Slow down, Lucy. He is amazing, but you need to use your head, not your heart.*

Little did she know that she may have distanced herself from Louis, but the paparazzi standing outside of Louis's flat may have just captured the photo of the year with Lucy kissing a mystery man.

CHAPTER 28

Louis

2026

Louis lay in bed and stared up at the ceiling, but his mind would not stop thinking about Lucy. He aggressively rolled to his side and grabbed his phone off the nightstand, then stared at the screen and thought about what to do.

You should text her and apologize. He stared at the screen longer, trying to decide what to do.

She is going to think you are a weirdo while texting her this late. He touched the screen on his phone to check the time. *It's not quite midnight. She left at 10:30, so it isn't that late. Plus, you could check that she made it back to her rental safely. Dude, why didn't you call her an Uber? You really should apologize.* His mind was a jumble of thoughts.

Louis

> I can't sleep.

Louis typed and accidentally hit send on this incomplete message. He sat straight up as though being in a sitting position would help him become a more competent texter. He ran a nervous hand through his hair. *My man, you seriously have no charm at all when you are around her. What kind of message is that?*

His nervous hands tried to recover by sending another message.

Louis

> I can't sleep because I was thinking I should have ordered you an Uber. Did you get back safely?

Louis could see three dots. He stared, waiting for something. She is awake.

Lucy

> I can't sleep either. I made it back safely to the rental. Don't worry about an Uber; I love taking the metro. Remember, I love train transportation. I don't get to take the Tube often at home without being recognized. 

Louis

> Is there anything I can do to make you not run away when you are with me? 🙂

Lucy

> No ... your charms are too powerful. 😏

Louis

> Who me? 😳

Lucy

Your smooth voice, your patience, great style, and hazel eyes. 😍

Louis

You do know you are speaking to Louis ... not some cool actor, right?

Lucy

 Yes!

Louis

What was keeping you awake tonight? 😕

Lucy

I had a couple of things on my mind. First, I found out the director wants to hear some of my voice work tomorrow morning.

Louis

Tomorrow morning?!? Did you know they would want to meet so soon?

Lucy

No. 🥺

Louis

You've got this. I saw a glimpse of you feeling the music tonight. Many in the industry don't know how to do that and you did it! 💪

Lucy

Thank you for being so encouraging. I really want to put myself out there professionally, so this is my chance. I just hope I do well.

Louis

You just need to give it up to God, and He will do the rest. 

Lucy

Yesssss!!!

Lucy

Can you meet me there tomorrow? I'll pin the address. I need to be there by 11:00.

Louis

Of course. Do you want to practice before your meeting? You can come back here in the morning if you want to rehearse.

Lucy

No, I don't want to overthink it if I don't sound great during our rehearsal.

Louis

Good point. I understand that.

Lucy

I need to go to bed. Thanks for being so great.

How can I pray for you tonight? You said you had a couple of things on your mind that were preventing you from sleeping.

It's not something you can pray for. I appreciate it though.

Are you sure? No judgment here. I am a prayer warrior. 🙏

I kept thinking about you ... you are what kept me awake. 🙈

Lucy looked at Louis's reply and laughed at his response while she was staring at her phone. She replied with a screen that was filled with floating hearts.

Good night, Lucy. 𝗓𝗓𝐙

Good night, Louis. 🌙

Both of them put their phones aside as they each lounged on their beds, Lucy at her rental and Louis at home.

Louis, how on earth is this talented, successful woman texting you?

Then, Louis rolled over onto his stomach and screamed into his pillow with excitement because she had been the best thing to walk into his life in a long time.

CHAPTER 29

Lucy
2026

Lucy was aggressively walking past the Parisians on the side-walk, because her mind was elsewhere. She wanted to just arrive. She just wanted to get to the building that housed the director who wanted to hear her sing. The anticipation of waiting another moment to sing, to do the thing that made her feel the most vulnerable professionally, felt like too much. *Why did he want an audition on such short notice? Did he want to see if I could withstand the pressure? Why was he asking for an audition with so little details given to Lucy?*

Even the encouraging text messages from Louis throughout the morning couldn't help her get out of her head. *I can't believe you told Louis to come. You are too far into your head about this. It hasn't been this bad in a long time.*

This is just a tryout ... this isn't even an audition, Lucy tried to tell herself. She had her baseball cap pulled low, nearly covering her eyes. She was wearing all black—something to match her attitude this morning as she was heading to her audition. Her mind kept returning to rehearsing the inevitable reality that she would not have what it takes, and it would be a spectacle for this tryout. *You are going *to embarrass yourself.*

Lucy took a deep breath, trying to steady her emotions and her overactive mind.

Lucy, why do you have such a negative attitude? You chose to do this. You chose to audition for this job. This opportunity is just that—an opportunity. It is a chance to try something new. You need to see this as an opportunity!

Just as she was trying her best to provide herself with some self-affirmations, Lucy accidentally bumped into another woman with her shoulder, causing the woman to stumble but regain herself.

"Pardon, s'il vous plait." Lucy held out a shaky hand while doing her best to apologize in French.

"D'accord," the woman returned with an unamused expression on her face and continued her stroll.

Lucy stepped aside on the sidewalk, shaking from head to toe, trying to catch her breath. Tears were stinging her eyes, and she was trying to force herself back into a better mindset. *Bloody hell, Lucy, what are you doing? Why are you putting so much pressure on yourself? Bloody calm down.*

She inhaled slowly, remembering a technique when she was overcome by anxiety or stress or whatever this was. Lucy rarely got anxious or nervous, or whatever this was: she just tried not to overthink but just go for it. This time, this opportunity, this thing she was committed to try had really gotten into her head.

"Hey there," she heard from behind her. A voice as soothing as any earthly voice could be for her. Lucy kept her back to him. *I don't want him to see me like this. I am a mess. I can't turn around and look at him.*

"I want you to try this. Imagine a box. You are going to slowly inhale like you are moving over the box." Lucy followed his directions in her mind, with her back still facing him. "Now, softly hold your breath, move over the box, now release your breath as you move down on the other side of the box. Finally, softly hold your breath one more time as you travel across the bottom of the box." Louis noticed that Lucy was slowly returning to her normal self.

"You are doing great. Is this, ok?" Louis put his hand on her bent elbow and stood behind Lucy as she continued practiced breathing while imagining a box. She leaned back into him as he stood behind her. Louis smiled to himself, thankful that she seemed to trust him in a delicate moment like this. He continued standing behind her and gently rubbed her arm in encouragement while Lucy continued to recover her breath.

Suddenly, Lucy turned around and threw her arms around Louis and nuzzled her nose into his neck. She took in his amber and cedarwood scent, nuzzling deeper into his neck. Louis brought his hand to the back of Lucy's head and rubbed the back of her head reassuringly.

"Thank you," Lucy whispered. "I am never nervous like this. I sometimes do my own stunts, and I don't blink an eye at that. I don't know what has gotten into me."

"Believe it or not, singing can be one of the most difficult things that people can try, especially if you don't feel like you have much control over your voice yet. Here is the thing: You are going to get more control the more you practice. Does that make sense?"

Lucy nodded into his neck and sniffled a bit.

"Father God, we come before you with this burden that Lucy is carrying. We know You have a plan for her. If this audition is meant to be, You will open the door for an opportunity. If the audition ends today, we know that You have a plan for Lucy that will be far better than what we could imagine. Father God, give her peace about Your plan for her. Flood her with confidence and reassurance that her worries end here on this sidewalk, and she can walk confidently in you as she auditions. Remind her that she is not alone. In Your precious son's name, we pray. Amen."

Lucy could feel the tension and pressure melt away from her. Between the embrace, the prayer, and Louis's presence, she was finally coming back to her usual self. She stepped away from Louis and continued holding his hand and breathing slowly, nodding at him as well.

"Are you good?" Louis asked.

"Let's do this," Lucy said with a newfound confidence.

"I think the building is just up here for the audition." Louis pointed at a building just a couple of blocks away.

Lucy and Louis began walking down the sidewalk when Lucy heard her phone ding. She glanced at the screen, just to make sure that nothing changed regarding her audition today.

Clara Whitmore

Is this you? If so, how do you want me to handle this?

Lucy clicked on the link that was added to the text thread from her agent.

"Oh la la, Paris is the city of love for Skye Reynolds" was the news caption, and she looked closely at a dark image of she and Louis kissing last night.

How? How could someone even know that she went to see Louis last night? We kissed just outside the door as I was leaving. How could anyone see?

"Everything ok?" Louis asked Lucy as they continued to walk, but he noticed the concerned look on her face, combined with the fact that her pace had slowed as she stared at her phone.

Another message from Dottie came across her phone.

Dottie

Hello, I hope you are having a lovely day. How should I respond to this news story? Sorry to bother you.

Another ding, with a message now from Liam...

Liam

Bloody hell, Lucy. Who is this bloke? Also, where was my fiancé when you were on your hot date????

Something in Lucy snapped, and she whirled around at Louis and held her phone screen out to see the new story

"What is this?" Lucy confronted Louis.

"What is what?" Louis calmly took her phone. He touched his glasses and looked closely at the image of the two of them in an embrace on his doorstep last night. He nervously pulled his hand across his beard and wondered how this photo had been captured at his house last night.

"I have no idea how this was taken." Louis took his eyes off the phone screen and looked at Lucy.

"I haven't had any run-ins with paparazzi throughout this trip. I find it ironic that while I am in the quietest neighborhood in Paris, suddenly paparazzi shows up at your door.   You don't find that strange?" Sarcasm dripped from Lucy's mouth.

"Well, yes, actually," Louis admitted.   "I don't know how or why someone would be in my area looking for celebrities." Louis remained calm and sympathetic, finally realizing what Lucy had to deal with while managing the demands of celebrity status.

"I can't imagine how difficult it must be to deal with this." Louis extended his hand in reassurance, but Lucy pulled her hand back.

"Who did you tell that I was coming to your place?"

"I wouldn't tell anyone intentionally if that is what you are suggesting." Louis stared at the sky, trying to rack his brain at how someone could have found out about it.

"Well, Louis, someone found out somehow, and it wasn't from me! If you wanted me to pay you more money for this job, I would have done it."

"Whoa, whoa, whoa, this conversation is going so far past what it should be. I didn't tell anyone." Louis extended his hand out again, only to be rejected by Lucy again.

"Now, I get to have an audition after all of this. I tell you what. I will go by myself. I just can't…" Lucy started walking away.

"I am sorry," Louis called to Lucy as she walked away. He seemed frozen by indifference. Would he let her go or intervene?

Just as Lucy was about to enter the door, she looked back at Louis standing on the sidewalk with a crestfallen look on his face, his hands in his pockets. Then, shame hit Lucy as she walked through the doors, feeling terrible about how she reacted.

What if he didn't tell anyone?

Then, she looked away and entered the building.

CHAPTER 30

Elle

2026

Elle texted Margaux, who was in Italy.

Elle

Wish you were here…

Margaux returned the message with a photo of an entire table full of Italian dishes at what looks like a party.

Of course, Elle thought to herself, *Margaux has found a way to make it a party in Italy.* Elle smiled when she studied the photo on her phone.

Elle

Are you at a party? How do you get invited to a party in Italy during a short stay there? You make friends everywhere.

Margaux

My roommates decided to go to a market last night. This was some of the food that was out for us as we did a paint thing. It was so fun, but my painting was terrible.

Then, she felt compelled to look around her rental and found herself being drawn to the balcony. As much as she hated to admit it, Elle was feeling lonely. She didn't realize that she would spend so much time by herself during her girls' trip in Paris.

Elle stared at her phone, struggling with a reply. Sure, she agreed to go, knowing that Lucy did have some work commitments, but she didn't realize that she would have this much down time … alone. Elle knew that she would have to return to her home in New York soon, but she and Liam were still working on the details of their life in New York together. She hated wasting time just sitting in a rental alone in Paris, and Elle was missing Liam. They needed to have some deep conversations about the transition to his move to New York. Elle just had this overwhelming feeling that she was wasting time here when she could be spending time with Liam.

Yes, I am fine. Sorry about being a sad sack. I can't wait to hear about your trip! Keep sending photo updates. 🖤

Margaux

Will do! Call if you need to chat. Hugs! 😊

Margaux stared at her phone for a moment, thinking about her best friend who clearly was struggling right now. She could tell by Elle's brief response that now was not the right time to have a deep conversation about feelings if she wanted to video chat with her. Margaux would catch up with her later.

Elle stared at her phone, contemplating if she should text Liam. She missed him so much. "Dear brothers and sisters, you have no obligation whatsoever to do what your sinful nature urges you to do," Elle said to herself. *Breathe and don't act impulsive. Liam will want to fix the problem, and you are fine by yourself right now.*

I am in Paris now. Get over yourself, Elle. You are going to sit here and enjoy the view and sip your coffee. Then, you are going to go buy some picnic items and go back to Luxembourg Gardens to have a picnic. You are going to invite Lucy to join you when she is finished. She did expect that she would be finished soon. If Lucy can't make it, then you are going to have the best picnic of your life sitting in Paris.

Elle took a deep breath and looked out from the balcony. She watched the riverboats glide down the river and people walk on the cobblestone sidewalk that ran on either side of the river. Some people could be seen sitting on the grounds of Notre Dame, eating a baguette while sitting on a bench, deep in conversation.

"The city of Paris is the living room for its people, and you are going to make yourself at home," she said to herself.

Elle finished her coffee and began gathering her things.

She went to her room and picked out black ankle-length pants, a black-and-white striped tank top and matched it with a white jacket. She chose white tennis shoes to match the ensemble. She changed her outfit and tied her hair into a messy but stylish ponytail and made her way to the door.

Elle pulled out her phone and text Lucy.

Elle

> Meet me at Luxembourg Gardens after your audition. I have a small surprise for you.

Elle dropped a pin of the location of the garden and sent it to Lucy. She opened the door to leave and found a very teary-eyed Lucy standing at the door.

"Are you ok?" Elle pulled Lucy into a hug and closed the door behind her.

The two friends stood in the door and hugged, and Lucy cried. Elle didn't ask her any questions but just let her friend cry and cry and cry. Elle rubbed the back of Lucy's hair, almost like an older sister would. "It's ok … it's ok," Elle whispered as Lucy continued to cry.

After some time, Lucy began to slowly stop crying. Her breathing began to slow, and she calmly stepped away from Elle once she was finally composed.

"Do you want to talk about it?" Elle asked.

"Not yet. I will cry too much," Lucy answered honestly.

"I know the perfect thing to help you feel better." Elle smiled conspiratorially. "Grab big sunglasses and your hat; we need to go touch grass."

Lucy looked confused but followed along with Elle's lead out the door. Elle had a large bag, which Lucy soon found would be used for today's adventure. They stopped by an adorable fromagerie and picked up some local cheese. They entered another charming shop, a patisserie, where they picked a baguette and some sweets. They visited a produce stand to pick up some fresh fruit. Finally, they stopped for a bottle of wine, which was the last thing to fit into Elle's tote bag. It required both women to take turns carrying the bags as they walked up the hill from their rental to Luxembourg Gardens.

Elle led the way and looked for her favorite spot that she visited last time in Luxembourg Gardens. Digging into her tote bag, Elle pulled out a blanket and tossed it across the grass for their makeshift table for their picnic. Lucy moved the bag to the center of the blanket and began unpacking their items for a picnic.

"When I was in medical school, before becoming a hairdresser, research suggested that touching grass and getting into nature will help reduce stress," Elle added as she laid down on the grass in the park. Lucy joined her after Elle patted next to her to encourage Lucy to join her in the grass.

"Hold my hand," Elle whispered as the two friends laid in the grass side by side, looking up at the sky. "Research also says that a gentle touch is a powerful impact to stress too."

This fact made Lucy emotional again. It made her think of how wonderful Louis had been on the sidewalk. His touch not only sent sparks through her veins but also could offer the best calming effect than she could ever imagine. Elle's reassuring comment made her think about Louis, and shame hit Lucy like a wave. Her nose started to run, and Lucy got that throaty feeling of fighting back tears.

"Want to talk?" Elle asked. "You don't have to pursue this singing thing. You are a talented actress without adding singing to your resume."

"It's not about that. The audition went pretty well, actually," Lucy replied.

Elle waited to see what else Lucy wanted to say.

"The director said I have some potential but need a bit more training."

"That sounds promising." Elle again waited to see what Lucy wanted to offer her.

"Have you heard from Liam today?" Lucy asked.

"We have been texting but that is it. Is he ok?" Elle had concern in her voice.

"He is fine … it isn't like that." Lucy paused, trying to form the right words. "I have been seeing someone … sort of."

Elle popped up on her elbows on the grass and lifted up her

sunglasses, as if doing both of those things would make her hear the rest of the story better.

"How? When have you had time…" Elle trailed off the last part of her question, thinking about the time that Lucy has spent with work stuff.

"Is he someone you met through work?"

"Yes … he is my voice coach. We haven't really gone on a date … well, I had ice cream with him after our rehearsal." Lucy sighed, thinking about the situation. "There was chemistry between us … that and he didn't have any obvious red flags like every guy I have dated. He was so thoughtful and such a gentleman. He literally is so calm all the time, it amazes me. He was the one who showed me how to deal with pushy fans calmly."

"What happened?" Elle asked.

"I think he notified the paparazzi that I was coming to his house to rehearse last night," Lucy said, sitting up even further. "We shared a kiss last night, and someone got a photo of it. We hadn't even kissed before, and someone happened to be lurking around just at the same time I was leaving his house."

"Why would he do that?"

"I know a photo is worth a lot of money." Lucy shrugged her shoulders.

"Do you think he seems like a guy who would do that?"

"I don't know." Lucy paused, her mind racing with scenarios.

"Honestly, I just don't know."

"There is something more you aren't telling me." Elle could already begin to read Lucy.

"I was horrible when I found out about the photos today. I scolded him. Even if he didn't do it, I just ruined any chance we had at getting to know one another better."

"Your phone keeps buzzing with text messages. Is he messaging you?"

"He messaged me a couple of times, but it is mostly my agent and my assistant wanting to know what we are telling the press about the mystery man photo. Liam messaged me as an overprotective brother and wanted to know who the mystery man was."

"I am glad I don't read that stuff," Elle admitted.

"I am glad you don't read it either," Lucy joked.

"In my gut, I think I overreacted and treated him like rubbish."

"If it makes you feel any better, do you remember when I overreacted with your brother, and he was able to get past it once I apologized? You even brought him to me so we could clear things up."

"That's true. I did help you find the love of your life." Lucy began to smile.

"What can I do?" Elle turned to sit up further, facing Lucy with her legs crossed.

"Actually, let's keep touching grass for a bit longer, then enjoy our picnic. I just want to stay in this bubble for a bit longer."

You stay in your bubble for now, Lucy, but I want to learn more about this mystery man because I love playing Cupid too, Elle thought to herself.

CHAPTER 31

Louis

2026

"Lucy, would you please answer your phone? I just have to let you know that I would never alert the news that you were at my house. I am sorry that it happened to you, but I wouldn't be the one to put you at risk like that. I'll admit that it is a bit coincidental, but it wasn't me. I just want you to know…"

"If you are satisfied with this voicemail message, press one. To rerecord the message, press two."

Louis pressed two.

"Lucy, I would really like to talk to you. I don't like how things ended with us today. I know that you were really anxious about your audition, plus you received the news about the photo at the same time, and I think it was just too much. I am sorry you are juggling so much right now, and I would like to be able to make things right. I just want you to know…"

"If you are satisfied with the voicemail message, press one. To rerecord the message, press two."

"Lucy, I am sorry about what happened today. Your voicemail

keeps cutting off my message, so I am keeping this short. Getting to know you has brought me so much joy in my life. I would not risk the joy you have brought to my life and my kids' lives by alerting the paparazzi. You mean too much to me to do that."

"If you are satisfied with the voicemail message, press one. To rerecord the message, press two."

Louis pressed one.

Mate, she is never going to call you back. She has far too many people in her life who will do a better job at keeping the paparazzi at bay. You are an amateur at this. You are an amateur at dating, let alone dating a celebrity.

"I have two questions." Noemie entered the room. "First, are you talking to yourself?"

"Yes, I was."

"Ok, then. Why do you keep calling Lucy to apologize to her?"

"Paparazzi found out about her visit last night and took a picture of the two of us on our doorstep. It's all over the papers. She was really upset about it. She thought that maybe I told someone she was coming to our house."

"I can see why she was mad. It is a bit strange." Noemie grabbed Louis's phone and looked up the photo. "Oh … it has been clear that you really like her by the way you look at her but based on this photo of the two of you kissing, I think she likes you too."

Louis took his phone back from her. "I didn't want you to see that."

"It's ok … I knew you would begin dating at some point. Plus, I like Lucy too. I was hoping you might start dating her."

"You were hoping I would start dating her, huh?" Louis pulled Noemie to him and gave her a hug. Louis was always amazed at how grown-up she was. She could see that he was feeling lonely and despite that it would be inviting someone new into their bubble, Noemie still wished that for him. His heart swelled with pride and gratitude for having such a sweet girl.

"Oh no," Noemie said. "I just remembered something for school tomorrow."

"What?" Louis asked as he pulled away from their hug to see Noemie's face.

"I was supposed to bring flowers for my teacher's birthday tomorrow. I can't let my class down. Everyone is bringing something for her."

"It's ok, I will go get some for you. I'll run upstairs to get my wallet and go … unless you want to come with me?"

"I'll stay here and work on homework if that is ok."

While Louis ran upstairs, Noemie looked up Lucy's phone number on his phone. Then, she quickly added her number to Noemie's own phone. Soon, he was back downstairs.

"Are you sure you don't want to go? Also, what color should I get?"

"No, I need to work on something." Noemie smiled, conspiratorially.

After Louis kissed her on the head and walked out the door,

accidentally left his phone on the kitchen counter. After Noemie heard Louis walk down the front steps, she texted Lucy's number. Noemie messaged Lucy and told her that she needed her help and to hurry.

Immediately, Louis's phone began ringing and ringing. Noemie smiled to herself and sent Lucy's call to voicemail.

Then, Noemie sat down on the sofa and began her homework, as Louis's phone continued to ring.

CHAPTER 32

Lucy

2026

"Noemie messaged about fifteen minutes ago." Lucy was trying to sound encouraging, but clearly showing signs of concern, while she and Elle rushed to Durant's home in an Uber.

"Since then, I have called five times and cannot understand why Louis is not picking up his phone either."

Lucy stared out of the window as they were travelling, inching closer and closer to Noemie. Elle put her hand on top of Lucy's hand as they sat in the backseat of the Uber. Elle could see that Lucy was distraught over this and must feel really connected to Noemie. The usually bubbly Lucy had become quiet and appeared to be deep in thought. Elle wanted to offer quiet reassurance but didn't really know what to say.

I am so surprised that Noemie reached out to me of all people to come get some help. Doesn't Louis have someone else who helps them? I know Louis mentioned that his boss helps out with the kids from time to time, but I'm surprised that she reached out to me. Then, Lucy's mind switched to worry, I hope everything is ok.

A pedestrian crossed in front of the car and caused the driver to come to a quick halt, mumbled something to himself as the pedestrian took their time crossing the street. Lucy looked around the headrest to see what was causing the delay and found herself growing even more impatient. Elle, again, tried to offer some reassurance.

"Could you tell by her tone if it seemed like an emergency? Perhaps, she just needed some help with homework?" Elle knew the effort was weak, but she wanted to try to make Lucy feel better.

"There is just something with this family that makes me feel protective," Lucy replied while keeping her eyes on the road and watching for their arrival.

"Could you move faster?" Lucy added.

The driver ignored Lucy's question and slowly began driving again.

Elle could see that Lucy was watching the driver's directions. "I think we are only one minute away," she offered as encouragement again.

Finally, the driver pulled up to the familiar house. "This is the place," Lucy said and quickly stepped out of the Uber and out on the sidewalk while Elle followed her lead. Within two large strides, Lucy was knocking on the door of Louis's home, while Elle made sure to finalize the details of the Uber and politely thanked the driver.

"Noemie, I am here." Lucy tries to keep her voice low, as to not alert neighbors. After the paparazzi situation earlier, Lucy didn't want to bring attention that she was back here at this house and didn't want to suggest there was an emergency in the event there were nosy neighbors. Elle finally joined Lucy in the front entry.

Lucy stood staring at the door, poised to enter the flat as soon as the door opened. Her hand on the door. After the turn of the lock and seeing the handle turn, the door opened to Noemie. Lucy walked to Noemie and embraced her. Elle followed in behind her, watching a version of Lucy she hadn't seen before. Lucy put her arms around the young girl, who returned the hug, without even knowing why Noemie called her.

Elle was watching the interaction. Lucy was in protector mode, and her connection to Noemie was so sweet. Elle found herself genuinely touched by watching Lucy embrace this girl. This moment was so tender and special. After seeing Noemie, it didn't seem likely that anyone was in danger.

"What is going on? What has happened?" Lucy asked, trying to sound calm. Noemie and Lucy still had their arms around each other.

Looking up at Lucy while still keeping her arms around Lucy's waist, suddenly, Noemie's guilt washed over her like a wave. Tears filled her eyes, and she buried her face into Lucy's stomach.

"It's ok." A beat of silence.

"What happened?" Only the sound of Noemie whimpering could be heard.

"How can I help?" Lucy persisted. Lucy rubbed Noemie's back to help offer some comfort. Noemie continued to cry, realizing that her poorly hatched plan was about to unravel.

Elle stood and watched, trying to be an observer. Normally, Elle would have tried to offer some help or find a way to assist the situation, but honestly, she didn't know the young girl.

Lucy heard the doorknob turn behind her because she was still just steps into their home. She pulled Noemie aside while still hugging her, thinking that there may have been danger or an intruder, which was why Noemie called her. Lucy turned her body so now she was facing the door. Elle stood closer to both Noemie and Lucy, trying her best to protect them. Everyone was on edge.

Much to her surprise, Louis entered the home with flowers in hand.

"What is happening?" Louis asked, with a completely confused expression on his face.

"I was just asking the same thing," Lucy added.

Louis walked over to Noemie and bent down to gauge why she was crying. He wanted to make eye contact with her … it was always the thing that they did when they needed to have a real understanding between them. Most days, Noemie tried to take on the role of adult; today, Louis needed to give Noemie reassurance.

Noemie finally was ready to share what happened.

"I heard you leave a message, well three messages, that you kept rerecording on Lucy's voicemail. I thought we weren't going to see Lucy again because you got into an argument…" Worry flooded Noemie again, and she began crying, which prevented her from finishing her story.

"We weren't in an argument, love." Louis pulled a piece of hair behind Noemie's ear in reassurance. "We just had a misunderstanding."

"I…I…I wanted to help." Noemie's breathing became unsteady,

and the tears started to flow again.

"It's ok." Lucy pulled Noemie tightly into a hug and held on as she continued to cry it out. Lucy was rubbing Noemie's back as she tried to reassure her. Louis gave the girls the moment they needed.

Louis heard the clinking of dishes coming from the dining area.

"Is Theo in the other room?" he asked, almost confused by the idea of Theo being in the dining room by himself while doing something with dishes.

Noemie nodded. "He is setting the table," Noemie added, slowly catching her breath after crying.

"I haven't prepared dinner or anything close to dinner yet," Louis responded, looking confused.

"I ordered something," Noemie whispered, "it should be delivered anytime. I had a little extra money of my own to pay for it."

"Why did you order dinner, and why is your brother setting the table?" Louis asked, clearly not connecting any dots to Noemie's sparse details of a story.

"Well, I wanted to help you two make up." Noemie began crying again.

"We aren't angry with one another; we just had a disagreement," Louis reassured her.

"I was just afraid that Lucy would go back to England without saying goodbye since your argument," Noemie explained. "I really like her."

Lucy and Louis made eye contact. Just a look that held between them and something inside Lucy burned inside; even this child can feel that there was more to us than just friendship. Just hearing sweet Noemie acknowledge their connection too made Lucy want to be standing closer to Louis. She wanted to take his face into her hands and apologize for how she reacted earlier today.

"I like you too," Lucy answered, still hugging her. "Why did you want my help?"

"That was the only way I could think of getting you here quickly." Noemie shrugged. "I knew you would come and help me." Noemie smiled at Lucy.

"You are correct. I would rush to help you." Lucy smiled. "I would rather you just ask though… don't scare me next time. I would have come to see you. Ok?"

"Am I going to be grounded?" Noemie had tears welling up in her eyes again.

"We will talk later," Louis said, trying to hide his smile as he rubbed both hands over this face in relief, confusion, and slight surprise.

There was a knock at the door as the group stood in the kitchen, solving the mystery of Noemie's non-existent emergency to get Louis and Lucy back in the same room together.

"Theo, come here," Noemie called. "I think the food arrived."

Theo dutifully came into the kitchen and took Lucy's hand as he entered the room. He didn't say hello … just offered a quick hand … then moved to answer the door.

Louis watched the warmth that Theo had for Lucy, and it warmed his heart. He just couldn't believe how quickly he had taken to her. There wasn't anyone else who he showed this kind of affection toward. With his specific type of autism, Theo used words sparingly and showed love in different ways. Typically, Theo never expressed himself physically like he did with Lucy by holding her hand.

Noemie walked toward the door and began reaching into her pocket for her money that she had to pay for the meal.

"Wait… wait… I will answer the door and pay for dinner," Louis added.

Louis answered the door and learned that Noemie had ordered a large salad and pizza for them to share. Louis paid the delivery person while Noemie began her role as host.

"Theo, will you go put this on the table?" Noemie reminded him, always acting older than her years.

Theo took the food and took the pizza and salad to the dining table.

"Lucy, will you please join us for dinner?" Noemie smiled, her eyes still bloodshot from crying.

"Of course, how could I refuse such a kind offer?" Lucy smiled.

"Elle, you are welcome to join us for dinner too. I am Noemie," she added while holding out her hand. "I am sorry for my manners."

Now that is the Noemie we know and love … the child who acts like an adult, Lucy thought to herself.

"I am Elle Bennett. It is a pleasure meeting you. However, I think I am going back to our flat. I appreciate the invite," Elle said formally, attempting to return Noemie's manner.

"I am Elle." She held out her hand to Louis too.

"It is a pleasure." Louis shook her hand.

"Lucy, I am going to go but take your time getting back to the rental." Elle hugged Lucy. "You didn't tell me Louis was absolutely beautiful and kind," Elle whispered to Lucy during her hug, then pulled away with a mischievous smile.

"I am going to get moving. I don't want your dinner to get cold. Good night." Elle made her way toward the door, then added, "I have a feeling that I may be seeing you again soon."

Lucy's eyes grew wide with Elle's comment. *Thanks Elle, you are completely putting my business out for Louis. I should be a woman of mystery!* Lucy said to herself.

Theo came back into the kitchen and grabbed Lucy's hand to guide her into the dining room. He then pulled a chair out for Lucy.

"Why, thank you, sir," Lucy added.

Then, Theo did the same thing for Louis as well.

"Noemie, before you sit down, do you mind putting the flowers in water for your teacher? I don't want them to wilt," Louis added.

"Lucy, would you like your flowers in water or take them with you like this?"

Louis was mid-sip and choked on his water from laughter after realization seemed to hit him. *She is a master at matchmaking,* Lucy thought to herself.

Lucy and Louis looked at one another, smiling at the effort the kids took to get them back together tonight. Their eyes met with longing and understanding that they both were eager to get today past them.

There is no other place I would rather be, Lucy thought.

CHAPTER 33

Elle

2026

Her heart was light and comforted by knowing that she knew her gut instinct was correct: Lucy had feelings for Louis. Although Elle couldn't put her finger on when this connection started, she could tell when Lucy was texting him the other day that she had some interest in someone. Now, Elle had met the man who had captured Lucy's attention.

I noticed that Louis doesn't seem like the guys that Lucy has dated in the past. First, he is a daddy, and his life seems to be focused on his family. He is a bit nerdy, which I love. I spent most of my formative years around the nerdy kids who were chasing their dreams of life in academia. Also, he is far removed from the entertainment world for the most part. He doesn't seem like someone who is immersed into that world. His world seems to be his kids. Liam seemed to be seeking that kind of person who was not focused on the entertainment world when I met him. I can relate to a man who wants the personal and professional life balance. Most importantly, he seems to have a strong faith.

Elle walked toward the metro, after leaving Louis's flat, and her heart was so full thinking of Lucy. *Lucy is falling for this man. I know it. This is a side of Lucy I had never seen in her life. Sure, she hasn't known him for long, but as I can attest to, when you know, you know. Louis offers a calm, softer side to Lucy's life. If he turns out to be the real deal, I think that even Liam would approve of him.*

Louis's arrondissement offered the quintessential family neighborhood Parisian aesthetic, Elle noticed as she walked the neighborhood while searching for the metro entrance. The lights from rooftop terraces illuminated the buildings. Families strolled around, and lovers were seen holding hands. Sounds of people's quiet voices, the clinking of silverware on plates at a nearby restaurant could be heard, and even some soft jazz music filled the street during her stroll. This stroll made Elle miss Liam so much.

Elle was so thankful for Lucy's idea to come on this trip, but she was not prepared at all for how much she would miss Liam. She was in the world's most romantic city, and she wanted to enjoy it with him so badly.

Elle, you are going to be back in London soon enough. You will be planning your wedding, and you will be able to spend time with Liam. You are going to be in your happily ever after soon enough, so just enjoy the time you have with Lucy right now. Elle was mentally giving herself her own pep talk as she came upon the metro.

She walked down the steps to her metro station and made her way onto the platform. Several more couples were enjoying a perfect late summer evening together. Shortly, the metro arrived, and Elle sat down near a window once on the train. She decided she wanted to stop at the St. Michel metro station and watch the Eiffel Tower sparkle from across the river while sitting near Notre Dame.

After arriving at the St. Michel Metro, Elle made her way up the stairs from the metro and walked down the sidewalk just far enough to get a good view of the Eiffel Tower from the grounds of Notre

Dame. The 4th arrondissement that housed Notre Dame was down the river from the Eiffel Tower, which is in the 1st arrondissement. However, Elle believed that if she sat in the park surrounding Notre Dame, she would have the perfect distant view of the Eiffel Tower. After finding what she believed to be the perfect spot, Elle sat down on the edge of the sideway that overlooked the Seine too. People used the city as their living room here. Friends and couples dotted the area with blankets, wine, and food. They were taking in the city too.

Taking out her phone, she took a picture looking down over the Seine, and the Eiffel Tower just became illuminated with lights. She loved seeing the structure "sparkle" with lights on the hour. Even locals who spoke French paused to watch the structure illuminate. Elle studied the photo and added a filter to make the lights shine more brightly. After she hit the forward button, she reconsidered the message after sending it because she didn't want to sound too lonely. Elle just wanted to remind Liam that she was missing him.

Elle

I admit it. Being away from you has been harder than I imagined. Seeing the Eiffel Tower sparkle just doesn't have the same magic without you by my side. Love you.

Liam's response was almost immediate.

Liam

You doing, ok?

Elle smiled at her phone. He was so thoughtful. Liam wanted his sister to have the best experience once he stepped away from his current role. He wanted to make sure that the new assistant was trustworthy and able to navigate some of the extra work that he always did for the best interest of Lucy. *He is such a great man,* Elle told herself.

Music could be heard from across the river. Just adjacent to where Elle was sitting, across the river, someone had set up a large speaker. Jazz music could be heard spilling out into the streets. Suddenly, a small group of people appeared around the landing where the speaker was housed and began dancing. They didn't just dance; they were doing variations of dances like the tango. Then, a slight change in music, the group began doing swing dances. It was almost like they rehearsed, but they were just enjoying a beautiful summer night in Paris. *Who wouldn't want to dance under the stars in Paris with the Eiffel Tower illuminated in the background? Someone pinch me now,* Elle thought to herself.

Elle took some photos of the group dancing. She sent two photos to Liam.

Elle

Now, I am really missing you. 

Liam

That looks like the night we had our first date in London, when we were dancing by the river.

Elle

It does remind me of that night. I don't think either of us dance as well as these people do though. 😄

Elle

You took me to see the Femme Frequency mural too.

Liam

That is when you knew I was the one, wasn't it?

Elle

How did you know? 

Elle stood up and looked around the area again. She didn't have many more nights in Paris and wanted to take in these final few moments.

The rental was just a short walk from there. She walked through the grounds of Notre Dame, walked through the park area that surrounded the historic church. She walked past the Shakespeare and Company store, and the music grew louder as she watched the groups of people dancing, a rollaway speaker playing and the cobblestone sidewalk their makeshift dance floor.

Elle continued walking to the rental, the lively music growing fainter. She could see a dark figure standing outside of her rental. At first, she was apprehensive, but she could see his face take shape. Soon, Elle could see Liam sitting on the step of her rental, and she began running toward him. Liam saw her and began speed-walking toward her. Elle threw her arms around his neck once he was within reach. Liam lifted her and spun her around with his face nestled in her neck. They were tangled, a combination of limbs and laughter.

Liam slowly set Elle down and looked into her eyes. "I heard you were missing me and I thought it would be a good idea to do something about that."

Elle put her hands on his face and looked into his eyes. "Oh, how much I have missed you." She brought her lips gently onto Liam's lips. Liam's hands lowered to Elle's back, and she pulled her body closer to him. Without a moment's hesitation, her kiss landed fierce and unpolished——too full of longing. Then, the kiss moved into something slower and softer. They clung to another in the moments after the kiss, as though they were overcome by time and distance.

They looked at one another, and both of them began laughing, so thankful and equally excited to see one another. Liam and Elle were almost giddy by the presence of the other but also had sheer gratitude that they had found one another after all the years of looking and longing for finding that special someone in this big wide world. Elle laughed so hard that tears began to well in her eyes. Liam wiped her eyes from laughter.

"Have you lost your mind or is it just me?" Margaux walked up to Elle and Liam.

"What are you doing here?" Elle was genuinely shocked.

"Well, I heard you missed me, and I always wanted to see Paris," Margaux deadpanned.

"Plus, I wanted you to meet Evan," Margaux added and then noticed that both Liam and Elle were standing outside of the rental, staring in absolute shock at her.

Elle hugged Margaux and whispered, "This is the guy who said he was your fiancé at the end of the fashion show in London. Is this your fiancé?" Elle was hugging Margaux and whispering all her questions in her ear.

"This is my friend, Evan." Margaux introduced a hulking dark blond-haired man with a warm smile who stood behind her with his hand out to greet them.

"It is nice to meet you. I have heard so much about you." Evan shook both of their hands.

"It is a pleasure meeting you," Elle said, but still clearly in shock with the surprise of the group.

"How did you all get here?" Elle looked around at her dearest people, suddenly standing on a sidewalk in Paris.

"Lucy invited us," Margaux added. "She gave me the information for the rental. She said she has been extra busy with work, so she invited us to come too."

Elle made a face.

"What is with the face?" Liam asked.

Elle paused. "Let's go inside because there is something you need to know about what has Lucy so occupied." Elle smiled conspiratorially, as she unlocked the door to the flat.

CHAPTER 34

Louis

2026

"You not only surprised me with this meal but also made it even better with great company." Louis lifted his glass and toasted Lucy from across the table.

Theo and Noemie took Louis's comment as a signal that they should begin cleaning up the table. Again, their coordinated efforts surprised Louis. He couldn't believe the effort both of his kids took to get Lucy here for dinner. *I didn't even know if the kids were ready for me to date. I didn't know if I was ready to date until I met her.* Louis's gaze fell on Lucy.

I am new at this dating thing. Is this even a date? Should I have let my kids get this close to her, knowing she is going to leave sometime soon? I need to research this kind of stuff before I go with my gut and begin having feelings for someone who is a celebrity. What was I thinking? Louis held his stare at Lucy from across the table and smiled, despite his apprehension. His eyes shared a longing to spend even more time with her. *Lucy looked so comfortable here in his house and with the kids. Could she really enjoy their company or was this part of being a great actress?*

"I have some homework that I need to do, so Theo and I are going to begin clearing the table." Noemie stood up and began taking the empty plates from the table. Theo followed suit and began helping his sister. As he was picking up Lucy's plate, he paused for a moment and leaned his head on her shoulder … almost a hug … clearly a sign of affection.

Lucy returned the gesture and leaned her head on top of Theo's. They stood in this position for merely seconds, but the moment was not missed by Louis.

I can't believe how taken Theo is with Lucy. He is never this affectionate with anyone, except our family. The interaction between the two made Louis's heart flutter and made him want to spend more time with Lucy even more. *If my sweet boy can trust her, he must know something I don't know. He doesn't trust easily.*

"You can just leave the plates on the counter in the kitchen. I will wash them," Louis called to the kids who had disappeared into the kitchen.

"Would you like to stay for some jazz music? I have a great record collection," Louis added, hoping that if spending time with him wasn't reason enough to stay, then maybe classic jazz on vinyl would be a better reason.

There was a beat of silence, then Noemie reentered the dining room.

"Good night, L," Noemie added while giving a hug to Louis.

"I love you." Louis kissed her on the head.

"Love you," Noemie answered.

Theo came to Louis and gave him a hug while Louis hugged him in return, whispering, "I love you, Buddy."

"Ok," Theo whispered with a smile.

"You love teasing me, don't you? I 'ok' you too," Louis said, which made Theo giggle.

Noemie gave Lucy a quick hug good night, but this time, Theo was happy to wave to Lucy as he was saying good night.

"Good night," Lucy called to both kids as they walked upstairs to their bedrooms.

"There is no pressure for you to stay–."

"I would love to stay and listen to jazz with you." Lucy smiled from across the room.

This is it. This is how a grown man gets his heart broken because I really, really like this amazing, confident, beautiful woman. And … the kids really like her too.

Louis's phone buzzed, and he glanced at the message. "I am sorry, but I need to reply to this," he responded. "Feel free to use the restroom down the hall if you like. Meanwhile, I will respond to the message and pick out some music for us."

Lucy nodded in approval and started making her way down the hall to the restroom.

"Would you like a glass of wine?" Louis called to Lucy.

"Sure."

He poured them both a glass of wine and sat the glasses on opposite sides of the table near the sofa. Then, Louis put on an Ella

Fitzgerald album on the turntable and began playing some music.

He picked up his phone and replied to his friend and former colleague, who happened to be the headmaster of Theo's school, James Johnson.

> Is everything ready to go for the show? It is our biggest school fundraiser of the year. I know most of what is happening for the show, but I don't know all the details because you have been helping so much. I am touching base with the team who is helping with the event. How are things going with your portion of the event? I can't believe that it is tomorrow night!

Louis looked at the lengthy message on his phone and had completely forgotten about the event tomorrow night. The last time he reached out to anyone on the team was the day before Lucy's job offer. Although he feels confident about the planning the team has done, the reality of silencing his notification from that group chat hit him like a ton of bricks.

James wasn't done writing though, as dots popped on the screen.

> I just need someone to be the "glue" for the event. The teachers know where their kids are set to perform, so it is just making sure the groups are where they are supposed to be. I know your work in helping with the musical performances was selected months ago, but I could use some extra hands tomorrow. Can you be there for the entire event in the evening tomorrow?

Louis stared at his phone while contemplating what he should do. What if Lucy needed his help tomorrow night?

"Are all French bathrooms so nice? I mean, the bathrooms are even stylish. How do French people do that? They make everything sophisticated," Lucy joked. Lucy must have noticed a strange look on Louis's face when she walked up.

"What? What happened? You have this worried look on your face. Did I miss something?" Lucy asked.

"I was just asked to be at an event tomorrow night as the annual fundraiser for Theo's school. I have been on the committee and just planned to stop in because most of my work has been completed. However, I was asked if I could help a bit more tomorrow night. I hope this doesn't mess up any of our plans."

"That's ok. We can rehearse tomorrow morning if that works for you."

Louis's phone dinged again.

"I may have to check my phone a couple more times just to firm up some details for tomorrow," Louis added, trying to do his best to not be disrespectful to Lucy and to show he was really interested in spending time with her.

James

Do you know any social media people? Our committee has tried to put some things out for fundraising outside of the school, but we haven't raised much money. Do you know anyone who may do some work for free?

Louis responded aloud to the last text message, "No, I don't know anyone in social media," but before he hit send, Lucy responded.

"I know all kinds of people in social media. What do you need?"

"We need someone to post some creative ideas just for tomorrow to get donations outside of the school. Oh yeah … they need to do it for free," Louis almost said with a chuckle.

"Tell the headmaster yes, you do know someone, because I know someone who will do it for free," reassured Lucy.

"Oh no, you don't have to do that," Louis reassured Lucy, but she was already on her phone texting someone.

"Would you like to have some volunteers to do some hair and makeup for kids if students wish to have it done?"

"Sure." Louis tried to hide a smile.

"You do realize that my soon-to-be sister-in-law is now a world-famous stylist who loves to help people." Lucy continued to text while also glancing back and forth from her phone to Louis.

"So, I can text Headmaster James that we have a social media person and some stylists to help with our fundraiser?"

"Yes and yes. Also, ask the headmaster to do some screenshots tonight of social media inspiration. Send me his number, too, please."

"Ok, done and done," Louis mimicked Lucy's response.

Lucy and Louis sat on their phones finalizing their plans for the fundraising event.

Lucy finally put her phone down when she noticed Louis was staring at her. She smiled and turned her attention to him.

"Can I ask you a very forward question?" Louis decided to be a bit brave.

Lucy nodded quietly, with a confused smile.

"Why aren't you married because any man would be blessed to have you in their life?"

Lucy smiled without saying anything.

"I am sorry. I am sure you get people asking all kinds of personal questions all the time. It is just you seem pretty amazing, and I can't believe you don't have men practically throwing themselves at you on a regular basis."

"Wow, you know how to make a girl feel special," Lucy teased, leaning over and bumping Louis with her shoulder.

"I am sorry. I usually hide behind an instrument, or I am spending most of my day with teens, so I am probably not the best at having a normal adult conversation."

"No, it is ok, but you give me far too much credit for being a great catch," Lucy admitted. "Truth be told, I have an uncanny ability to pick the least reliable and trustworthy people to date. So much so," she continued, "that my brother has taken on the job as driver, bodyguard, and personal assistant so that I steer clear of trusting the wrong people."

Lucy fought that tingling, burning sensation in her throat when she was about to cry or get emotional. Her chin gave a tiny wobble that she hoped that Louis didn't notice. Her mistakes bothered her much more than she cared to admit, but she wanted to be honest.

"Well, you and I have the opposite problem. I just never have the time to date. I work two jobs. I have no idea how to even talk to adults, let alone have the ability to entice a woman to spend more than a few minutes alone with me." Louis ran a shy hand through his hair, then slowly stroked his well-groomed beard nervously.

"I think you are more charming than you realize," Lucy whispered, slipping her shoes off and putting her feet up on the ottoman in front of her.

Lucy, do you know how absolutely beautiful you are? Louis looked at her lips as she sipped on her glass of wine. Louis desperately wanted to say something, but instead, he hid behind a nervous smile.

There was a beat of silence.

"I am sorry for the way I acted earlier today," Lucy said quietly. "You didn't deserve that when I heard about the paparazzi."

"Thank you for saying that." Louis put his hand on Lucy's hand. "I can promise you that I would never put you in danger to earn a dollar."

"Thank you," Lucy whispered and saw that Louis was looking at her again.

"You aren't convinced of my sincerity, are you?" Louis asked.

"It isn't you, but I have a history of…"

"Trusting the wrong people," Louis finished Lucy's sentence.

"Yes," Lucy whispered.

"I hope to get to prove to you that I can be trusted," Louis whispered and gently put his finger under her chin so that their eyes met.

Suddenly, the wall between them vanished, and Lucy couldn't hold back any longer. She placed her hand behind Louis's neck and brought his mouth to hers. She was uncontrolled and grabbed for Louis hungrily, with her other hand bringing his body closer to hers. She didn't have anything between them. Louis's mouth responded to the initial soft touch of her lips, but the kiss quickly deepened, bringing them closer together. She quickly repositioned herself so that she was facing him on the sofa. They were all elbows and limbs, embracing and searching one another. Both of them were eager, almost too eager for this moment. There was no control, both aching for more. Then Louis pulled away.

"I …I…" He had to restrain himself, standing up and distancing himself from Lucy, who was still sitting on the sofa.

"I am so sorry." Lucy looked confused and disappointed.

Louis came back to her. "No, no, noooooo … there is nothing to be sorry about." Louis paused. "I want to be the man who earns your trust, and starting like this won't do it." He continued to hold Lucy's hands and took each one of them to his lips and kissed them gently while keeping eye contact with Lucy.

"I want to spend so much time with you, but I need to earn your trust first."

Lucy looked up at his hazel eyes, and a small smile spread across her face.

"Ok?" Louis replied.

"Ok." Lucy smiled.

Louis, you need to show her you are a man she can finally trust. You have to find a way of telling her everything but now is not the time.

CHAPTER 35

Lucy

2026

"I need to know when you realized Liam came to Paris." Lucy entered the dining area of the rental where Elle and Liam were already sitting at the table.

"Good morning, Sis." Liam stood up and gave his sister a big hug.

"It was the best surprise, Lucy." Elle stood up and joined the brother-and-sister hug. "Thank you so much for encouraging him to come. It was the sweetest surprise."

"Are you bloody kidding me? I had to practically change my phone number during our visit because he was asking for updates about you," Lucy teased.

Elle broke the hug to look at Liam's face. "Did you really bug your sister about updates during our trip?"

"Not really," Liam said nervously. "Maybe, I did just a bit." Then, Liam ditched his sister to pull his fiancé into a hug.

Lucy watched the two lovers and thought, This is why I encouraged Liam to come to Paris. They are the sweetest together.

It is a gift to spend this time together before we are busy with life. Lucy stood watching them and was so thankful that her brother had found a lovely, trustworthy woman.

Liam noticed that Lucy was watching the two young lovers hugging when he remembered something he wanted to ask his sister.

"So, Lucy, who is this Louis guy that I have been hearing about?" Liam smiled, glancing at Elle, but really trusting his sister with a new person in her life.

"Well, he is my incredibly talented voice coach." Lucy tried not to gush. "That is how we met. He is a Godly man who is incredibly gentle and patient." Lucy paused for a moment.

"He sounds wonderful," Liam added.

"I know that I am just getting to know him, but we seemed to get on so well. I will admit that it is new though," Lucy continued. "I am taking my time with him."

"It sounds like you are being level-headed about it," Liam encouraged her and showed a relieved look on his face.

Elle and Liam had already returned to the table to enjoy their coffee while Lucy began making her coffee.

"I do have one more thing to share about him," Lucy reluctantly added.

Liam suddenly revealed a frown, unsure of what Lucy was about to tell him.

"He is a single dad."

"Isn't he the first single dad you have dated?" Elle asked.

"That is a big responsibility," Liam added, always being the rational one. "You have to think about the kids who may get attached to you if you are just dating casually."

"I get that completely. I met the kids on the first day I met him, which was before there was any connection between us, so I got to know them in a different context. Honestly, I already have a soft spot for his kids." Lucy smiled. "The kids are so…so… lovely." Lucy took a moment to find the right word because she hadn't been in this situation before and really enjoyed spending time with the entire family. *I still can't believe that his ex would leave the entire family. I am falling for all of them, and she would choose to leave them all is unfathomable.*

"I am happy for you, Lucy. Just take things slowly, especially with kids involved with the dating situation," Liam added.

"Good morniiiiiiiiinnnnnnnng." Margaux entered the kitchen as she announced her arrival. "Did you know we were coming to Paris? I can't believe we all have our own rooms! This rental is huge!"

"Hey there, love," Lucy added and greeted Margaux with a kiss on either cheek.

"Who is ready to take on Paris while simultaneously offering our styling services to a school fundraiser?"

"Here, here," Elle called back to match Margaux's enthusiasm.

"Oh, I have missed you," Margaux said to Elle, her co-worker and best friend, while placing her arms around a seated Elle's neck. Elle returned the hug with patting Margaux's arms that were surrounding her neck.

"Me too." Lucy walked over, joining the girl hug.

"Group hug!" Evan entered the kitchen and joined the group, immediately covering the girls with his long arms while joining the group hug, still with Elle sitting at the table for her breakfast.

"Nice to meet you, Evan," Lucy called with her mouth covered by someone else's arm in the group hug.

"Nice to meet you too," Evan answered while still hugging the group of women. "Please tell me there are some real Parisian pastries nearby that I can go buy," Evan added.

"This is your first breakfast in Paris, isn't it?" Liam asked Evan.

"Yes, it is. Do you want to go find some pastries with me?" Evan asked Liam. "Margaux, do you mind texting me what all the ladies would like from the bakery while I run back upstairs to change?"

"Roger that," Margaux called back to Evan as he headed toward the stairs.

"Hey Evan," Margaux called to him again, causing him to pause at the bottom of the stairs. "Can you even believe we are about to have real French pastries in Paris? Who are we?"

"I know, right? Who are we right now?" Evan smiled a goofy but pleased grin as he bound up the stairs.

"He is a force," Lucy said to Margaux.

"You have no idea," Margaux smiled.

"Give coffee orders to Elle, please. I will get coffee for everyone." Liam gave Elle a gentle kiss before walking to change and go out with Evan.

"Ok ladies, we need to start planning for this fundraiser tonight." Lucy joined Elle and Margaux at the dining table. "Margaux, did you contact your friend about doing the socials for the event?"

"I did contact her. Her name is Amelia Harper, and she is doing some work right now with a non-profit in Barcelona, but she said she could do most of her work remotely. She is already communicating with Headmaster James."

"Perfect," Lucy responded. "What kind of theme is she doing? Maybe you guys can work with it?"

"We are on it," Margaux added. "Amelia, Elle, and I did a video chat last night when you reached out to us, so we have had some time to plan a bit. Amelia is doing a 'Be a Hero for a Hero' theme for the event. She is thinking a superhero theme."

"I love it," Lucy added. "Do you guys think you can incorporate any hair or makeup ideas with the theme?"

"Of course, Elle has already made a list of some fun props and accessories for the mini-makeovers we are doing with any of the students who wish to have one. We also received Headmaster James's number as well, so we are able to ask questions. I think we are going to visit the school after breakfast so that we can see our workspace for the event."

"Fancy that, the dream team has figured out so many details in a few short hours. You two are incredible. After the event this evening, I need to treat you all to dinner for all of your effort to make this happen."

"Ok ladies, we are heading out to get some breakfast and coffee." Evan and Liam reentered the kitchen. "Please text us your orders."

"Thank you, guys," the girls called.

"Now, let's see that supply list for tonight so I can have my assistant get all of the items sent to the school for you." Lucy began reviewing the list. "You birds are incredible. You literally pulled off a very successful event for one of the most in-demand fashion designers in London, and you haven't hesitated to help with this school fundraiser. You are incredible," Lucy repeated.

"We are so happy to do it." Elle took Lucy's hand.

"Who is ready to find some heroes for the fundraiser?" Lucy chimed in and the women set to make their final plans for the fundraiser.

CHAPTER 36

Louis

2026

L ouis picked up his phone and sent a text message to Lucy as soon as he returned from taking the kids to school.

Louis

Good morning. ☀️

Lucy

Good morning to you. 💤

Louis

I am dragging too because this amazing woman kept me up talking late last night. 😜

Louis smiled at his screen, waiting on Lucy's reply, watching the three dots.

Lucy

I don't have a good reply to that one. Guilty as charged. I think flirting via text is our thing. You make me smile. 😌

Louis

You bring it out of me. 

Lucy

See, there you go again.

Louis

Ok, then. What time do you plan on showing up to rehearse? Do you want to go to a new place to rehearse or to my home? I have a location in mind where we could go if you want a change of scenery.

Lucy

Is this a date? Is it the ice cream place because we have already been there. After all, ice cream makes everything better.

Louis

We will celebrate with ice cream then.

Lucy

Celebrate what exactly?

Louis

The moment you are offered the role as the famous jazz singer.

Lucy

See ... there you go again. ☺

Louis

Could you meet me in about thirty minutes to rehearse one more time?

Lucy

Sure! 👍

Louis

I just pinned the address. Let's meet here. The acoustics are amazing.

Lucy

See you soon!

Louis smiled at his phone for a moment before he began collecting his things. He also took the flowers that Lucy forgot at the flat last night.

After about twenty minutes, Louis arrived at the Jardin des Tuilerie ... the "Garden of Tile." He walked around the grounds, looking for one of the semi-private alcoves that were perfect for acoustics. Plus, the park was nearly empty, so most likely no one would notice them as they practiced. It isn't uncommon for people in Paris to have music playing or to be singing in public spaces, not for busking but for the pleasure of it.

Lucy

I am here! Where are you?

Louis pinned his exact location and texted it to her.

Lucy pulled up the directions and saw Louis at a distance, looking for her, eagerly holding the flowers that she left at his flat. She did her best to steady herself and not rush to him, but she felt the urge to run and give him a hug. Just seeing him holding flowers for her with a big smile across his face made her heart skip a beat. She could feel her stomach drop in anticipation of seeing him again.

Lucy tried her best to keep her pace slow and steady, but her heart wanted to run into his arms.

"You are adorable," she said and took the flowers from Louis as he stood inside one of the alcoves.

"Well, thank you, miss." Louis brushed off his shoulders.

"You brought me to a public park to sing?" Lucy's voice could not hide the panic she was feeling.

"Yes and no. We are in a garden, and we are going to sing, but these alcoves have amazing acoustics. Surprisingly, passersby shouldn't hear us either. The tiles are great for sound but also keep it private too."

"Really?"

"You can trust me on this." Louis took her hand and kissed the back of it.

"You wouldn't believe it, but the first day I started singing professionally, I was so incredibly nervous. I remember my first time singing at the Le Chat Bleu. It was June of 2019. I was so nervous that I got sick before I took the stage. The Paris jazz scene has always been a big goal for me and to finally actually perform on stage was surreal. I even told the audience that night how nervous I was before I started performing."

"When did you first perform there in June?"

"It was late June, the last weekend actually. I won't forget that date because it was the start of my professional life as a jazz musician in Paris. Why?" Louis turned his head slightly. "This is not a question I thought you may ask about my being nervous."

"I was there that night! I just realized it was you. You were the man I saw that night I visited Le Chat Bleu for the first time."

"Wait, what?"

"I came to Paris that weekend; I was in the club. I remember you now. You sang a song that I felt was meant for me that night. You sang 'Almost Wasn't Enough,' and it was like you knew exactly the song I needed to hear."

"I did sing that song," Louis admitted, but still looked skeptical. Then a light of understanding hit him.

"Were you sitting in the back of the jazz club at the only back round table?"

"I sat in the back; I am sure you couldn't have noticed me. I was discreet. I was feeling heartbroken during that weekend, but to answer your question," Lucy answered, almost mesmerized by this moment, "yes, I was sitting at the round table, hidden in the back."

Lucy fought emotions that took her back to that evening and that weekend but then surprised herself by meeting the beautiful man who performed the song she needed to hear that night.

"You were in the back corner. I saw you come in the club. I remember you too." The moment was like deja vu for Louis. He remembered her but didn't realize until now that Lucy was that woman he remembered so well from that first night that he sang professionally. He was sitting in awe at the moment that they both clearly remember, for different reasons. Yet, each of them remembered the other so well.

"You were wearing a green sweater vest," Lucy added. "Am I right?"

Louis laughed and held her hands while kissing each one on top of each one and looking up at Lucy in amazement.

"I keep the old sweater because it was from my first gig there. I am nostalgic like that." Louis smiled, mesmerized by the fact that Lucy really did remember him too. *I can't believe sweet, beautiful Lucy who has seen the world, yet she remembers hearing me sing at Le Chat Bleu.*

Both Lucy and Louis stared at one another, taking in the serendipitous moment. They had crossed paths before now, and they both remember one another. This was a God thing. They stood for a moment, staring at one another, in awe at this beautiful moment and reality of the beautiful thing that they shared. They couldn't deny that it felt like they were almost meant to be—right here and now.

Louis sat down and patted the bench that was across from him. Lucy sat there across from him. They were facing one another, knee to knee. With encouragement and slight uncertainty of singing in a public place, they began to warm up as they normally did together.

"Wow, you were not kidding about the acoustics. This place makes me sound amazing," Lucy said surprised.

"You actually sound so great, even outside of the enclave, but don't worry; no one can hear you."

"Do you want to practice your song again?"

"Sure." Lucy took a deep breath and began her song. She was calm and confident as she sang. Lucy closed her eyes again and was feeling the music. She swayed as she sang and used one of her hands to help her keep the rhythm by tapping on the side of her leg. Louis just observed her in awe. She was such a fast learner and coachable. She listened so well and clearly had been doing her breathing exercises too because she was able to hold out her notes. When she finished, Louis couldn't help but stand up and applaud, which caused Lucy's face to turn various shades of red.

Louis was literally cheering for her and was amazed at how far she had come so quickly. "You are incredible." He sat back down to face Lucy and patted her hands.

"You are going to do well at your audition."

"You are embarrassing me because I know that I am not quite good yet, but I can tell that I have improved," Lucy admitted.

"Love, when I tell you that you are amazing, I mean it."

"Really?" Lucy asked with uncertainty.

"Really," Louis answered.

"Well, because I properly caused a right scene, I will embarrass myself too."

Lucy looked at Louis skeptically.

"No, you didn't really embarrass me, but I am just not confident with my singing."

"You are not confident about your singing ... yet," Louis corrected.

"Yet." Lucy smiled, leaned over, and gave Louis the sweetest, most tender kiss. She pulled back and looked into his eyes for a moment.

"Do you mind if I share something with you?" Louis said, a twinkle behind his hazel eyes.

"Sure." Lucy looked confused.

"I started working on a song last night." Louis smiled and pulled out a piece of paper.

"Wow, you wrote the song on paper? How 1990s of you," Lucy joked.

Louis offered a nervous smile, and Lucy could see that he truly was nervous, which is something she hadn't seen from him yet.

"You don't have to share it because I was embarrassed earlier. You don't have to put yourself out there because I did by singing in public. It is ok." Lucy patted his hand.

"No, love, I want to share it with you because you inspired it." Louis's Adam's apple bobbed nervously. "It isn't finished, but I thought I would share some of what I have with you."

Louis cleared his throat and began singing quietly.

"Lucky you … lucky me,

You beautiful you,

I didn't think you could be true,

I thought I had what I need,

You came and I realized I am incomplete…"

Louis's voice cracked as he became emotional. Lucy leaned in again and placed her hands on either side of his face, looking into his intoxicating hazel eyes and whispered, "Lucky you … (pointing to Louis) and sang, "lucky me" (pointing to herself).

This woman is so incredible. My man, I think you have already fallen for her.

Louis stood up and pulled Lucy into his arms, his face buried into her shoulder as he held her a foot off the ground, slowly turning as they held their embrace, nestled in an enclave in a garden in the heart of Paris.

CHAPTER 37

Amelia
BARCELONA • 2026

"Hey, darling." Margaux emphasized the word to sound like "dahling" when she answered the video chat call, doing her best to mimic her British friend, who was video-calling her.

"Hey, love, it is so good to see your face again!"

"I know … when can we escape back to Italy again?" Margaux teased.

"How are things going in Barcelona?"

"Well, the city is absolutely charming. The art here is top notch, but I haven't had a chance to really explore much yet," Amelia said with a disappointed expression.

"Are you busy with your work there?"

"I am busy trying to figure out the director of the non-profit."

"Who is she or he?"

"The director is a he, and he doesn't like any ideas from anyone other than himself. I think this organization has some great potential to bring in some money for their programming, but he doesn't seem to want to hear any of my ideas yet. Clearly, they could use the fundraising because the building can use some upgrades."

"I am so sorry to hear that … maybe over time, he will warm up to the idea of your creativity."

"Maybe?

"I don't feel like I really have a purpose yet, which makes me feel a little crazy. I like to stay busy," Amelia explained.

"You have only been there for a couple of days though." Margaux tried to sound reassuring.

"That is true, but my dad made it sound like I was needed immediately when I was scheduled to come after our trip to Italy, but I am really not that busy."

"Well, thankfully, we need your expertise!" Margaux reminded Amelia.

"Yes, yes, yes!" Amelia replied. "Thank you for thinking of me for this event. Is Lucy there? I would love to introduce myself to her."

"She is out for a work thing right now, but I will make sure you meet her while we work on this project. She has some connections everywhere, and I think you will have some great connections after this gig."

"That would be amazing!"

"So, how can we help you? How can we collaborate? Elle and I have decided to go with your theme of 'heroes' with our mini-makeovers. We are getting capes, masks, gloves, shields, and utility belts. We want the kids to feel like superheroes too.”

“I bloody love that so much,” Amelia added. “I have been communicating with the headmaster. I just sent him a grid where people circle the amount of money that they are to donate and to tag their friends to help on their socials.”

“Oh, sorry to interrupt, but I want to introduce you to Elle Bennett.”

“Hi Amelia,” Elle called from behind Margaux during her video chat.

“Hi, Elle, I have heard so many wonderful things about you,” Amelia called out.

“I have heard so many wonderful things about you too! I am so excited to work with you for this project!”

“What are some of your other plans for social media? Well, I received photos of the students, and I covered their faces with superhero masks to protect their privacy. I worked all night on this and gave each of the students a superhero name and a superpower. Each hero will be featured and shared on the school’s social media throughout the day. The photos are darling.”

“That sounds adorable,” Margaux replied. “What a great idea.”

“The headmaster has some audio from students describing their musical heroes and the sound bites that are bloody adorable. So, I am going to take a photo of some famous people and use the audio of the students talking about their musical heroes. I am hoping I can get you two to share these because I think we will have the most buzz with these. Hopefully, Lucy may share them too."

"It sounds like you have this really planned. I know we picked the right person to help with this last-minute project. Honestly, I don't think the school has ever done anything like this so these funds will be so helpful."

"I do have a few other ideas that I am working on, but I don't want to share those yet because I am still collaborating with the headmaster on them."

"Is there anything we need to do?"

"I don't think so. I am so excited to be part of this. I could use some prayers for my current job now. I see so many opportunities to grow the program here in Barcelona, but the director is a major grumpy curmudgeon. I hope to get some guidance from him soon because I am desperate to start working."

"I will absolutely pray for you," Margaux reassured Amelia.

"Reach out to me if you need to video chat again before the event tonight."

"Sounds great."

"Hugs, sweet friend," Margaux smiled.

"Toodles," Amelia called back.

Now, if my time here working in Barcelona for this non-profit could only be that easy.

CHAPTER 38

Elle

2026

"I need to get to the school to see our setup for the event," Elle told Margaux after taking a bite of a croissant.

"After looking at this complete spread of pastries, you are going with a croissant? There are so many options in front of us that you probably have never tried." Margaux tried to persuade Elle to be more adventurous.

"You are correct, but who said that I am only enjoying one pastry?" Elle joked and took another, larger bite of her croissant, while her eyebrows did a little cha cha.

"After breakfast, I can take you to the school," Liam offered, always the driver and protector in getting his girls where they needed to be.

"What can I do besides deliver food?" Evan offered assistance as he held two different pastries, one in each hand, eager to try all the things since arriving in Paris, much like Margaux.

"Believe me, these two ladies will forget to eat most of the day once they start working," Liam offered some advice to Evan.

"Doing our royal duty, keeping our queens happy." Evan made the Brit in the room chuckle with his royal reference. Evan held up his coffee cup and cheered his coffee with Liam's cup.

I love seeing the two men in our lives getting along so well. Now, I understand why Margaux held so much guilt and shame with breaking up with Evan before their reconciliation. He seems like a great guy, and they are both hype people for sure, Elle thought to herself.

"I am running upstairs to get ready." Elle jumped up from the table and began heading up the stairs.

"My girl never stops," Margaux added.

"Elle, do you mind heading there by yourself, and we will catch up with you in a couple of hours? This is our first time in Paris, so I think we want to do some sightseeing, if you don't mind," Margaux explained.

"That works for me. Have fun," Elle called from the top of the stairs. "I'll send you some notes once I see the venue."

"So, Liam, you have been to Paris before, right? Where should we go first?" Evan asked.

"After I take Elle to the school, I am happy to take you to the Eiffel Tower, which is the obvious choice for your first visit. You should go to the Sacred Heart church because it has the best views of the city. Notre Dame is amazing to see because it is iconic and historic but is located near some of the most charming neighborhoods in Paris, where you can grab lunch or walk around and be a Parisian."

"Thanks, mate." Evan looked up from his phone. "I used that word right, didn't I?" Evan asked.

Liam chuckled. "You did."

"Where can I find some tacky shirts that say I heart Paris?"

There was a beat of silence.

"Oh … you are serious," Liam replied.

"I know they are hideous, but it is an inside joke with Margaux," Evan continued and shot a loving glance at Margaux.

"Hey, no judgment here. You should be able to find them just across the street from Notre Dame. There are tourist shops there."

"I am ready." Elle returned and was eager to check out the venue for the event tonight. She learned that she loved doing this kind of planning. Her recent work that brought her to London for the fashion show surprised her in how satisfying she found this type of creative, event-focused work. She was ready to do more.

"I am ready when you are. Let me get the car keys." Liam stood up and headed upstairs.

"Do you mind sending me Amelia's number? I may have an idea for her," Elle asked.

"Sure" Margaux grabbed her phone and sent Amelia's contact information.

"Hey love, I am ready to take you." Liam walked up to Elle and kissed her head. "I will come back after I drop her off at school," Liam confirmed with Evan and Margaux.

"Have fun exploring!" Elle called over her shoulder as they walked out the front door.

After a short drive through the city, Elle arrived at the school. Headmaster James was thrilled about the support for the event.

"Hello there, it is an honor to meet you. After doing such well-respected work in the world of fashion, it is an honor to have you supporting our small school. Because of the needs of our students, it can be difficult to get much support because many of the families struggle to meet the varying needs of their own children. This event truly helps in many ways," Headmaster James explained.

"The honor is mine. My name is Elle Bennett." She held out her hand. "This is my fiancé, Liam." Liam shook his hand too.

"Nice to meet you both," Headmaster James stated.

"I would like to see the space we are using for hair and makeup. Also, I would like to know a bit about most of your students. Do you think most students will take advantage of our work or will most avoid getting a makeover?" Elle inquired.

"We have a large group of girls who attend our school, and many of them have their own style. I think many of the girls will take advantage of it. Some of the boys may be indifferent, so I would allow them to approach you because most of them are on the spectrum and prefer limited physical contact with only people they know."

"Duly noted. I do have superhero props that I thought may be a fun option for the theme." Headmaster James's eyes widened. Suddenly feeling unsure about her idea, Elle mumbled, "It was only an idea; we don't have to do that."

"That is a great idea to help bring some of our students out of their shells for the mini-makeover. I love the creativity for the event!"

Headmaster James gushed.

"That is wonderful to hear. Do you mind showing me our workspace so that I can be prepared as possible for tonight?"

"Of course, follow me. Did I mention that our donations have already doubled as of this morning since our event last year? Most of the donations have been through Amelia's creative ideas on social media. We have people donating funds for this event that don't even have kids at our school, and some have come from different countries," Headmaster James continued as they approached the room.

"I know it is a relatively small space, but it is just adjacent to the stage and easy for our students and teachers to navigate in and out of easily. I hope this will work for you."

Why does he seem nearly apologetic for the work we are doing here? Elle, you need to remind him that his work is valuable, and it is an honor to have a role in it. It is God-honoring because it clearly is his calling. Elle stopped quickly and turned to face Headmaster James.

"Headmaster James," he looked at Elle with uncertainty as she began speaking, "the work you do here is so important. I assure you. It is an honor to be just a tiny bit of help for your program. I hope that our efforts are a blessing to you and the students here."

An initial surprised expression fell on his face, which quickly morphed into a slight sense of emotion. He took a moment to compose himself and whispered, "Thank you." After that affirmation, the headmaster stood taller and looked more reassured.

"Thank you. Very well then, I will leave you to this space so you can start planning. I will come back to check in and see if there is anything I can do to help you prepare this room."

"How much time do you need here?" Liam asked Elle, once the headmaster left the room.

"I could use an hour. Do you want to drop off Evan and Margaux for some sightseeing for a bit?"

"Yes, I will come back and get you in an hour," Liam reassured Elle.

"I can take the train back to the rental. I have been exploring here the past few days. I think I know the metro pretty well."

Liam stepped closer to Elle. "I want to spend every moment with you that I can," he whispered and put his arms around her waist for a quick hug, but Elle's legs almost felt like Jell-O. She practically melted into him with that hug.

Seeing that he made a swoony impression on his fiancé, Liam kissed her on the cheek and made his way out of the door with a playful smile on his face because he planned to come back and make her swoon again.

CHAPTER 39

Margaux

2026

"Hey Margaux, Liam is here," Evan called upstairs as he awkwardly attempted to slip on his shoes while balancing on one foot.

"I'll be right down," Margaux called back.

"Don't forget your list of places you want to see," Evan called up again after successfully slipping on his shoes while attempting a balancing act.

"Got it." Margaux walked down the stairs and waved a journal in the air as a gesture to Evan.

"I didn't realize you were bringing the list." Evan smiled as he saw Margaux tuck her journal into her oversized bag.

"Of course, I am bringing this list. This is my most precious list. The list that has guided all my big dreams since I was a pre-teeeen," Margaux emphasized the last syllable.

"Thankfully, you upgraded the journal. The original journal was looking pretty ragged, as I recall." Evan smiled as he followed Margaux, who was leading the way toward the door.

Evan quickened his pace so that he could reach the door before Margaux and quickly opened it in a gentlemanly manner.

"Thank you so much for dropping us off for some sightseeing," Evan said as he saw Liam leaning against the car outside, scrolling on his phone. Evan shook Liam's hand as he approached.

"It's no bother. It gives me something to do while Elle is at the school making her final plans for tonight's show." Liam put his phone away and placed it in his pocket as he greeted Margaux with a short hug.

"What would you like to do … whoa, whoa, whoa … do you have an entire book of things to do because I don't think you have that much time?" Liam responded.

"Sorry to scare you with my book life's wish list that I have carried around since I was a preteen," Margaux answered as she made the entire sentence one word. "Don't worry, I have only a few things I would like to do today. As much as I want to experience all that Paris has to offer, I do know that we have the opportunity to help an amazing school today too," Margaux beamed.

Liam made eye contact with Evan as though they were speaking a secret language for guys, who adore women who have so much they hope to accomplish.

"I know I am a lot," Margaux said and again was beaming, saying the thing that both men were thinking.

"I wouldn't have it any other way." Evan leaned down and kissed Margaux on the head, and she smiled up at him.

I can't believe I am looking into the eyes of a man whose heart I had broken when I left for New York. I didn't break off the engagement with him because I didn't love him, but I broke up with him because I was scared. Then, I left our town and moved to New York. After some time, he found me in Italy after the fashion show that I worked on with Elle. I couldn't believe he found me, and he has been doing so well since the breakup. I harbored so much unnecessary guilt. I would have never guessed that God had a plan for us to be back into each other's lives.

I don't know exactly where this relationship is headed, and I am not trying to figuring it all out, but it is such a joy to have him back in my life. Now, we get to experience a city that we dreamt of seeing since we were dating as teenagers. We are about to do another experience together, and I am in awe at what God has done in our lives, Margaux reflected as she was looking at Evan in amazement.

"I really want to take Margaux to the Eiffel Tower, even if that takes up most of our time waiting in line," Evan added and again Margaux looked up at him, adoration in her eyes.

"I thought you would say that, so I purchased tickets for you already. If you turn on your Airdrop, I will send you the tickets," Liam added nonchalantly.

"Wow, mate, I don't know how to thank you." Evan gave Liam a pat on the arm, again trying his best to use British terms in his American accent.

"I used to do things like this for Lucy all the time with her work, so it is no problem at all. The Eiffel Tower is in the seventh arrondissement, so you may want to sightsee in the area, but you can easily navigate the metro system here. Just be mindful of pickpockets," Liam explained. "The Musee D'Orday and Rodin Museum are located in that neighborhood. If you continue back toward the rental, you will go to the sixth arrondissement that has Les Deux Magots, which is an iconic cafe where literary and musical greats congregate. There is also Luxembourg Gardens, where you can lounge like a local. It doesn't sound exciting, but you feel like a Parisian when you lounge at a park on a beautiful day like today. Finally, if you keep heading toward the rental, you will find Notre Dame nearby.

"I would also suggest going to the Le Sacre Coeur church, but you will need to take the metro there. It has the best views of the city."

"Liam, it seems like you have your own little life's wish list in your pocket with all of these suggestions," Margaux teased.

"I have been in Paris for work-related things for Lucy on a number of occasions, so I know how to navigate the city pretty well, and I like to have suggestions for people who visit," Liam answered with a smile.

Margaux couldn't help but be consumed by her thoughts on their drive through the city. *A month ago, Elle didn't have her fiancé Liam, who is driving us to the Eiffel Tower. Evan and I were not speaking, and I was wracked with guilt about the breakup. The only place I had seen Lucy was in celebrity magazines, which I no longer really consume anymore now that I feel like I have my own life. God has surprised me in so many ways in the last few weeks, it is humbling … and amazing … and awe-inspiring,* Margaux thought to herself.

"Do you have any other must-see items on your list?" Liam asked.

"I would like to see the Arc de Triomphe," Margaux added.

"I can drive you by it and take you around it. I believe you can tour it, but it is up to you. At least I can take you to see it, and it can check half a box. What else?" Liam smiled.

"I have a tour of the Catacombs." Margaux smiled. "I know it is a bit creepy, but I am intrigued and Evan loves history."

"You may want to do that one tomorrow. After I drop you off, I am happy to look up some ticket options for you, if you like. I think you should have some time tomorrow to sightsee. How long do you plan to stay in Paris?"

Evan and Margaux looked at each other shyly.

"We don't know." They both shrugged.

"You don't know how long you plan to be here?" Liam, who was clearly a planner, was completely kerfluffled by this answer.

"We are going to leave obviously, but we aren't in a hurry to head back to the States. We both feel like we have an opportunity of a lifetime to be here and travel together. Plus, I just earned an entire year's salary from the fashion show we did in London, so I feel like I have a little time to not rush back to work. After all, my boss Elle is here in Paris, so I don't know that I need to hurry back." Margaux smiled sheepishly.

"That is understandable. I lived in New York, and it was not as easy to travel to different areas like it is here. You can hop on a train and see four countries in a short period of time," Liam added.

"Ahem," Evan added.

Margaux laughed.

"Margaux does have a pilot at her disposal who is eager to take her to some places too." Evan smiled proudly.

"That's true. I didn't even think about how you have your pilot's license. Is that how you arrived here?"

"Yes," Margaux gushed. "He is such a great pilot. I am so proud of him."

Evan beamed at the compliment.

"If you don't mind though, I have really discussed the topic with Elle regarding extending my stay in Europe. Please don't mention to her yet because I want to talk to her about it. I am not hiding anything, but I want to discuss the topic after the event tonight. I would like to take advantage of being here in Europe with Evan."

"Sure, I understand that. Actually, Elle and I have quite a lot to discuss regarding our future too. It isn't every day that you get engaged to someone who lives in a different country and you are navigating your future." Liam smiled sheepishly. "I will go wherever she wants to be. Initially, it was going to be my immediate move to New York, but lately, I get a sense of uncertainty from her about it. I could be wrong, but we have some things to discuss," Liam added.

"I completely understand," Margaux added.

Liam, you were speaking to a couple who just reconciled in Italy and live in two different states in the U.S. We aren't really a couple again, but we are dating again and traveling together. If you want to discuss complicated, I think we may be equally complicated, Margaux thought to herself.

"It sounds like we all have things to discuss with Elle," Liam said again.

The group stared at one another, thinking of all their possibilities of their future, but not one of them wanted to think about it today.

"Are you ready to go see the Eiffel Tower?" Evan beamed when he asked Margaux.

"You have been waiting to ask me that, haven't you?" Margaux replied.

"You have no idea how long I have waited," Evan replied with a knowing grin.

CHAPTER 40

Lucy
2026

"Are you ready to go?" Lucy called impatiently up to Liam, who was grabbing his keys to the car.

"I am coming straight away, but you do realize that we are really early for the event," Liam answered back to his sister. "Plus, I can't wait to formally meet this man that I have been hearing so much about." Liam came down the stairs and had a playful grin on his face, anticipating that his sister was excited to see Louis even more than she wanted to leave for the fundraiser.

"I know we are a little early, but…" Lucy paused because she didn't know what to say to Liam about being in a hurry. *I can't wait to see Louis. I don't want to be late. I am nervous about my over-protective brother meeting the first bloke that I have really, really liked for the first time in forever, or I don't want to be needed and not be there,* Lucy thought to herself.

Liam touched Lucy's arm. "I know. I want to spend as much time as I can with Elle too."

The brother and sister shared silent smiles … both of them thankful for having found someone special in the most unexpected way. Both felt more with these two people than they have felt in a lifetime, and it was so unexpected. The quiet smiles that they share said more than they could have articulated aloud.

"What is that in your hand?" Liam asked when he noticed the large tote that Lucy was holding.

"I wanted to bring a few things for Theo for his performance." Lucy paused. "Is it customary to bring a gift for a boy during a performance night? I know I have received a performance night gift on several occasions, and I thought I would bring something for him, too." Lucy shrugged, and Liam thought her reaction was so endearing.

Liam looked confused. "I have no idea," he said with a shrug.

"Well, I picked up something for Theo as a token if it isn't too weird." She smiled nervously.

"That is so kind." Liam smiled at his sister, seeing his sister's effort to make a good impression on Louis's kids, despite never having dated a single parent before now. In his opinion, she always gravitated toward the bad boys who were fun at first but were completely unreliable. Louis was a breath of fresh of air, compared to the previous men she dated.

"Are you sure you don't mind driving me back to the school? I know you just took Elle back to the school for the big event. I can't believe how quickly she was able to pull so many ideas together so quickly. Then, she set up the style space earlier today." Lucy paused. "She is incredible."

"I know … it is one of the many things that I love about her."

As they approached the car, Liam opened the door for his sister and smiled. "I know she is incredible and sometimes I just don't feel like I deserve someone like her. She is amazing."

"Don't get all lovey-dovey on me," Lucy teased, buckled up, and began gazing out of the window as Liam began driving.

After a short time, they were already arriving at the school and could see that a few more people were entering the school.

"Are you staying?" Lucy asked.

"I have to get Margaux and Evan from Notre Dame, and I will be back shortly. I will attempt to help in any way that I can."

"Do you feel like you are being my driver all over again after driving all of us around the city?"

Liam smiled. "I don't quite have the same talent that you guys do, so I am happy to help in any way that I can."

"You are the best big brother a girl could ask for," Lucy stated and began making her way out of the car. *I don't like to see my brother write himself off so easily. I think he is pretty incredible too. He and Elle are so fortunate to have found one another.*

"Don't forget your bag."

"Thank you." Lucy turned back to the car and grabbed the small gift for Theo.

Lucy spun with extra pep in her step, which made Liam smile again. She seems almost giddy. *She just may be falling for Louis,* Liam thought to himself.

Lucy walked into the main entrance where she was greeted by

Headmaster James, who eagerly shook her hand.

"It is such an honor to have you help with our fundraiser!" Headmaster James shook her hand a little too enthusiastically.

"It really is my pleasure. I am so happy that I was able to help during my visit." Lucy smiled and looked around the room for a familiar face.

Lucy could then feel a hand thread itself through her hand. Based on the size, she could tell that it was not Louis, but someone much smaller.

"Hello, Lucy." Noemie smiled and stepped closer to her. She rested her head against Lucy's arm with her sweet hello.

"Hello there, pretty girl." Lucy rested her hand under Noemie's chin so that she was looking up at Lucy's face. "You look like a movie star," Lucy emphasized.

Noemie did a small twirl for Lucy to show off the red dress that matched her red bows in her hair. Her natural curls were twisted into high space buns with coiled wisps that had just a hint of sparkle that enhanced each curl.

"Did I notice some glitter in your hair?" Lucy asked with feigned surprise.

"You did." Noemie smiled, completely pleased with herself. "Elle said that she had time to do my hair too."

"I am so happy to hear that. Did Theo get a makeover too?"

"He is getting his makeover now. Want to go see him?"

"Of course." Lucy smiled. "I will head there straight away."

"Headmaster James, is there anything I can do?" Lucy asked in an attempt to help her transition to a room with a more familiar face.

"If you could contact Amelia because if she is available, I would love to have her be included in our final fundraising count. She has done an incredible job with her social media presence today. I don't know how you had someone of her caliber agree to do this event, but she has been outstanding."

"I will absolutely touch base with her. Let me talk to Elle to see if she has some ideas on how to include Amelia seamlessly into tonight's event remotely."

"Sounds great. I can't believe we only have an hour before the big event, and we already have blown our fundraising goal out of the water!" Headmaster James said, almost giddy as he walked into the room.

"I am so happy to hear that."

At this point, Noemie was eager to lead Lucy to the makeover space where Margaux had just arrived and was setting up her space.

"Hey there, beautiful," Lucy called to Margaux. "How did you sneak past me?"

"I am stealthy like that," Margaux joked. "Wait… wait… wait… who is that diva behind you?" Margaux asked about Noemie.

"This is Noemie."

"You are stunning," Margaux cooed as Noemie did a small twirl for her new friend.

"It is nice to meet you." Noemie held out her hand to shake Margaux's hand. "Thank you for taking the time to volunteer for my brother's school."

"You are welcome." Margaux tried to hide her surprise by the mature manner in which Noemie communicated.

"Hey there, Theo." Lucy noticed him sitting at Elle's station. He was smiling as he looked at his reflection in her mirror. He was wearing a red cape, red mask, and red socks. Lucy wasn't sure if he would want to partake in the mini-makeovers because she didn't know the extent to him getting overstimulated, if at all, but Theo looked so pleased with himself.

As Lucy watched Elle finish up with Theo, he turned his head, and a huge smile spread across his face when he saw Lucy. She waved to him, and he hopped down from the chair and made his way to Lucy.

"Hello there, have you seen Theo? You are a superhero, correct? I am sure you can help me." Lucy feigned confusion about Theo's identity while speaking to him.

He removed his mask and his smile grew wider, and he leaned toward Lucy.

"There you are." Lucy leaned down and gave Theo a hug. "I brought you something for you to celebrate your big performance tonight." Lucy handed a bag to him.

Theo took the bag and investigated its contents. He pulled out a hat with a train on it that matched Lucy's signature baseball cap that she wore often.

"You seem to like my hat," Lucy explained.

He smiled and nodded.

"I can keep it for you because you already have a cool look with your costume now.   Wouldn't you agree?" Lucy bent down and cupped Theo's chin with her hand.

Theo whispered, "Yes."

"Yes to what?" Lucy heard behind her and felt the brush of a hand graze the small of her back. Her stomach fluttered just by the mere proximity of Louis.

This time, Lucy's smile widened. Despite her back being to Louis, she knew it was him.

Theo grabbed the hat out of the bag Lucy was carrying and showed Louis his new gift. Theo was beaming.

"What a happy surprise!" Louis explained, knowing that Lucy had purchased a matching hat for Theo. Theo seemed to constantly steal Lucy's hat any time she wore it in his presence. Now, they had matching hats.

Oh Louis, Lucy thought, *the sweet look on your face knowing that I found something for your sweet boy. Sure, the gift may have been for Theo, but I think you are equally surprised.*

Theo put the hat back in the bag for safekeeping while Louis approached Lucy and whispered in her ear.

"I need some direction please because I would love to take you in my arms and give you the most tender, loving kiss," Louis whispered, "but I want to do whatever makes your professional life easier too. I don't want any affection to cause a fury of unwanted attention from the media or to whomever may be watching us. How am I supposed to act in public around you?"

Lucy turned around and faced Louis with a mischievous smile on her face. "Well good sir, I don't think we have to worry too much about paparazzi following us while I am here for this event." Lucy placed her arms around Louis's neck. "Plus, we are backstage with only closest family and friends for the moment. I am going to enjoy the quiet for just a few moments." Lucy stepped closer to Louis, feeling a little awkward with such a public display of emotion, especially in front of Margaux and Elle.

"Elle and Margaux, have you formally met Louis?" Lucy asked while placing her arms around Louis's neck and staring contently into his eyes.

"Yes, we have met," Elle answered and gave Louis a wave. Elle was clearly pleased to see Lucy so happy and to learn more about who had been keeping her so busy during their trip to Paris.

Suddenly, it was Louis who paused the adoring hug so that he could give everyone his attention.

"I am so honored to have you here for this fundraiser. When I mentioned to Lucy that I could use some help with the event, I didn't even think that she would have an entire community that would be eager and willing to share their expertise. It is quite humbling. Thank you isn't enough, but I do want to tell each of you 'thank you' from the bottom of my heart."

Lucy rubbed Louis's back as he shared his heart for their work.

"God brought every one of you into my life this week," he added, in awe at God's work in his life in the last week.

"He is good," Elle responded to Louis's comment.

"All the time," the group responded, then broke out in laughter because all of them were thinking the same thing about God's work in their lives. It was one of those "you know if you know" moments for church people.

"Excuse me," Headmaster James entered the room, "we have several students who have arrived for their makeovers. Are you ready for them?"

"Of course, send them our way," Margaux responded.

"I'll greet and help with costumes when they arrive," Lucy called while they wait.

"Perfect, then you will send them to either one of us who is ready for their five-minute makeover."

"I think we have a plan." Elle smiled, looking at the girls that she had become so close to and was so thankful for.

"Who is ready for a big night?" Noemie asked the group of ladies, a way of offering encouragement but sounding beyond her years as usual.

"We are!" they cheered excitedly.

Louis and Noemie left the room and helped in the main hall as more people began arriving.

"I have decided that I want to be Noemie when I grow up because she is far more sophisticated than I am," Margaux teased, acknowledging Noemie's poise and maturity.

"I know … she is so wonderful," Lucy gushed.

"I can't believe I have met such a special family." Lucy smiled, her heart felt emotion, overwhelmed by gratitude for this unexpected week in Paris.

"Oh hello, you are here to help with our school event?" a woman interrupted as she brought her child for the hero makeover.

"Hello, would your kiddo like to come with me to pick out their costume?" Lucy responded, doing her best to underplay her notoriety. The woman answered, but still looking shocked that a celebrity was here for their school fundraiser.

"At the risk of sounding forward, but how did the school have a celebrity like you at our fundraiser? This is incredible to have your influence for this event."

"You are so kind," Lucy replied, trying her best to navigate the pushy woman that she was not prepared for at the start of the night.

The woman stood there, waiting for Lucy to answer how she learned of their school fundraiser.

"Oh, you are serious," Lucy replied, offering a hint at the all-too-nosy woman. She replied simply, "I am a friend of one of the organizers of the event."

"I have been on the committee in the past," the woman replied, but still looking perplexed, trying to figure out who could have known Lucy, also known as the actress Skye Reynolds.

"I am friend of the Durant family," Lucy finally said, just to avoid any further tension because another family had arrived for a makeover. She didn't want to make the moment awkward.

"I served with Mrs. Durant on the committee … absolutely lovely woman. The kids have been handling everything well … despite it all. Thank you for being here," the woman added.

Suddenly, this conversation had gone into very strange territory. *Lucy, did you just now realize you don't know anything about Mrs. Durant as this woman called her? A lovely woman, as she described. You are falling for a man whose past you know nothing about. Noemie and Theo's mom was "wonderful," and you don't even know who she is. You are entering into a blended family situation, and you know nothing. How did you do this to yourself again?*

Lucy's stomach was no longer filled with butterflies, but it had turned to knots in the pit of her stomach. Why doesn't she know anything about the kids' mom? She waited for Louis to say something, and he had never mentioned his ex-wife. When she had mentioned it a couple of times, it was clearly something he was not eager to discuss. Standing here listening to another woman gush about how wonderful she was suddenly made Lucy feel uneasy. She didn't feel jealous but felt like Louis hadn't been completely honest with her about his past. *Lucy, you don't need to know everything, but you should know something about the kids' mom.* A familiar uneasiness fell over her. The same uneasiness that came to her after time with her previous relationships.

Lucy was trying to hide her apprehension and her shaking hands. She looked for another child to help, to distract her mind that was suddenly racing, trying to add up some details of Louis's past that she may have missed.

"Hello there, would you like to pick out your costume?" Lucy smiled widely.

The smile was just hiding the feeling of uneasiness that had overcome Lucy. *Is there a reason Louis had been hiding his past with the kids' mom? Lucy, how are you falling for a guy this quickly? What are you doing?*

All the hope and excitement Lucy had been feeling had suddenly been replaced by the old feelings of doubt and uncertainty that she had felt with her past. She was suddenly questioning her ability to be a good judge of character and wondered what else she may have missed about Louis.

CHAPTER 41

Louis
2026

"This was incredible." Louis smiled as he walked up to the group of friends at the end of the night. The group was standing around and talking while waiting by the exit of the school. Louis made his way around the group and shook the hands of Elle, Margaux, Evan, Liam, and saved Lucy for last, but pulled her in for a hug. *These people have improved my life in so many ways this week. I am so thankful for them, even if a handshake is all that I can offer.*

"It was so much fun," Margaux gushed. "I honestly cannot pick a favorite moment. I thought the makeovers were the best, but then I saw all the talent here at the school, and it was amazing!"

"I agree," Evan added. "How did kids make music out of banging some kind of sticks together?"

"I know, that was one of my favorite moments too," Liam added.

"I think the ukeleles were my favorite," Elle added.

"What about you?" Elle asked Lucy.

"I loved what Amelia did with the fundraiser theme. Given our time frame and the fact that she was simultaneously working on a project in Spain, she was able to find a way to make this vision come true. She rocked it really. Plus, she acts like she doesn't have much experience with big projects, and she could have fooled me because she surpassed any expectation I had."

"Then, she joined us for the final announcement for the total amount raised, and it was clear that she was shocked by it too."

"You know what I would love even more? I would love to get something to eat," Evan admitted. "I am in one of the most iconic, gastronomic cities, and I am starving. Who wants to find some food?"

"I will drive." Liam smiled and held his keys up.

"Noemie and Theo have gone home with my sitter because it is a late night, so I am game for late-night dinner." Louis smiled, doing a little groovy move to show his excitement for such a great night.

"I have so much to celebrate," he whispered in Lucy's ear. *This beautiful, talented woman has done so much for your family in such a short time. God has been so good to you,* Louis thought to himself. Louis stared at Lucy, but she seemed to be mentally somewhere else, so he tried to avoid overthinking it.

"I have the perfect place for us to go. Give me five minutes to make some calls." Liam stepped away from the group and quickly started making a call.

"This is one of the many benefits of having a fiancé who worked as a driver, bodyguard, and planner of some sort." Elle smiled, clearly enjoying the chance to be the passenger princess.

"I hope he works his magic because I am starving," Evan stated.

"I see that nothing has changed because I remember you were always hungry," Margaux teased.

"True … completely true," Evan deadpanned.

Liam returned. "We are all set. Let's go have dinner."

Elle put her arms around Liam. "Thank you for taking care of us." Elle beamed while looking at her fiancé. She was so thankful to have a man in her life who helped her just relax and to not have to always be in charge all the time, like she felt before she met him. She felt like she can finally breathe for once.

"I was able to park just around the corner, and my car can accommodate our group … with a little creativity." Liam smiled playfully.

With some creativity and patience, the entire group was able to finally maneuver themselves in the car and head toward Isle St Louis. Although the restaurant was on an island, it had the perfect ambience for the group and had been recommended to Liam previously. They pulled up on the street just adjacent to the Isle St Louis, which was a pedestrian-only island.

"I am going to drop you off and I will meet you in ten minutes after I park the car at the rental. You know what a hassle parking is here in Paris. It is not too far to walk back to the restaurant from the rental."

"I'll head back with you," Evan offered. "I am glad to walk back with you. Plus, it will keep my stomach occupied from thinking about food."

"Louis, do you mind walking with the ladies to get our table?" Liam asked. Clearly, Liam was used to being the one to make plans as when he used to work for Lucy and was always having to think ahead.

"It would be my pleasure." Louis beamed. "What is the name of the restaurant?"

A horn blared behind Liam's car.

"It is called Le Pont des Saveurs," Liam called. "Ask for Tomas."

"Got it," Louis called.

Liam and Evan pulled away, and the group started making their way to the restaurant.

"I really love the charm of this area," Elle added. "I spent some time exploring this island during my visit, and it is delightful. I actually think I have seen the restaurant while I walked around here. I think it is just ahead and down the way on the right after we cross the bridge, but first I want to show you something."

Elle led the group across the bridge to a small, raised sidewalk that held a small band. The music poured out onto the street and played some French jazz music.

"I know it isn't probably the level of jazz that you are used to hearing, but I just love it so much," Elle added as they stood and enjoyed the music. "Liam and I danced to music like this when we stopped while we were in London. It was the first time I realized I was really beginning to like him."

"You did? Who knew my brother was so romantic!" Lucy teased.

"It was a perfect night," Elle said quietly as she watched the band.

"What kind of jazz is this?" Lucy asked Louis as he put his arm around her as they listened to the band.

"It is called jazz manouche or gypsy jazz," Louis answered. "This type of jazz was my brother's expertise."

"Really? He loved playing it?"

"He taught it at university. He played, studied it, and taught it," Louis answered quietly.

"Where does…?" Lucy began to ask but was soon interrupted by her brother Liam.

"You didn't make it to the restaurant yet?" Evan asked as he and Liam joined the group.

"I am so sorry, darling, but I just had to stop and listen to the live music. It reminded me of our first dance together," Elle answered Liam, even though he wasn't the one who asked the question.

"May I?" Liam asked and held out his hand.

Elle walked toward Liam, taking his hand, then moving closer to him. Soon, they were both swaying to the music. Each couple followed their lead. Evan and Margaux came together, but with Margaux's small statue, she actually slipped off her shoes and stood on top of Evan's shoes. This looked almost rehearsed or most likely done so often when they have danced together previously.

Then, the newest of couples came slowly together, but everything about Lucy seemed rigid when Louis brought her closer. She tried to fight it, but her intrusive thoughts were too overwhelming; the self-doubt was too strong.

"This is an incredible night," Louis whispered as he lowered his hand to the small of Lucy's back.

"It was," Lucy responded in a monotone voice.

"What is going on?" Louis whispered, trying not to bring attention to them.

"Can you tell me about your ex?" Lucy just blurted it out.

Louis was confused. "My ex?"

"The kids' mom … where is she? You never talk to her or about her."

"Where is this coming from?" Louis asked, turning the couple slowly so that no one else could hear their conversation. Then, another couple joined the dancing, then another couple who had been walking by and decided to join the spontaneous dance.

"A woman at the fundraiser was gushing about the kids' mom and how wonderful she was and … and…" Lucy couldn't find the words.

"It isn't like that," Louis added.

"I am sorry." Lucy looked confused, like he was purposely being evasive.

"I just realized that I adore your family and know nothing about their past. I think this is an important conversation to have." Tears welled in Lucy's eyes, and she swiped her eyes quickly so that no one would notice.

"This can be easily explained, but I think we should talk after dinner," Louis replied.

"It is not jealousy, but I just want to know the situation that I may be entering with your ex. I think it is a fair question to ask if we move further with this." Lucy tried to defend her feelings and struggled to fight the feeling of insecurity of her past that had turned to bitterness before meeting Louis.

"That's not it," Louis whispered, still dancing literally and metaphorically.

A worried crease showed between Lucy's eyebrows, and she contemplated Louis's responses. Lucy wondered why he was being so vague and almost dismissive.

Louis's mind was reeling too. *I had been meaning to tell Lucy, but it never seemed like the right time. I had planned on telling her before she left. There was never a good time alone to talk about it.* Louis took a deep breath. *You need to tell her, but this isn't the time. She is the best thing that has happened to you, and you may lose her. You just need to tell her now.*

"There is no ex because I am not the kids' father." Louis's words stumbled out of him in order to explain his vague responses so that Lucy would understand.

The music stopped.

Everyone stopped and clapped.

Lucy dropped her hand, and her face said everything. Louis had confused and crushed her with his quick response. She looked like someone who had been deceived, and she wasn't entirely wrong.

Louis was not ready to share the truth. His heart ached because he could see the hurt on her face.

Louis, she doesn't trust you now. You have hidden the one thing that you weren't ready to tell her. You have proven to her that you are exactly the man she wanted to avoid.

CHAPTER 42

Elle

2026

"Dinner was incredible," Margaux cooed.

"Thank you for arranging it for us." Elle leaned in and gave Liam a kiss on the cheek for once again being the man with a plan.

"I can't believe Tomas kept bringing out entrees for Evan to try," Margaux added. "I think he has never seen anyone rave about every dish as much as you did, babe."

"Every dish was perfection," Evan said. "Literally, every bite I had was the best food I have ever tasted." Evan shook his head in disbelief.

"You must have the metabolism of a teenager because you can eat so much food and not gain weight," Elle added. "How do you do that?"

"It is a gift," Evan deadpanned.

"Louis, did you enjoy your dinner?" Elle asked Louis.

"Who knew that curry chicken could be so indulgent and rich?

It was phenomenal. I will have to return there and hang out with Tomas again," Louis joked. "Despite living in Paris, I have never been to the restaurant. I love how well the owners take care of their customers at the restaurants in Paris."

"You are quiet over there," Liam said to Lucy. "What did you think of it?"

"It was lovely, quaint, and quintessential Paris. Plus, the food was outstanding too. Personally, I loved ending the meal with a sweet crepe. The honey drizzle with the creamy filling was otherworldly. Great recommendation, big brother."

Liam beamed after her compliment.

"I am going to miss having you plan my life for me." Lucy's face seemed a bit serious. "I know you have left me in good hands with Dottie. She has been reaching out to me all day today."

"Would anyone be willing to go listen to some live music in Paris? Louis has a sitter, and I am visiting for the first time," Evan asked the group.

Margaux pulled Evan in for a hug. "You are really embracing this adventurous lifestyle, and I am here for it." Evan beamed at Margaux for the compliment.

"I am game for anything," Elle added. *It doesn't look like Lucy is up for anything, though. She has been so distant since the fundraiser. She was pretty quiet at dinner,* she thought to herself.

"Pooky Bear, you know that I will go on any adventure with you," Evan said to Margaux.

There were some audible groans by some members of the group when they heard Evan's nickname for Margaux.

"My man, what did you just call your love?" Louis leaned in and had to confirm what he heard as Margaux's nickname.

"Oh no, it is true that Americans have nicknames like Pooky Bear and Lovey. I only thought it was in the movies," Louis added.

"It is true," Evan deadpanned. "Margaux is the original Pooky Bear, so all others pale in comparison."

"You are so good with smolder," Louis joked and held out a hand for a handshake. "I need to take notes."

Evan and Louis jokingly shook hands to congratulate Evan on his smooth nature.

Elle was soaking up this moment. I cannot believe that I am in Paris with a group of friends who have quickly become like family in the past few weeks. I want this to last forever, but I can't help but notice the change with Lucy. Something must be on her mind.

"I do have a place in mind that we can go for some fabulous jazz," Louis added.

"Is everyone game for a little live music?" Evan asked.

There were some head nods, and the group began to follow Louis's lead.

As they were walking the cobblestone streets toward the venue, Elle moved closer to Lucy. She was determined to find out more about what was going on with Lucy.

"What is on your mind?" Elle whispered.

"I am just tired," Lucy added.

"And…" Elle asked. "I know you aren't only tired. You were quiet through the meal, and I could tell that you sort of tolerated being there. What is going on?"

"I will talk to you later, but it isn't the right time."

"Promise?" Elle asked.

Lucy nodded quietly.

"Is there anything else I can do?"

Lucy showed an appreciative smile for the concern that Elle was showing her and shook her head no.

"We just cross this bridge to go off of the island and go into the neighborhood called The Marais. The venue is just down the street on the left. Just be sure to mind your step on the cobblestone." Louis had slowed down and was by Lucy now. He was doing his best to be attentive to Lucy, but she remained somewhat distant, based on Elle's observation. As much as she was trying to be discreet, Elle was still paying close attention.

"Here we are, this is our sister club to Le Chat Bleu. It is much smaller but still attracts some great talent. Welcome to the Green Dog." Louis reached the door and pulled open the small venue in almost dramatic fashion.

As they entered, the small group nearly took up half of the tables. There were only 20ish tables for 2 scattered around the venue, and all of the tables were incredibly close to one another. In Paris, most tables are placed only inches apart from one another. Green velvet was tastefully placed around the room to elevate the space but not overwhelm it.

Louis led the group to their table as he received several waves, and one man came up and gave Louis a hug. The hug was so endearing that he lifted Louis off the ground for a big hug.

Louis was chuckling to himself after the warm reception from his former manager. "This is my mate, Harrison Winstead, who hired me to work here after I first moved to Paris."

"This bloke only lasted here for a couple of weeks and soon realized that his talent was being wasted because he was quickly upgraded to the Cat soon after arriving. Meanwhile, the peasants are still down here trying to make a name for themselves," he joked.

"These are my friends: Evan, Margaux, Liam, Elle, and Lucy," Louis introduced the group to his friends.

"I will send our signature drinks your way.

"Nice to meet you. There is some incredible talent here tonight. Let me know if you need anything," Harry said as he left the table.

"Who is he?" Margaux asked.

"He is the manager here. He is a great guy. He … helped me so much when I first moved here," Louis paused mid-sentence, but didn't finish his thought. "I was really struggling when I first moved here."

"Here we are … the Green Dog specials." Harry passed out the drinks to everyone at the table.

"Let me know if you want to sing anything tonight. We will make time for you for a couple of songs. It would be an honor." Louis stood up and gave Harry a hug and handed his credit card to him.

"I want to thank this group of people. They have done something incredible for me tonight," Louis whispered to the manager.

"Tonight is on me, mate. I am glad some good things are happening to you. It is well-deserved." Harry patted Louis on the back and made his way toward the back of the small stage. "Perhaps, one day, you will dare to grace my stage again."

Louis watched Harry walk away as he turned his attention back to his friends. He couldn't help but take in the small space as it felt like the size of an auditorium when he first began performing in Paris.

The stage could hardly be called a stage; it was more of a small platform that held just enough room for a small group to perform. The lighting was positioned to make the small platform the center of the venue. Typical to many jazz venues in Paris, the lighting was dark and selective. Tables were illuminated by small gold lamps with green shades that covered each light.

Each of the couples sat at their own tables, but close enough where everyone could be heard. Out of the group, Margaux and Evan sat in the middle because they were much more outgoing collectively than the other couples. Elle and Liam sat on the outside with Lucy and Louis on the other side.

"Hey there … are you doing ok?" Louis whispered to Lucy. He finally felt like they could have a semi-private conversion with the other two couples in conversation.

"No, I am not ok right now. Why didn't you tell me that you aren't the kids' father? Don't you think that this is an important detail to leave out during our time together?" Lucy's voice began to rise ever so slightly. She made an effort to compose herself.

"Was this part of some kind of plan? Did you intentionally mislead me?" Lucy's voice returned to a shout whisper, but it still seemed to go undetected to the group.

Louis looked confused. "You think I would make up something like that? You think I would pretend to be their father to manipulate you in some way?" A look of hurt fell on Louis's face.

"You didn't answer my question. All you did was basically tell me what I did wrong with misunderstanding your intentions."

"Do you think I am the kind of man who would pretend to be someone's father to attract you? Would you be drawn to me if I wasn't their father? Do you really think I am that manipulative?" Louis was trying to understand how their connection became so fractured so easily. He was thinking that she could be the one potentially and now, there was nothing but distance and uncertainty.

"It doesn't matter what I think. I just want to know the truth. I feel like an imbecile after the woman at the fundraiser shared information about the man I really care about, and it was information that I had no knowledge of. I felt humiliated by not knowing something so basic. It made me realize. Do we really even know each other?" Lucy fought the urge to tear up. "Plus, you still haven't answered my question."

"Lucy... I."

"Ladies and gentlemen, we have a special visitor in the house tonight. We have award-winning Louis Durant here tonight." The manager stood on the stage and had a mischievous smile across his face.

Suddenly, the small venue seemed to grow louder with applause. After realizing that Louis was being encouraged to perform a song on the stage, the group of friends began cheering for Louis to perform something for the crowd.

Louis looked at Lucy as though he was apologizing for having to leave the conversation because now was not the time. It was never the right time, or so it seemed. Lucy didn't have any expression, not disdain or excitement.

Louis stood and silently mouthed, "I am sorry" to Lucy.

Finally, he stood up, and the small crowd grew louder with their applause. Evan rose from his seat in a playful manner and took his cloth napkin and playfully wiped off the tops of Louis's shoes as though he was part of his entourage.

"Here he comes," Harry spoke into the microphone. "Ladies and gentlemen, please welcome Louis Durant to the stage."

As Louis made his way to the platform, Harry asked, "Do you think you may have time for one song for us tonight?"

Louis smiled at the crowd from the stage, where the audience burst into enthusiastic applause.

"Sure, I will play a song that I have been working on but haven't quite finished it." Encouragement in the form of more applause broke out throughout the venue.

Louis played some notes on the keys as he sat down at the keyboard.

"I began writing this for a special person in my life. It is called 'Lucky Me.'" Then Louis began playing the song that he wrote for Lucy.

Lucky you … Lucky me,

You beautiful you,

I didn't think you could be true,

I thought I had what I need,

You came and I realized I am incomplete…

Everyone was staring at Lucy in complete awe of the moment. The venue was filled with admirers who were witnessing a man serenade a beautiful woman.

Lucy wiped a tear that had escaped the corner of the eye as she listened to Louis sing her song.

Despite such a beautiful moment, Elle could see something different in Lucy's expression. The crowd wasn't seeing the face of a woman in love, but a woman who had been hurt.

CHAPTER 43

Louis

2026

Clearly, your song was not the right time in the jazz club. Lucy did not seem to be impressed with it. Plus, she looks like she is far past angry. She seems hurt and you, my man, are the reason for that. You are the reason that the woman is hurting … the very woman who has brought you more joy in your life in just a matter of a few short days. You need to tell her tonight … even if she has already made up her mind about you. You need to tell her.

Louis's intrusive thoughts were interrupted by Margaux gushing about her experience in Paris.

"I have to admit that my evening in Paris tonight couldn't have been any better." Margaux shrugged her shoulders in awe, as though she was having a conversation with herself. She continued to shake her head slowly to herself, just trying to convince herself it was not a dream but real life.

"Seriously, I can't believe I am walking around the streets of Paris, after having one of the most incredible dinners I have ever tasted. Then, I was practically serenaded during our post-dinner visit to a charming jazz club." The group just kept quiet with smiles on their faces, soaking in Margaux's excitement.

"Then…then…," Margaux paused for melodramatic effect, "the chef treated you like royalty and kept bringing you new dishes to try!" Margaux gave Evan's muscled arm a tap with the back of her hand.

"I know … it was incredible," Evan agreed. "You need to add our memories in your life wish-list book."

"Of course, I am experiencing things in my life that I couldn't have even imagined that I could have wished for…" Suddenly her cheeks turned pink when she saw the expression on Evan's face. Suddenly they both realized that their recent reconciliation was so unexpected, even if they were unsure exactly where their future was headed. They didn't want to label or put too much pressure on things right now. For now, they were really enjoying being back in one another's lives.

"Wait… wait… how can you add an item to a wish list after you have experienced it? Isn't it not really a wish?" Liam seemed intrigued by this concept.

"Actually, I think these moments are like God winks, Liam. They are beautiful moments that God has given me. They are beyond what I ever imagined that I could experience." Margaux thinks for a moment and retorts dramatically. "It would be unlawful to not add them to my wish list because I didn't even dream that I could experience. Besides, who says that I can't have wishes that I have already come true added to my list?"

Evan nodded. "She is right."

"How so?" Liam pushed but was teasing at this point.

"She is right because she is always right," Evan deadpanned and gave Louis a high-five.

The entire group laughed because it was clear that most men understood the importance of keeping their ladies happy.

"I don't know about you guys, but I am exhausted after such a busy day. Honestly, I love being this tired though. It is not a complaint in the least. Plus, I am so thankful to have all of you together here," Elle said to the group.

"I am glad I came." Liam took Elle's hand and led her into a twirl that spun her into his arms.

My man, you need to hold her hand. Show her some affection. Do something or at least say something.

"We need to talk," Louis whispered to Lucy.

"I know," Lucy whispered back without looking at Louis.

"You know you can trust me, right?"

Lucy's gaze suddenly turned to Louis, and she didn't respond. She just gave him a steely stare.

"Here we are. I will get the code." Liam stepped ahead of the group as they approached the rental.

"I am going to stay out here so that I can say goodbye to Lucy," Louis responded. "It was so good hanging out with you all tonight. I don't think I can truly ever thank you or show each of you how much today meant to me. What you did for my boy and his school."

Evan came over to Louis and gave him a one-armed man hug where he pulled him close and slapped him on the back.

"My man, I didn't do much today, but we must hang out some more," Evan answered and broke the ice from the emotionally tender moment. He pulled Louis in for another hug while Louis laughed and wiped his eyes, not sure if it was from emotion or laughter.

Elle gave Louis a hug. "I am so thankful we could help Theo's school. It meant so much to me. Thank you for giving us a chance to make a difference. Oh wow, I sound like an advertisement." Elle laughed at her comment. "You know what I mean."

"I am sure I will be seeing you again soon." Elle smiled and patted Louis on the shoulder.

Weird, does she know that Lucy is upset with me? That's an interesting comment given our distance for the evening.

Liam gave Evan a handshake, then Margaux offered Louis a hug before telling him goodnight.

"Thank you, Margaux for all your help tonight. You were the superhero," Louis added, and it made Margaux chuckle.

"Is he always this corny?" Margaux asked Lucy.

Lucy shrugged her shoulders with a smile.

Slowly, the friends made their way into the rental, except Louis and Lucy who remained outside.

"Can we talk?" Louis asked Lucy.

"That is all I wanted was honesty. I told you that when we met. So, what is your story?" Lucy said matter-of-factly.

Louis started to get emotional again, like he did earlier when he thanked the group. He took a step away from Lucy to hide his emotions and compose himself, then took a deep breath and wiped the corner of his eye.

Louis, just tell her.

Lucy just stood there. When Louis turned around, he did see a note of concern on her face, but she was still very stoic.

"I am not Theo and Noemie's dad. I am their uncle." Louis took a deep breath again, fighting back tears.

"I came to Paris to watch them while my brother and his wife went on a trip of a lifetime to his wife's home country in Africa." Louis's voice started to get unsteady, and he slowed his words.

"My brother, my best friend in the world, and his wife were killed in a car accident on their way back from the trip." Louis walked away again, beginning to sniffle and wipe his eyes with his back turned to Lucy.

"I became the guardian to those beautiful kids … my kids. They are my kids, but I am not their father." Louis's voice broke, and he felt a reassuring hand rub his back. He kept his head down while he let tears flow but remained with his back to Lucy.

"I am so sorry," Lucy whispered. "I didn't…"

Louis turned around and hugged Lucy with his face buried into her neck.

"I didn't tell you about the truth because it is so hard to talk about. I didn't mean to hide anything from you," Louis whispered. "I lost my best friend that day. The kids lost both of their parents, too."

"I am so sorry." Lucy continued to hug Louis, feeling for the man who had lost so much.

After several minutes, Louis's breathing began to return to normal. He wasn't sobbing, but he was hurting.

"I am sorry that I hid that from you." He looked up into Lucy's eyes. "Are we able to get past this? I wasn't being manipulative."

"I know," Lucy whispered. "It's just…"

Louis looked confused. "What?"

"I just…" Now Lucy was the one fight back tears. "I just don't know about us."

CHAPTER 44

Dottie

2026

"Hello there," Dottie said in a whisper, suggesting that the early call was more excusable if she whispered a hello to Lucy.

"Yes…" Lucy answered with a gravelly, morning voice. Seeing the call come through on her phone took away any mystery as to who would be calling her this early.

"I am so, so sorry to call you this morning, but I have received several urgent messages last night. The director wants to see you today."

Please say yes, please say yes, Dottie was thinking to herself because she wasn't looking forward to contacting the pushy assistant again to negotiate another time.

"Let me think." A very groggy Lucy rolled over in bed and stared up at the ceiling of the rental. She was trying to think about what her plans were today, and all she really had planned was saying goodbye to Theo and Noemie before heading back to London. Lucy's stomach twisted just thinking about not seeing those sweet faces so often. Even if things didn't work out with Louis and her, she really, really cared about those kids. They were both amazing.

"Did he say what time he wanted me to come and audition again?"

"He was hoping for early afternoon," Dottie replied promptly, with a bit of overexaggerated enthusiasm, hoping that it would make the request a little bit easier for Lucy. Dottie doesn't know Lucy well enough yet to really know her preferences, and she was assuming that this last-minute request wasn't ideal for a well-known actress.

"The last-minute request isn't ideal," Lucy responded.

Yes, Dottie, you do know what you are doing with this job after all. You are only new to the job. You aren't an imbecile after all, Dottie said to herself. *You will be an amazing assistant to Lucy one day; you just have to give yourself some time to learn the ropes!* Again, Dottie was doing her best to fill her mind with self-affirmations instead of doubt.

"Would you also contact Callum Jones, who is the assistant for Axel Scott? I know that I need to do some follow-up promotional work with the designer, so could you please contact him for more information?"

"Absolutely."

"I think I can do that last-minute audition," Lucy said. "Also, I need to get a train back to London late this afternoon. I have some things I need to take care of. Would you purchase my train ticket and send me the information?"

"Straight-o," Dottie replied with even more exaggerated enthusiasm.

Why do I always say such strange things when I am nervous? Dottie, why can't you act like a normal person?

"How has your trip been?" Dottie asked weakly, trying to shed some light into the personality of her new boss. "I hope you enjoyed having a group of friendly faces join you." Dottie smiled to herself. She would have loved to have a group of friends surprise her in Paris. First, she would love to have a group of friends, but then to meet them in Paris would be icing on the cake.

"It was one of the most unforgettable trips I have ever had," Lucy said with a smile, even though the knot in her stomach grew tighter after speaking the words aloud.

"I am so pleased to hear that. I know that Liam told me how hard you work, so I am so happy you had time for fun. It is well-deserved," Dottie explained.

A smile spread across Lucy's face. "Thank you for all that you have been doing from London while I have been out of town. I am sure it isn't easy juggling so many people when you are trying to learn the ropes of a new job."

Dottie tried to hide the giddiness in her voice when she received the acknowledgement from Lucy. Her last boss offered nothing but insults most of the time, so those kind words made Dottie want to jump up and down in excitement like a teenage girl.

"What a lovely thing to say," she squeaked out. "Aside from your brother, I hope to be your best assistant yet."

"Brothers can still be a pain, even when they act as your assistant sometimes, so don't feel like you need to fill those shoes." Dottie could hear the warmth from Lucy's voice, and it made her smile.

Speaking to Lucy had given Dottie hope and confidence with this job that she hadn't had yet. Dottie was finally feeling the self-imposed tension release a bit after chatting with Lucy.

"Thank you so much," Dottie replied, finally beginning to understand that she had a pretty amazing boss. She could leave her old worries from her previous job behind her.

"Is there anything else I can do for you?"

"No," Lucy replied. "Just send me my travel information once you book it."

"I meant to ask … will anyone be traveling back to London with you? Should I book their transportation as well?"

"No, I will be traveling back alone," Lucy replied. There was almost a sadness that Dottie detected in Lucy's voice.

"Very well, I will get the information to you straight away. I will confirm the time of your audition through text message as well."

"Thank you."

"Thank you, Lucy."

Dottie pushed the end call button on the phone and fell back on the bed. She kicked her arms and legs in delight after their conversation. This was the first time she felt competent and confident about her new job. She was also excited to learn that Lucy Hall was going to be a great boss to have.

CHAPTER 45

Margaux
2026

Amelia

Wotcha? 

Margaux

What did you call me?

Amelia

WHAT ARE YOU DOING? 

Margaux

Is that some kind of British phrase? If so, I am so here for it. Remember, I am a small-town girl who just moved to the big city! Hey girl hey is how I say hi!

Amelia

What was the final $$ from the fundraiser????

While Margaux waited for her friend's reply, she saw the three familiar dots, anticipating a response. After a short delay, Margaux was distracted by another text from Evan.

A smile spread across Margaux's face when she saw the response from Evan. She was absolutely amazed by his new adventurous spirit. Years ago, when they dated in high school, he was overcome by his anxiety. He had panic attacks that were triggered by small spaces or airplanes or a number of things that made him feel like he was losing a sense of control. But now, Evan had done so much work on himself. He was like a new person. The adventurous partner she always hoped for in the previous years they dated was right there, and she was absolutely soaking in these moments with him.

Margaux was doing her best to not think of the logistics of their recent reconciliation while he still lived in Indiana and she was in

New York City. This time together in Italy and Paris was like a dream. She then thought of her reply to his response.

Amelia texted Margaux back, pulling her from her chat with Evan.

Suddenly, Margaux remembered that she was in the middle of texting Evan.

Margaux started to reply to Evan when a text from Amelia came through.

Evan interrupted with another text message.

Then Amelia popped back up in her notifications.

Margaux was so impressed by how much Amelia was now expressing her faith. When they met in Italy, Amelia didn't seem very strong in her faith; if anything, this experience had helped her lean into her faith more.

Margaux

> God is using this time to bring you closer to Him. I know it sounds like bumper sticker talk, but I promise you, I can see it through your texts.

Margaux switched back over to her conversation with Evan to see a new text pop up.

Evan

> Should we go see her??

Margaux

> Don't tease me with a good time. 😐

Evan

> You know a guy with access to an airplane...

Margaux

> We could explore one more day in Paris, then we head to Spain?!?!? You're serious, right?

Evan

> I would never, ever joke about traveling with you because that would be a death wish. Traveling is your love language!

Margaux

> Do you mind if I tell Amelia we will come see her?

Margaux could express her sassy and joyful attitude even through text message.

Margaux's phone screen was suddenly filled with a cascade of hearts.

CHAPTER 46

Elle

2026

Elle looked down at her phone as she was waiting for an opportunity to speak to Lucy about last night. She could hear Lucy rumbling around in her bedroom that morning, but she hadn't made an appearance yet. She continued to relax in the kitchen and scroll on her phone.

I just know something was going on between Lucy and Louis last night, Elle thought to herself. *They seemed to be getting along so well, and he seems like a great guy. I can't imagine what happened.*

Elle heard Lucy's door open and heard footsteps in the hallway upstairs, which suggested that she might be making her way downstairs.

"Good morning, sleepyhead," Elle cooed to Lucy, after seeing Lucy make her way down the steps. "Actually, erase that, you look amazing. I thought that you had a late night and decided to sleep in, but it looks like you are ready for the day."

"I have to go to another audition for the director. The director contacted my agent yesterday and requested another audition, which I was expecting technically, but I was hoping to have more notice," Lucy explained as she went directly to the coffee machine and immediately hit the start button.

Elle looked around to see if anyone was around the rental who could hear their conversation. "How are things going? I could tell that things were a little tense between you and Louis last night." Elle paused for a moment to see how Lucy would receive her question, afraid that she might get defensive if she thought Elle was prying.

Lucy turned around to face Elle and leaned back against the kitchen cabinet. Lucy let out a deep breath … then her face crumpled.

Elle walked over and gave Lucy a hug. She held her friend, and Lucy buried her face into her hair and cried.

"I am so sorry things didn't work out with Louis."

"What did he do?" Elle asked, then noticed that Liam had quietly entered the rental with a box of pastries. Lucy lifted her head to see Liam standing there, looking completely confused about what was happening, but trying to sway the girls with some yummy pastries.

"What did he do?" Liam asked. Elle and Lucy looked at one another and laughed at Liam and his overprotective-brother reaction to seeing the women embracing in the kitchen. His mind went immediately to the cause, and he wanted to fix it.

Lucy wiped a tear from the corner of her eye and started to speak, but she felt the tingling feeling in the back of her throat. The distinctive feeling right before you are about to cry, but she fought the impulse. She was determined not to cry about this situation.

"I cut things off with Louis," Lucy admitted, while Elle and Liam stood in the kitchen in complete confusion.

"I am so confused about this, Lucy," Liam replied and put down the pastries on the table.

"I am confused about it too," Lucy half-cried and chuckled at the same time.

"What happened?" Elle asked. "Why don't you go to the table, and I will finish making your coffee for you? Tell us what happened. I thought you both seemed to be getting along so well, that is until the fundraiser." Suddenly, a shocked expression fell across Lucy's face.

"Did he completely hate the fundraiser for some reason?" Elle asked in mock inquisition mode. *I mean, who in their right mind would be disappointed by a successful fundraiser?*

"Wait… what… no," Lucy answered in the confusion, but did realize that Elle was trying to lighten the mood a bit.

"I realized that I just can't trust myself to be in a relationship, even if he does seem pretty amazing," Lucy confided.

"How did you come to this conclusion?" Liam took a bite of a chocolate croissant, with a confused expression on his face.

"Here is your coffee." Elle brought the coffee to Lucy who was seated across from her brother at the table.

"Thank you." Lucy held the warm latte up to her mouth and sipped lightly.

"During the fundraiser, a woman approached me and gushed about the kids' mom, and it completely made me realize how much

I didn't know about Louis's past. I literally know nothing about their mom! It made me feel uncomfortable that I was really clueless when it came to that aspect of Louis's life. I don't need to know everything, but I should know some things."

"That is true. You are so busy, and you are about to start a new movie." Liam began to give Lucy reasons that he understood her perspective completely, but he seemed to be more distracted by his croissant.

Liam, what are you doing? Elle thought to herself. *Everything I know about this guy has been great, and he makes Lucy happy. Plus, she seems to really care about his kids too.*

"You realized all of this when the woman talked about his ex?" Elle tried to hide her confusion because Lucy had seemed so excited about Louis.

"Not exactly. I asked Louis about the kids' mom, and he evaded answering my questions most of the night last night," Lucy explained very matter-of-factly.

"That's weird," Elle replied, then found herself crossing her arms, trying to decide what she really thought about Louis.

"We didn't get to talk until we were all back here last night."

"What did he say?" Elle kept asking questions. *Elle, you are losing your gift of reading people because you really thought Louis was a great guy.*

"He told me he wasn't the kids' dad," Lucy said.

Then, Liam started choking on his croissant when he heard what Lucy said. Elle walked over and started patting Liam on the back.

He gave Elle a thumbs up and finished his chewing.

"I am so confused by everything right now," Elle said. "Did he say more after that?"

"He is their uncle. He became their guardian when his brother and sister-in-law were killed in a car accident."

Liam and Elle looked at Lucy in shock.

"That's just awful. My heart goes out to him," Elle almost whispered. "Did you cry when he told you that? Those poor kids."

"We both cried," Lucy said, finally showing some signs of that usually empathetic person that she was.

"You really don't think this is worth it?" Elle asked, trying to hide the hope in her voice. The kids adored Lucy too.

"I really do care about him … and the kids, but I just don't trust myself. I think back to the circumstances when we met, and I was taken by his charm, talent, faith, and personality. I just dismissed some internal questions I had, and it makes me not trust myself. I need to work on my instincts more. I am not angry at him for not being upfront about his situation, but I am angry at myself for blindly falling for someone who I didn't really know."

I knew it, Elle thought to herself. *Lucy does care about him, and she was falling for him. Any perceived dishonesty she feels makes her uncertain about herself, not him.*

"Are you going to say goodbye to the kids?"

"I am."

"I bet that is going to be hard."

"It will be, but I hope to stay in contact with them. I adore them so much." Lucy smiled, thinking about Louis and the kids.

"It breaks my heart thinking about what he had gone through with his family," Elle said.

"Me too," Lucy whispered, clearly hiding her emotions, not revealing how she really felt.

Elle stood up and walked to Lucy and gave her a hug. Elle could hear Lucy sniffle quietly, trying to fight back tears.

Elle and Lucy joined Liam at the table while they sat quietly eating their breakfast and sipping coffee.

After a few moments, Lucy stood up rather suddenly. "I have to get going." She made every effort to maintain her poise in front of Elle and Liam.

"We will see you later, but are you sure you don't want me to go with you back to London by train?"

"No, the two lovebirds can have some time together going back to London. Besides, you know how much I love riding the train. It is a little treat to myself." Lucy's smile beamed, but Elle noticed that the joy didn't reach her eyes.

Lucy grabbed her bag and made her way to the door.

"I can give you a ride to the audition," Liam offered.

"No, thank you. It is just a fifteen-minute walk." Lucy's smile faltered a bit.

Liam and Elle walked to the door with Lucy as she made her way outside. Once the door closed, Liam asked, "Do you think she is hiding something?"

"Yes, I do," Elle answered.

Elle looked at Liam, and there was a mutual understanding without saying a word.

"The question is, what are we going to do about it?" Liam smiled conspiratorially.

CHAPTER 47

Lucy

2026

I need to find a restroom so that I can make sure I don't have mascara running down my face, Lucy thought to herself after finding herself getting emotional during her walk. *You promised yourself that you would not get emotional or cry because this is your choice. You need time to think and pivot. You do not need to be charmed by a man again.*

Lucy made her way down the hall toward the loo. Just as Lucy turned the corner, she found herself face to face with Louis.

"Hello there." Louis's throat was dry, and his mouth was having a hard time forming words, his mind was distracted by last night's conversation. He didn't sleep at all because that conversation that had been on replay in his head since last night.

"Hi there," Lucy said, almost shyly. *This is going to be much harder than I thought. How am I going to tell him that I am heading back to England today? How am I going to tell the kids that I am leaving today? You will come back to see them. You adore them. Plus, they don't need to experience any more loss in their lives. You will remain in their lives.*

"Sorry, I didn't mean to block your way," Lucy replied. She tried to reassure herself, *you don't need to be so awkward about this. Don't make eye contact with him because you will melt into those hazel eyes.*

Both Louis and Lucy stared at one another awkwardly for a few seconds. *Louis ran a nervous hand through his beard, which is what he often does when he is deep in thought,* Lucy thought to herself.

After the initial shock of nearly walking into one another, the nerves started to fall away, and they looked at one another warmly this time. Some of the shy, awkward feelings started to slowly disappear. The couple looked at one another, a short glance, but full of longing, full of everything they could not change and everything they wished for. They remained in the stillness of the moment. Finally, Louis was the first to break the silence.

"No, it was me who was in your way just now," Louis said. "Would you like to run through the song one more time?"

"Sure," Lucy said. "Just give me a few minutes. I can meet you in the room."

Lucy walked into the restroom and found the nearest stall, entering as quickly as she could. She took a deep breath, trying her best to keep centered and focused today. *You've got this; don't let his hazel eyes distract you, even if he is so bloody beautiful and talented.* Lucy stood in the stall, taking cleansing breaths, trying to regain her confidence about what she needed to do.

She finally left the stall, walking across the room to the sink. She turned on the faucets and washed her hands, for no particular reason. She grabbed a paper towel and stared at her reflection in the mirror. She looked into her own eyes, like she was looking at a stranger. *Are you ready to go sing your goodbye song with the most amazing, genuine, kind, and wonderful man you have ever met?* she thought to herself.

Lucy took another deep breath, thinking about the irony of the situation. *Oh, and why don't you sing this heartbreaking song for an audition for a part you are already nervous about? Are you ready to show what kind of actress you really are?*

Lucy finally stopped staring at herself in the mirror and threw away the paper towel. Her personal pep talk was over, and she had to move now. She walked out of the restroom and made quick steps to the audition room. Lucy hesitated for just one more moment, then turned the handle and entered the room where Louis was already seated at a piano.

Another man was standing at the piano with his back to Lucy while he was chatting with Louis.

"Lucy, you aren't going to believe this, but this man has performed with me before today."

Finally, the man turned around and smiled eagerly at Lucy. "Hello Lucy, my name is James Wilson. I was sent by the studio to run the audition. I hope this doesn't put too much pressure on you, having a new face here." James held out his hand.

"No, not at all." Lucy tried her best to show a confident smile. "I mean it isn't a problem at all. When did you work together before?"

"We worked together in London on a jazz album," Louis respond with a wide smile, clearly recalling a special time from the past. His smile had reached up to his eyes, which made Lucy happy.

"John was with us when we cut the album, too. He was so incredibly talented. By the way, I am so sorry about … everything," James added. James said so much without saying much at all.

Lucy smiled at the men, who were not just reminiscing about a time that included Louis's brother, but clearly a special time in both of their lives. She listened to the men reminisce a bit longer, sharing stories and rolling with chest-deep laughter. Lucy couldn't help but smile, even if these stories weren't her own. She adored seeing this moment with Louis, while getting a glimpse of his brother's character. Lucy listened and smiled, as quiet laughter erupted into hands-clapping laughter as one story after another unfolded.

After some time, Louis realized how quiet Lucy had become while they recalled the early years as musicians. "Oh, I am so sorry that we were so sidetracked." Louis stood up and walked to Lucy's side and offered a gently pat on her arm, friendly, but not forced.

"Are you ready to start?" James asked Lucy.

"I am ready as I will ever be," Lucy answered. She held her hands awkwardly so that she wouldn't fidget as she answered him.

"Are you sure you don't want to rehearse your song? I am happy to step out for a few minutes," James offered.

"I am happy to go through it one more time." Louis used the statement as a question to Lucy.

"I think I am ready." Lucy smiled.

Louis sat back down at the piano and began the music. When they first began working on the song, they didn't know that this song would be so poignant as their final song together for their audition. They didn't realize how heartbreakingly beautiful and torturous these words would be right now, today of all days.

Initially, they avoided eye contact when Lucy began her song,

"My bags are packed and I am ready to go

My heart is the only thing that truly knows

As I sit - waiting on the train to depart

I know the man I am leaving still has my heart."

They avoided eye contact until that line. Then, Lucy and Louis's eyes sought one another. The room disappeared, and all that remained were the two people who cared deeply for one another. Lucy had tears well up in her eyes as she sang the last line, her eyes fixed on Louis.

The music stopped.

The room was completely silent.

Their eyes stayed fixed on one another.

Applause fractured the silence. "That was amazing!" James approached Lucy and shook her hand and moved to Louis to shake his hand too. Lucy discreetly wiped a tear from the corner of her eye.

Then James eagerly began discussing details of the logistics of the collaboration. He added more details about the movie, rehearsals, and contacting Lucy's agent. Lucy had hoped to finally expand into music in her career. It sounded like finally this goal, this dream, was coming to fruition. However, while her mind was celebrating, her heart was elsewhere.

The details of the new collaboration that were falling onto deaf ears because Lucy and Louis knew this this wasn't an audition—this was goodbye.

CHAPTER 48

2026

"Oh dear." Dottie checked her phone as a series of text messages from Lucy began to fill her inbox.

"Right-o," Dottie reassured herself, once she saw the stream of text messages come through to her phone.

Lucy

Schedule a follow-up...

Contact Axel Scott's fashion house.

Follow-up with voice lessons in London.

Filming will begin...

Forget Axel Scott, contact Callum Jones.

Thank you for scheduling my train...

"Oh dear," Dottie told herself again. She grabbed her trusty tote bag and glanced at the infographic she designed to better understand all of Lucy's primary contacts and their roles.

"Callum Jones…" Dottie was speaking to herself while trying to find his name on the infographic.

"He is the assistant to Axel Scott." Dottie noted on her infographic. "What do I need to contact him regarding?" Dottie cross-referenced her notes with her text message to ensure that she would sound informed during her initial contact with him.

"Should I text him or call him?" Dottie pulled out a pencil and tapped the pencil on her chin as she was thinking. Dottie grabbed her phone again and Googled Callum Jones with Alex Scott Design.

"Well done, Nancy Drew, you were able to find out that he is just a thirty-year-old bloke, so I am going to text him. He would probably be put off if I tried to give him a call."

Dottie picked up her phone and sent Callum Jones a message.

Dottie

"Good golly," Dottie said to herself. She sent the message before she meant to send it. Her hands began to shake because she was already making mistakes with sending a bloody text message too soon.

Her phone dinged.

Callum

???

"Humpf," Dottie said to herself, with a slightly irritated look on her face.

Dottie

My apologies, I am writing to ask for a time that Lucy can meet with Axel Scott regarding their collaboration.

Callum

You need to talk to Axel.

Dottie

Should I always contact him for his own appointments, or do you do that?

Dottie reached into her trusty tote bag and pulled out a notepad. She opened up the notepad and wrote down some details.

Callum

You need to ask.

"Crabby McCrabs," Dottie whispered to herself. *Should I thank him? After all, I may need to contact him again in the future. I should keep it pleasant.*

Dottie looked back at her notes to see what information she should gather for Axel Scott when her phone dinged again.

"Oh boy, another one." Dottie glanced at her phone and saw Callum's message of a scull emoji.

So strange, Dottie mentioned to herself. *Who even knows what that emoji means? Oh well, onward and upward, Miss Pemrose, but first, we are going to see what that emoji means.*

Dottie quickly found the meaning of the scull emoji. *The scull emoji means laugh out loud or an embarrassing moment, she read aloud to herself. It could mean death. Bloody hell, am I supposed to be embarrassed? I shouldn't be embarrassed. He should be embarrassed. Pushy bloke. I am not starting my new job with having other assistants push me around.*

How about that, Mr. Jones? she thought to herself.

Dottie stared at her phone and saw the familiar three dots with what appeared to be Callum's response.

??

So, he can send a scull emoji, but I can't?? What a numpty. She sent three question marks back to Callum.

Dottie saw the three dots, waiting for his reply. Then, another text message came in for more tasks for her day.

Do you always have to have the last word? Plus, is it your first day ever using emojis?

Yes and no. 

She added a scull emoji again, just to push his buttons.

Dottie, you now have a million things to do before Lucy arrives this evening, and you are trying to push buttons of some random numpty that you may never see. Get to work, bird. Yet, she found herself waiting on his response.

The three dots disappeared.

Ha! I won. He has given up, she thought to herself. *I had the last word … or emoji. You are not being childish; you are establishing boundaries with your new job. Onward and upward, Dottie Pemrose.*

Almost giddy with this tiny victory, Dottie looked through her detailed planner and began adding color-coded items to her to-do list. She used her favorite office supply table to place next to each task and would soon have the satisfaction of removing the table to indicate a job complete. Plus, she would draw a line through the item, just to appreciate the satisfaction of a task complete.

"Contact Callum Jones," she said aloud to herself and drew a line across his name.

Contact Axel Scott, Dottie added to her list. She continued her list while scrolling across the text messages to see what had been added to her list.

Dottie, I hope you enjoyed your down time with Lucy in Paris because your job has finally become demanding. She smiled to herself, so excited for this next chapter. Then, she heard her phone ding again with yet another task.

She saw a message from Callum, and she stabbed the screen with her finger, just waiting to see what he had to say. Then, she saw the world's longest text message filled with scull emojis.

Bugger, she said aloud, seeing her once-held-texting-the-last-word-victory being stolen from her. *If you like games, I am the master of games,* she said to herself conspiratorially.

CHAPTER 49

Elle

2026

"**A**re you sure you don't want me to come with you because it feels weird having you go on the train by yourself? I really don't mind. I am sure Liam can handle not seeing me for a few hours while we travel," Elle asked a very somber Lucy.

"No, it is fine," Lucy said nonchalantly, as she stared out of the window of Liam's car.

"Did you get a chance to say goodbye to Margaux and Evan?" Elle asked, attempting to change the subject, but also fishing for information on all the people that she said goodbye to today.

"I did say goodbye to both of them. They are absolutely adorable." Lucy finally showed a glimpse of the happy–go-lucky woman she met weeks ago in New York City.

Wow, Elle, you met Lucy just weeks ago in New York, which led to you meeting the love of your life. Then, it led to an amazing opportunity, and now you are engaged to the most amazing man and caretaker you have ever met … well compared to your dad, she thought to herself. Her thoughts made her admire her engagement ring. She watched the beautiful stone sparkle as she held out her hand, then glanced at Liam, who was watching his fiancé admire the ring he chose for her. They shared a smile, no words needed; both were thinking of how unexpected this engagement had been.

"You are thinking about your engagement, aren't you?" Lucy smiled at Elle.

"I am." Elle smiled and turned to look at Lucy, who was in the back seat. "I can't help myself. Who would have thought that I would become one of those giddy women when I got engaged? I used to be so serious."

"That is true," Liam added. "We didn't start off on the right foot when we first met."

"But look at you now," Lucy cooed, and Elle leaned over and rested her head on Liam's shoulder as he continued driving.

"Going back to Margaux and Evan, they are staying at the rental one more night, so you two are welcome to stay, too," Lucy offered.

"As much as I love Paris, I think Liam and I have some details to iron out regarding the wedding and where we are living in the coming months. So back to London for us, too." Elle smiled nervously.

"So, you just have some small easy conversations to have," Lucy joked.

There she is, Elle thought, *there is Lucy coming back to us.* She had been so indifferent and confused the past couple of days. The last time I saw her happy was when she first started spending time with Louis, and their future looked bright. I wonder how things went saying goodbye to the kids.

"How did it go saying goodbye to Theo and Noemie? Are you doing ok?" Elle asked hesitantly. "You don't have to talk about it if you don't want to…" Elle's voice trailed off.

"It was hard, but I am going to be in their lives. I adore those kids." Lucy's face lit up. "I took both of them some gifts to open for the next couple of days. You should have seen Theo's face when he saw the train wrapping paper. He is so bloody adorable. I think Noemie sensed some tension between Louis and I because she acts like an adult most of the time. She loved her gifts too. She really needs to have a strong mother figure in her life to take pressure off her trying to be in charge all of time." Lucy added. "I will stay in contact with the kids and Louis, too."

"You plan on staying in contact with Louis, too?" Elle asked, again trying to avoid sounding like someone who was prying, but Lucy and Louis seemed to have a real connection. However, staying in contact after moving in different directions may be difficult too.

"Of course, I would love to have him as my voice coach for the work I am doing with the film, but I just don't know. I fully trust his ability to give me confidence to do the work. I fully trust him with the project," she added. *I just don't trust myself not to muck things up for both of us,* she thought.

"I will pray for you to have discernment. I know it is hard but just try to listen to the right voice. One of my favorite Bible verses that I tell myself when I am indecisive is Romans 8:12: 'So dear brothers and sisters, you have not obligation whatsoever to do what your sinful nature urges you to do.' In other words, avoid following your sinful ways and, in this case, pay attention to the voice you are listening to in your head. Is it the voice that build you up or fills you with fear?" Elle explained.

"I love that so much," Lucy said, whose facial expression revealed that what Elle told her made her wheels start spinning.

Liam looked at Elle. "I hope to get to that point with my Bible studying."

"You will." Elle squeezed Liam's hand.

Watching the two lovebirds, Lucy had a hard time not getting emotional watching such a tender moment. She would always be thankful having a front-row seat to her brother's love story.

"Here we are." Liam pulled up to the train station.

"Dottie was sure to book the private cabin so I would be safe," Lucy added as she was sliding across the back seat of the car. She knew that Liam and Elle worried about her traveling alone. Before exiting the car, she put on her trusty train baseball cap.

"I will see you both in London and thanks for the ride." Lucy went around the car and gave Liam and Elle a kiss on each of their cheeks.

"Thank you for taking my bags to London, so I can just enjoy the ride. I love you both. I will see you there." Lucy smiled and gently tapped the side of the car to emphasize their goodbye.

Slowly, Liam began pulling away from the train station and asked Elle, "Are you buying this story that she is trying to give us?"

"No," Elle whispered.

"So does that mean I should respond to the text that Louis sent me?" Liam asked.

CHAPTER 50

Louis

2026

"I want to go say goodbye again, too," Noemie demanded.

"I don't even know if Liam will tell me about her train details quite honestly. I don't even know if saying goodbye at the train station is possible if I don't hear from him. Plus, we already said goodbye earlier today," Louis admitted. *Why are you even telling Noemie this stuff? This is why she acts like an adult; she doesn't need to know details like this. Then again, you are sharing this with Noemie because she really likes Lucy, too,* Louis responded to his own self-doubt.

Theo stood next to Louis and took his free hand that wasn't holding his phone. Louis just noticed that Theo was wearing the hat that Lucy had given him that matched her own train hat. Theo smiled shyly at Louis.

"So, that is your not-so-subtle-way of telling me you want to come too?"

"Yes," Theo whispered.

Louis smiled. "Sometimes, I think you like her a bit more than you like me."

Noemie's face made a funny "well…" expression, and Louis brought her into a hug. "I don't know if we will get a reply from Liam before her train leaves. Plus, she does travel often for work, so we may not be able to see her anytime we want to see her. You understand that, right?"

"I do understand that, but she is literally in our town, still." Noemie had a quick counter to Louis's reasoning.

"That's true, so I guess we just wait until we hear from Liam," Louis added.

"I say we just go to the train station. We know that Gare du Nord is the station that uses the Chunnel. Plus, I looked up the trains that leave for London this afternoon, and there are only four options. I think we just may be able at least wave goodbye to her train from the platform," Noemie explained.

"You, my dear, are a force. I think you should be a solicitor, or as the French call them avocats, right?" Louis's French was still spotty from time to time when the term was very specific.

Noemie smiled widely. "Thank you, but are we going or not?"

Meanwhile, Theo walked over to stand by Noemie, showing that he was in solidarity to find Lucy at the train station rather than just sit there and think about her leaving.

"It looks like I am outnumbered," Louis added.

Noemie squealed, and she and Theo hugged one another.

"Put on shoes." Everyone ran in different directions in their home, looking for any and all items that they were taking to the train station with them. Within minutes, everyone returned to the front door, ready to go.

"Let's go." They all piled out of the front door and were walking quickly toward the metro and began descending the stairs. In fifteen minutes, they would be ascending the stairs from Gare du Nord.

"Noemie, where should we go first? What train is leaving next?" Louis asked the girl, who clearly had a better game plan than he did. They sat together on the metro, creating their game plan as they were making their way to the station.

"It looks like the next train leaves in 15 minutes from platform 3." Noemie was staring at Louis's phone.

"Perfect. Are you ready for an adventure?" Louis asked Theo. He replied with one satisfied nod.

"Just so you know, we may not find her, ok?" Louis was doing his best to prepare the kids for possible disappointment.

"We know," Noemie answered for both of them. "It may be disappointing, but we both understand that."

"Yup," Theo added quietly with a nod.

Just as they arrived at Gare du Nord, Noemie saw a message from Liam on Louis's phone that she was still holding.

"Liam replied to your text message." Noemie handed the phone to Louis once she saw the notification.

Louis took a nervous breath.

"How are you doing?" Louis read aloud.

Louis

Actually, I would love Lucy's train information because we are just arriving at Gare du Nord to say goodbye to her.

Liam

You're there now?

Louis

Yes.

Louis smiled at Theo and Noemie, who were looking at him with hopeful eyes.

Liam

Her train just left.

Louis's heart fell, but he tried not to show his disappointment.

He saw three dots on his phone, indicating Liam was still commenting.

Liam

Would you like a ride to London instead?

Louis

What??

Liam

I am in my car with Elle. We can come get you.

"What is happening?" Noemie was growing impatient.

"Lucy's train just left," Louis added, "but Liam and Elle are going to drive us to London to say hello, instead of goodbye. Do you want to go surprise Lucy that way instead?"

Noemie and Theo began jumping up and down while they hugged one another.

"Now, we have to ride back home to grab our passports."

"This is like a rom-com," Noemie cooed. "I always dreamt of going after a love in another country."

This comment made Louis laugh as they made their way back onto the train that they had just exited just moments ago.

As they took their seats on the metro back to their home, Louis asked Theo, "Are you ok with going on a last-minute trip to London?"

Theo reached into his pocket and took out a wadded-up piece of paper and unfolded it and showed it to Louis.

It was a picture Theo had drawn of Lucy and he riding a train together with their matching hats.

"In that case, I hope we are able to find her because you need to give Lucy this work of art yourself."

Theo beamed and held Louis's hand as they continued their way back home.

CHAPTER 51

Elle

2026

"Who is ready to go to London?" Elle called out of the car, with the window down, as they pulled up to Louis's place.

"Are we arriving much later than Lucy?" Louis asked as he began putting bags in the back of Liam's car.

"Actually, I think we can make it about thirty minutes behind her," Liam said confidently. "It takes most people longer, but I have driven it so many times, I have my ways."

Meanwhile, Theo and Noemie were scooting into the car with all their quickly-prepared-travel gear.

"Wow, you can pack quickly," Elle noted, as she stood outside of the car to help Louis and the kids.

"We travel to London from time to time, too. The kids know how to travel, that is for sure."

Elle marveled as the kids had their neck pillows, headsets, and blankets that they brought with them.

"This is your captain speaking. We will arrive in London in just over four hours. It should be a smooth drive. Please relax, take a nap, and enjoy the drive," Liam said from the front seat, in his best pilot impersonation, as everyone buckled their seats and got comfortable for their drive.

"That was actually pretty good," Noemie called from the back. "You really sounded like a pilot."

"That's a really nice headset," Elle complimented Theo.

"As you recall," Louis explained to Elle, who was at the cafe when they first met, "Theo needed a new headset, so this is a gift from Lucy."

"I like your train hat, too," Elle added, while Theo beamed at the compliment.

"Even though Theo loves trains, he doesn't like how loud they are, do you, Buddy? This headset was a godsend," Louis added.

"Your hat looks like Lucy's hat," Elle added.

"Yes," Theo whispered and nodded.

"Well, I am going to play some quiet music, and I would encourage everyone to relax for a bit because we are going to be on the road for a little while. Maybe you can enjoy the countryside?" Liam added.

After twenty minutes of being on the road, everyone in the car was settled and began to grow quiet. Elle looked in the vanity mirror and saw that Noemie had put a mask over her eyes, and, based on the relaxed position of her mouth, she had fallen asleep. Theo had his train hat pulled down over his eyes, and his bulky headset was over his hat. It looked like he too had fallen asleep.

Liam looked at Elle, who was checking on the kids in the back. He appreciated her ability to keep tabs on everyone.

Elle looked at Louis last. Louis was staring out of the window, clearly deep in thought and was watching the beautiful countryside pass by.

Elle said a silent prayer to herself. *Lord, if it is Your will, it would be wonderful to give these kids a break. If caring about each other was enough, I think they would have worked things out on their own. Lord, help them find a way.*

CHAPTER 52

Lucy
2026

She took the steps off her train and took in the familiar scenery of London. She walked through the familiar St. Pancras Station but stood in the middle of the station with crowds of people passing by her. Lucy was just taking it all in and honestly felt a little lost too.

At least no one is expecting the actress, Skye Reynolds, to come through the train station, Lucy thought to herself. *Most celebrities would take an airplane, which is another reason why she loves taking the train.* Lucy sat down on one of the benches, just to think.

I don't really want to go home to my empty flat, Lucy told herself. *I just need to sit and think a minute. One would think I would have had plenty of time to think on the four-hour train ride. So, Lucy, where do you want to go?*

Lucy stood up and pulled her bag over one shoulder and made her way toward another area of the station that would take her back toward her neighborhood, but not home yet. She walked toward a connecting train and made her way down the steps and took a seat on the Tube.

She watched patiently as she approached the Notting Hill

neighborhood. Then, she stepped off the Tube and took the stairs up into her neighborhood and made her way to its charming streets. She found another bench and sat down on it. Lucy needed to think. She needed clarity. She needed peace.

This spot. This very spot was where the first boy that ever broke her heart saw her for the last time. She had, for years, questioned what she had missed. She questioned how could she have possibly misunderstood his intentions when they planned their trip to Paris. They walked the streets that day before the trip, planning in excitement for time together, and then he didn't come. It was shortly after that she began her descent into self-preservation. Any time things went south when she dated, her thoughts would always return to what she could have missed to get the wrong impression. How could she have been so naive? How could she have chosen that guy? This was where the seeds of self-doubt were planted, and it would bear fruit for years in her mind. This is where it started. A young Lucy with stars in her eyes, who bore the responsibility for every broken relationship she has ever had.

This was the spot, now the spot where she was no longer feeding this need for her to take on the full responsibility of any mistakes in a relationship as her burden to carry. She was not feeding this self-doubt and bitterness any longer. Elle's words really resonated with her before she made her way into the train. *This sinful nature of feeding my self-doubt when it came to relationships ends here. This is the spot where my life begins now, finally free.*

If only she was still in Paris when she came to this realization and could go to Louis and apologize for her overreaction and attempt to make their way through the muck of what their connection had become.

Oh well, Lucy, she told herself. *At least, you can move forward now. You are officially saying goodbye to it.* Lucy said a prayer, "God, thank you for making me see things clearly. Please just give Louis and the kids the happy ending they deserve. They are lovely people and have been through so much already. Amen."

She sat alone on the bench for a few more moments, finally feeling lighter.

I want to celebrate this moment with ice cream because ice cream always makes everything better, she thought to herself. Lucy stood up and began making her way down the sidewalk to her favorite local ice cream shop. In just a short walk, she opened the door to the ice cream shop.

"Hello, Darry," she said as she walked into the shop.

"Lucy, my dear, I haven't seen you in a while. To what do I own this honor?" Darry was wiping down the counter because the shop was about to close for the night. His Irish brogue was distinct when speaking.

"I just arrived into town and knew that I needed to get some of the best scoops in town."

"My lasse, you have made my night. Do you want your usual?"

"Of course." Lucy smiled as she felt a lightness overcome her. She felt different, knowing that she would live differently now. She was finally letting go of these chains of doubt.

"The Lucy special." Darry put a cup in front of her with a tiny spoon.

"Cheers." Lucy held up her cup of ice cream to Darry who held up an empty cup.

Lucy sat and quietly ate her ice cream as Darry made some small talk. Lucy finally felt her shoulders relax; she just wished things worked out differently with Louis. *Who knows, maybe he will want to work together and do more voice work,* she asked herself.

The chime rang as another customer entered the shop, but Lucy continued to quietly enjoy her treat. Plus, Lucy didn't turn to look so that she could be discreet with her "celebrity" status.

"Ice cream fixes everything." She heard a familiar voice say, and she saw Louis standing in the ice cream store.

Lucy jumped up and walked to him, stopping just shy of touching him.

"How?"

"How am I here in London? How am I in the ice cream shop? How am I standing in front of you asking if we can start again?"

"Yes." Lucy stepped closer to Louis and gently took his hands in hers.

"I need to say some things first," Louis continued. "I am sorry that I betrayed your trust by not being completely honest about everything. I promise I was not trying to hide things, but I just didn't want to have some difficult conversations, honestly."

"I…" Lucy began, but Louis continued.

"I just want you to hear me say this. I wish I wouldn't have let you go without begging you to stay. Without coming up with a plan for us, without trying to fight for the good thing we have," Louis added, then let out a nervous breath.

"I am finished." Louis smiled sheepishly. "I am sorry. What were you going to say?"

"I am sorry," Lucy said, "I overreacted." She paused again. "I really overreacted."

"Let me show you that you can trust me. I want to show you that I am a man you can trust with everything," Louis whispered and took her face into his hands.

Lucy stared at Louis's lips. *Are you going to kiss me or not?* Lucy thought to herself. The distance between them was too far, so she stepped closer and put her arms around his neck.

"Can I kiss you?" Louis whispered to Lucy.

"I thought you would never ask," Lucy whispered and brought her lips to Louis.

Louis kissed her in return so gently, like he was holding glass. His hands cradled her face, like he couldn't believe she was here right now. His soft lips touched hers so gently, so softly, but his kiss deepened and lingered, showing how much he ached for her. He slowly pulled his lips away and put his forehead to hers, grounding both of them in the moment. He wasn't demanding but silently asking for them to begin again.

The chime rang again, and Lucy was surprised to see Theo and Noemie walk into the shop.

"I have no words," Lucy said. "I can't believe you are here." She immediately walked over and threw her arms around Noemie and Theo. Lucy kissed them both on the tops of their heads.

"I am so happy you are here." She continued to hug both kids.

An overzealous Theo pulled out a wadded-up paper out of his pocket and handed it to Lucy.

"Well, let me see." Lucy opened the paper and saw an image of Lucy and Theo on a train together.

"This is just perfect, Theo." Lucy hugged him again, and Theo put his arms around Lucy. Louis watched this special moment in awe at how Theo had opened up so quickly to Lucy. Noemie stood next to Louis, taking in the moment too. They both understood how special it was to see Theo not only trust someone so quickly, but to express how much he cared for her.

"Thank you so much. I will cherish this always." Lucy held the wrinkled paper up to her chest. "I love it."

"Ok," Theo responded and smiled widely.

"Wait, did you just tell me you love me? I know your code words for 'I love you.'" Theo smiled at Lucy while also laughing quietly to himself.

"What about you?" Lucy turned to Noemie and hugged her. "Do you think I am ok?" and Lucy tickled her and pulled Noemie to her.

"Ok, ok." Noemie finally giggling like a girl her age instead of an adult. Noemie too was letting Lucy know that she loved her too.

Then Lucy turned to Louis and made a curious face.

Louis responded by putting his hands up like he was innocent. "I have no problem with telling you how ok you are to me."

Louis pulled Lucy into his arms in another embrace. Lucy put her arms around Louis, and he moved his mouth closer to Lucy.

"Ok?" Louis asked quietly.

"Ok," Lucy answered.

Louis pulled Lucy into one last kiss, so gently and tender while both Noemie and Theo covered their eyes and jumped up and down for this new beginning for all of them.

EPILOGUE

Paris to Barcelona

"A re you there?" Margaux asked Amelia as she held her phone to her ear, while she plugged her other ear with her finger. The noises of a small, working airport filled the air.

"Yes, love, I am here," Amelia called out as best as she could.

"We are going to be taking off in a few minutes. We have received clearance, or something like that." Margaux laughed out loud because she couldn't believe that she was someone waiting on her own airplane to get clearance for take-off. Well, Evan's airplane that she had now become the passenger princess of.

"I can't believe you are coming to Spain." Amelia was fighting back the emotions, just thinking of seeing a friendly face was more than she could even communicate.

"I will message you once we land, and we will come your way. Thank you for using some connections to get a rental so last minute."

"No problem at all. I am so thankful to see you both. What happened with Lucy and Louis?" Amelia was practically yelling in her phone so she could be heard.

"I have so much to tell you. Just a quick update: Louis and Lucy worked things out, and he and the kids are spending a couple of days in London. Elle and Liam are in London planning their future. Then, you have the world-trotting duo who is packing up to see you in Spain." Margaux was practically giddy talking about all that was going on the lives of her friends.

Amelia seemed really quiet.

"Amelia?

"Yes," she asked.

"You are so loved."

"Thank you," her tiny voice replied.

"I am going to let you go, and I will see you in a few hours, ok?"

"Sounds a-mazing," Amelia emphasized amazing.

Amelia stared at her phone, like she was willing Margaux to transport her fun-loving self to Spain right that minute. She stood in the hallway of the non-profit and looked at their miserably looking walls and haphazard paint. *If Santiago would let me get rid of this miserable, peeling paint, it might actually be one of the many things that are making people run from this organization rather than signing up their children for their programs. It is no wonder this place is dying a slow death. It needs life.*

Just as Amelia finished her thought, she noticed that a piece of student art, the one that had given this space any sort of life, had fallen halfway down and was barely hanging onto the wall. It was literally the one cute thing in this hallway, surrounded by years of neglect.

Amelia looked around for something to help her reach the art so that she could take it back into place. She saw a stool in the adjacent room, which should do the job. *This isn't the most secure stool I have ever seen, but I weigh next to nothing, so I am sure it is fine. Plus, this is one productive thing I am trusted to do at this point.*

Determined, Amelia picked up the stool and placed it in the hall. Then, she shifted her weight and took a large step so that she had one foot on the stool, making sure that she was balanced before pulling up her other foot on the stool. She made sure she was feeling balanced and steady before reaching on her tiptoes to tack up the one piece of student art that brought joy to this community center.

Surprisingly, the adhesive was still tacky, and the art easily reattached to the wall. Amelia placed both hands on the art and smoothed out the winkles of the page. She smiled at the image of kids playing outside of this organization and would have loved to have known the story of this moment. *Clearly, this organization was in a different time when this art was created because the only thing this building is doing well is sagging into disrepair,* she thought to herself.

It was at that moment she heard a crack from the stool, and all of the sudden, her mind went into overdrive, and she was not thinking clearly. She thought, this is going to hurt and try not to hit your head. Real time turned into slow motion, but her brain was in even slower motion too. She held out her hands Superman-style to grab something, but there were only smooth walls. Amelia began tumbling backward, and she closed her eyes; her brain wouldn't allow her to do anything but hope for the best.

As Amelia continued her slow-motion descent, she felt arms surround her back and legs. Suddenly, her head was tucked up to a chest, and she was spun in a circle. It was like the momentum of catching her caused both she and some random hero to spin in a circle. Finally, the momentum slowed, but Amelia's heart was still racing and so was the superhero's heart.

Soon, she realized it wasn't a superhero, but it was Santiago holding her protectively in his arms. Their eyes met, and both of them stared at one another breathless; no one could speak. They just stared, processing what happened, and Amelia noticed that his eyes weren't brown but seemed to have specks of gold too. *Wait, he has been nothing but a headache since you have been here. Why are you letting him hold you?* Reality came rushing back with a vengeance.

Suddenly, she felt the urge to squirm out of this awkward position and out of his arms.

"What are you doing?" she asked in frustration.

'What do you mean what am I doing? I was saving you from breaking your neck!" Santiago explained.

"What were you doing?" His eyes narrowed, and his hands began moving expressively.

"I was trying to fix your dangling art that you have neglected because it is the only nice thing in this hallway." Amelia also narrowed her eyes and crossed her arms, so that she could hide that her hands were still shaking from the fall.

"So, no thank you for helping you not break your neck?" Santiago asked again. He was now crossing his arms too, determined to make her realize that he actually did something to help her.

"So, no thank you for trying to make this place look like a place where children actually want to be?" Amelia spit out, but the words were just a little too personal. *That was unnecessary, Amelia, that was a low blow. Play nice.*

The two stood there, glaring at one another. No one was going to be the first to cave. They were at an impasse. After what seemed like several minutes, Amelia was the first to break the silence by spinning on her heel and marching out of the hallway, deep in thought.

I always notice details, but how did I just notice the gold specks in Santiago's eyes? Too bad he is such a jerk. He may have gold in his eyes, but his heart is stone!

As Amelia walked away, Santigo's thoughts betrayed him.

Why, why did she get sent to come "help" me because I am doing fine here on my own. I just need time to rebuild this place, and she is just a distraction!

READ THE
LOVE ON THE ITINERARY SERIES!

Michelle Tibbs-Brown

Michelle Tibbs-Brown is the author of the Love, on the Itinerary series, which includes Love, Styled and Love, Discovered. Michelle plans to continue the series and will release Love, Composed in June of 2026. She "fell in love" with love the moment she watched the Cinderella movie at a drive-in theater as a child. When Michelle isn't working or writing, she is planning another budget-minded trip for her family, volunteering, making a quick trip to Disney, or enjoying the cafe life in her pretty little city. She calls beautiful Saint Petersburg, Florida, home with her husband and daughter.